Walls of Fear

Walls of Fear

A Kristin Ginelli Mystery

SUSAN THISTLETHWAITE

RESOURCE *Publications* · Eugene, Oregon

WALLS OF FEAR
A Kristin Ginelli Mystery

Resource Publications
An Imprint of Wipf and Stock Publishers
199 W. 8th Ave., Suite 3
Eugene, OR 97401

www.wipfandstock.com

PAPERBACK ISBN: 978-1-6667-3585-7
HARDCOVER ISBN: 978-1-6667-9342-0
EBOOK ISBN: 978-1-6667-9343-7

JANUARY 25, 2022 4:18 PM

The nature of the criminal justice system has changed. It is no longer primarily concerned with the prevention and punishment of crime, but rather with the management and control of the dispossessed.

—MICHELLE ALEXANDER, *THE NEW JIM CROW: MASS INCARCERATION IN THE AGE OF COLORBLINDNESS*

It is said that no one truly knows a nation until one has been inside its jails.

—NELSON MANDELA

Contents

Preface

After thirty years of writing social justice theology, I have turned to fiction to try to evoke the emotional, physical, psychological, legal and cultural elements of the great evils of our time.

One of those great evils, though clearly not the only one, is systemic racism. For people of color who are daily on the receiving end of the abuses of racism, identifying this evil is not difficult. But, when someone is perceived as white, they do not experience these assaults on their bodies, minds, and spirits directly. For them, the way our society functions can just seem normal and any racial problems are caused by "just a few bad apples."

The question I have posed to myself in writing this novel is "How can I help break through this normalization of racism for white folks so they can 'feel' it too?" I also asked myself, "How can I authentically represent what racism does to people of color?"

I have created my main character, Kristin Ginelli, to be a white woman of considerable white privilege. She has been trying to understand systemic racism, but she does not really start to "get it" until she is thrown into the blatantly racist structure of our society by teaching in the prison system. At one point in the book, as she learns more and more, she ponders "the toxic spider web of prisons that covered the country, catching people and holding them in filaments so strong and sticky they could not escape it. The web was made of so many connecting strands: corrupt cops and prosecutors, judges and politicians, and a society that spooled out racism like a spider spooled out silk."

I crafted that image to impress on the reader (and on myself!) how interlocking racism can be and how hard it is to struggle against it. In addition, I have crafted an extended metaphor on the body to convey the way in which white supremacy dehumanizes people of color.

Alice Matthews, a central character in this novel and others, is an African American woman. She works as a campus policewoman and the structures of racism both on the campus and in the larger society are clear to her. Alice and Kristin have forged a friendship across many barriers, but it is not easy and the task of unspooling racism can divide as well as unite them.

I have used the framework of what is called "Womanist" theology and ethics to provide a deep dive into these issues and point ways we can move forward. I have listed books on Womanism and other topics in the "Recommended Reading" section at the end of the novel.

The term "Womanist" was developed in 1983 by African American writer and activist Alice Walker in her collection of essays, *In Search of Our Mothers' Gardens: Womanist Prose*. She crafted the definitive definition of Womanist: "A Womanist is to feminist as purple is to lavender." To me that has always meant that the term "feminist" was not only inadequate to describe the experiences of African American women, but also it was not sufficiently intense.

This field of Womanism has grown and changed over the years, as living, vibrant things tend to do and some of those developments are reflected in the reading list as well.

Kristin, while a white woman of privilege in many ways, also lives with the many contradictions different women's lives can entail. As I was writing out the Table of Contents, I recalled how much I have her driving west and east along a major Chicago highway, teaching at a women's prison one way and heading to take care of her elderly, former in-laws the other way. Meanwhile, she also has to take care of her twin boys and fit in writing her doctoral dissertation. Years ago, Dr. Mary Pellauer, a feminist ethicist, and I reflected, in a recorded conversation on healing and grace that was constantly interrupted by our children, how interruptions are just the way many women have to work and care. And indeed, that better reveals the movement of the spirit. It's messy.[1]

And I have included some humor. Sometimes you need humor in life to temper the stresses and strains of all that evil conspires to do.

The one thing the Devil can't stand is to be laughed at.

---

1. Mary D. Pellauer with Susan Brooks Thistlethwaite, "Conversation of Grace and Healing: Perspectives from the Movement to End Violence Against Women," in *Lift Every Voice: Constructing Christian Theologies from the Underside*, eds. Susan Brooks Thistlethwaite and Mary Potter Engel (New York: Harper Collins, 1990).

1

"I want my lawyer, my kids, my fiancé, my dog, and my wedding planner," I said as loudly as I could as the door to the interrogation room opened. I hated that my chattering teeth made me sound weak.

Two men entered but did not answer me.

"I want to make a phone call," I said, trying to control my shivering.

I was freezing, and it wasn't just from having been locked in an ice cold room. The cold came from inside.

I wrapped my arms around myself and felt a twinge in my bandaged hands. My cuts had been stitched and my bruises examined in the emergency room, then I had been whisked away by these cops and taken to this interrogation room.

I was beginning to get very angry. That was good. It was warming me up some.

2

Decaf coffee only works if you throw it at people.

—ANONYMOUS

Two months earlier

"What the hell is a wedding planner?" Alice Matthews asked me in an irritated voice. I tried to cut her some slack. She'd just started on a nicotine patch and withdrawal from cigarettes was setting in. I was suffering from withdrawal too, only from caffeine, not nicotine.

Alice was my best friend and a campus policewoman at the university where we both worked. She and I had made a pact. She would quit smoking, and I would quit mainlining coffee. Our pact had started January 1. We were two weeks into it now. It seemed like two years.

Back in our halcyon nicotine and caffeine days, we would have been sitting outside even in the January cold so Alice could smoke, and I could drink my jumbo cups of French Roast. Now we were sitting inside the campus coffee shop that Alice preferred. It was right off the path that bisected the main quadrangle where she normally patrolled.

It was warm in the coffee shop, a little too warm if you asked me. The high-ceilinged space was painted a sunny, golden color that was intensified by those "full spectrum" light bulbs that mimicked sunlight spilling down on the patrons. It always reminded me of the set of that TV show Baywatch, but it probably was a good idea to mimic sunlight in Chicago as there was almost no real sunlight to be had, especially in the winter.

Without the fake lights, I guessed students, faculty, and staff would be so depressed by sunlight deprivation, they would stop functioning altogether. We'd find them stacked like cordwood in the halls, classrooms, and dorms, having lost the will to keep moving.

The delicious odor of coffee pervaded this space, and that made it even harder for me to bring my cup of herb tea to my lips. The tea smelled like a stewed selection of weeds.

I didn't take a sip. I just put it down again and focused on Alice's question.

"That's someone who does all the stuff about pulling the wedding together so I don't have to go taste a dozen types of fondant. I don't have the time, and Tom really doesn't have the time."

"Hunh," Alice said, but she knew that Dr. Tom Grayson, the man I was marrying, was a surgeon and barely slept as it was. She wasn't buying it for me.

"But you and all, you're not teaching now, right? And not doin' that so-called consulting for us on the campus police, so how come you need to get somebody else to do it?"

Before I'd changed careers to teaching philosophy and religion at the college level, I'd been a Chicago cop. I quit after the murder of my first husband, Detective Marco Ginelli. I had also quit because of the corruption and sexual harassment. In addition to teaching as an instructor now, I had gotten a contract to consult part-time for the campus police. When I'd started this new, combined career, I'd naively thought a college campus would be less violent than the Chicago streets. I'd found out differently and had helped solve a couple of crimes on campus in the last two years together with Alice and her partner, Mel Billman.

I looked over at Alice, trying to tamp down my own irritability while sympathizing with hers.

I watched her fingers twitch on the table for a second, and then she ran her hands through her now very short hair. I thought she'd cut it to keep from pulling on her dark curls. Her brown eyes closed for a moment, and the smooth, mocha-colored skin of her face was pulled upward by her hands on her scalp like she was doing her own facelift.

I really did empathize. I'd been cycling through the full gamut of caffeine withdrawal. Before I'd quit, I'd been up to about eight, large cups a day and giving it up cold turkey like I had meant I'd had headaches, fatigue, depression and a generalized anxiety. The only thing that helped was running on the indoor track at the university gym but getting myself there had been a huge challenge. I'd invited Alice to come run with me on her lunch break, and she'd told me what I could do with that idea in no uncertain terms. As a campus policewoman, Alice walked all day. In my caffeine-withdrawal haze, I'd paid no attention to that.

"Alice," I said, in the most neutral tone I could muster, "you know I took this sabbatical to finish my doctoral dissertation. I've put it off too long, and Adelaide has really gotten on my case about it." Dr. Adelaide Winters was my department chair and a friend but she was also one tough cookie about the standards in her department.

"And I can't manage to plan the wedding, take care of the boys and find time to write. It just won't work." I had twin boys who were nine. They were the spitting image of their father, Marco, something I cherished, and that could also tear at my heart as I still grieved for him.

"So your plan is to just show up for your own wedding that somebody else fixed up?" she said, frowning at me.

"Right," I said, going a little past neutral in my tone.

"You got a preacher at least?" Alice asked, pulling a wrapped stick of gum out of her shirt pocket and twirling it between her fingers like she used to twirl her cigarettes.

"Yes, Jane. She's agreed, and she has booked the date." Rev. Jane Miller-Gershman was the college chaplain, and she'd become a good friend.

"So are you gonna keep that date a secret, or let anybody else know?" Alice said coldly, her gum packet whirling faster and faster between her fingers.

What an idiot I am, I thought. I hadn't yet shared the date with Alice. Yes, getting Tom's schedule and Jane's to match with when the campus chapel was available had required a ton of negotiation, but we'd just hit on a date. And I hadn't yet asked Alice.

"We just figured it out this past weekend, Alice. I planned to tell you today," I said, and I could hear the defensiveness in my voice. I had just totally forgotten I had planned to bring that up with Alice.

"Hunh," she said, glaring at me. "So, when is it?"

"Saturday, May 22," I said, not needing to consult my phone calendar. The date was burned into my brain after all the back and forth negotiation.

"And Alice," I said tentatively. "I wanted to ask you to be my Matron of Honor."

She looked at me for a long moment, her brown eyes giving nothing away.

"I'll need to check with Jim," she finally said. Jim was her husband. He was a long-haul truck driver and frequently gone from home. It was hard on Alice and their daughter Shawna who was the same age as my boys. They did have family close by where they lived in a southwest suburb, so at least Alice was not on her own when Jim traveled.

"Thanks," I said, kicking myself inside. "Shawna and Jim are both invited too, of course. There will be several children. It will be quite informal." I could hear myself babbling. This is what came of not having any coffee for two weeks. My brain felt like it was made of cottage cheese.

"Yeah, yeah," Alice said shortly. Then she glared at me. "You gonna let some stranger pick your dress and what the honor attendants wear?"

"No," I said swiftly. "I'll get her to make a book of samples, and you pick what you like. And I'm paying for all the dresses and the suits. No argument."

"The hell you are," Alice said, starting to rise.

I wasn't giving on this one.

"Yes, Alice, the hell I am."

"Hunh," she said, now standing and looking down at me. "Stubborn meets stubborn."

"Exactly," I said, and smiled.

She didn't smile back. She just buttoned her dark, navy, wool pea coat, slapped her winter, duty cap on her head, ear flaps up, nodded to me and marched out. It had to be below zero for Alice to put those ear flaps down. She claimed she needed to "hear what those idiot students are saying" when I challenged her on exposing her ears to Chicago winter weather.

I watched her through the window. At least she was pulling on her gloves as she headed down the main path. Distracted by that, I took a gulp of tea.

I shuddered.

I took my phone out of my pocket. I'd silenced it when Alice sat down.

There were six messages from the wedding planner.

3

If I cry at my wedding,
it'll be because I'm overjoyed the planning is finally over.

—ANONYMOUS

I started to listen to the messages from the wedding planner as I walked back to our Prairie Victorian house that was only blocks from campus. I'd bought this huge, nineteenth century monstrosity for its location, but it was turning out that its rambling, enormous size was now essential.

I had a very large trust fund inherited from a great-aunt. I'd used some of that money to buy the house after Marco's death. When Marco and I had married, the trust had been a bone of contention between us, so we had lived on our salaries. But when he'd been murdered, and I had quit the force, I had just used the money to help me and my babies survive and get support. In those first few years of widowhood, I had cared for my children and not much else.

A live-in couple, Carol Allen and Giles Diop, had occupied a separate apartment on the third floor for several years. Carol mostly helped with childcare and Giles did a lot of the cooking. Carol was a student at the School of Social Work and Giles, an international student from Senegal, was a math PhD candidate at the university. This arrangement had worked very well for several years now, and I had assured Carol and Giles nothing would change for them.

But there was change, no doubt. Tom and his daughter Kelly had moved in. Tom had been widowed for two years, and his daughter Kelly, a sixteen-year-old, had come to live with him. To say Kelly's and my relationship was complicated was like saying the previous president had been merely "difficult."

I had offered to have Kelly's bedroom done to her color specifications to make her feel welcome, and she'd jumped at that. She'd chosen purple for two walls, orange-accented wallpaper on two and black furniture. There were Art Deco, pendant lights. The area rug was black and white stripes. Thank God it had a door that was closed all the time. The room gave me mild vertigo if I had to enter it.

I had asked my boys if they'd like to each have their own bedroom (yes, we had enough rooms for that) and decorate it themselves. They'd said, "No way!" to the separate bedrooms. They had shared a room since infancy, and they liked it. Thinking they'd still need something special, I'd bought them each a loft-type bed with a desk underneath. The first night of the new sleeping arrangement had seen our Golden Retriever, Molly, crying piteously because she could not climb the ladders and sleep with each boy in turn. We were all awake until midnight; Tom and I had finally just lifted the single mattresses from the top of each platform and placed them on the floor. The next day, we used screwdrivers, adjustable wrenches, and a drill to re-make the bed-desk assembly. Each bed was now only twelve inches from the floor and each desk attached to the foot of it. The bookcases became headboards. Molly immediately jumped from one bed to the other, rolling around on the covers with joy.

I was now on message four of the six the wedding planner had left, and the tenor of the messages was rising in pitch, something about "the groom's cake." My mind wandered to my groom.

Tom was a surgeon at the university hospital. We had met when a knife-wielding assailant had put a long gash in my arm that required stitches. Tom had sewed me up in the emergency room and driven me home. My grief for Marco had warred with my growing love for Tom. I had come to terms with that, knowing I would always love Marco too. Tom's feelings for his deceased wife were different as they had been divorced, but of course also very complicated. Tom, it turned out, had substantial investments of his own, so the trust fund was not an issue for him. Still, there were plenty of other concerns for both of us, and we had talked through a lot of them both together and with Jane when we'd met with her several times. Tom was a very reserved person, but quite insightful as well. I had taken solitary walks along the lake after each of these sessions, however, just shedding the tears that needed to be shed.

I realized with a start that the voicemail messages from the wedding planner had finished. What was the problem with the groom's cake? I couldn't remember. I sighed and replayed the first one. Oh. She wanted to know if the groom's cake should be the same flavors of cake and icing as the wedding cake. I stopped walking about fifty feet from the house, stood on the sidewalk and typed "We don't care" into the text box. Then I stopped before pressing "Send." Was that too abrupt?

The lack of coffee tempted me. I pressed send.

❀ ❀ ❀

I ENTERED THE HOUSE, empty except for Molly who looked at me quizzically when I opened the door.

"What are you doing here?" was written on her tawny, expressive, doggy face.

"New schedule for us both," I told her as I rubbed her ears. I dumped my purse on the desk in my small study room that was just off the foyer and let her out in the yard for a few minutes. She followed me back into the room and settled down on a dog bed I kept there for her.

I pulled my cell phone from my purse to set it on the desk, and I was horrified to see there were four more messages from the wedding planner. I ruthlessly deleted them without listening.

I opened my computer, but my mind was on what a hassle this wedding planner was turning out to be. I'd gotten a list of wedding planners from Jane that people had used for weddings at the university chapel. She swore she had weeded out what she called the "Wedding Nazis," the control freaks who gave pastors such trouble. The rest she had deemed "okay."

But ten calls down the list of planners, I'd found almost everybody was booked already for May. Who planned so far ahead? Everyone but me, apparently.

Victoria Layne of "Glorious Day," however, had been available. I'd interviewed her just before Christmas over coffee (in the truly glorious day when I was still drinking coffee). She seemed quite young, but maybe that was the long, brown-with-copper highlights hair and the big, brown, innocent eyes. She had reasonable credentials. She had been mentored by the people who had been my first choice, Harrison and Glen of "Simply Fabulous," two guys who seemed terrific on the speakerphone, but who turned out to be booked. So I'd hired her, and she'd given me an extensive form to fill out with our preferences. I'd asked Tom if he had any preferences, and he'd replied, "Yes. I'd like to be legally married by the end of it." Me too, really.

I'd thought filling out the form would be the end of it for me as well, but I should have paid attention to the emphasis on Victoria's website of her "gift for communication." This apparently meant calling and texting me incessantly. I really should deal with it, I thought, but instead I shoved it aside.

I had hours to begin work again on my doctoral dissertation. Crunch time.

I opened my computer to the file on my revised dissertation topic, "The Abuse of Power in Institutions." The proposal had barely squeaked by my doctoral committee for approval at the end of last semester. Since it was my third proposal, I could why several of the faculty were dubious about me and my apparent dithering. I didn't think I was dithering. I was trying to give a damn about what I planned to research and write about.

The abuse of power interested me. I'd seen its machinations both in the police force and in the academy. It mattered a whole lot who got abused and who got to be the abusers. That's what the Black Lives Matter folks were saying.

I knuckled down and started to re-read what I had submitted in the late fall. I was relying heavily on George Orwell. You honestly couldn't beat Orwell for displaying how power was most effective when it combined seduction and threat. How did abusive systems of power get people to submit, seemingly willingly, at times almost ecstatically? And Orwell knew and showed in chilling detail how the purest form of power is its ability to inflict pain on others and how that fosters the hate that the system needs for energy.

I made notes in the margins of my proposal. I wanted to drill down further into the ways in which gender and race played into this dynamic.

I was so engrossed, I nearly jumped six inches off the chair when my phone rang.

It better not be that wedding planner, I thought as I pulled my mind back to the moment.

I looked at the phone display. No, it was Jane.

As I answered, I hoped nothing had happened to mess up our wedding date in May.

But as it turned out, Jane said she wanted to meet "on a totally different topic." We agreed to get together in her office at 10 am the next day.

I got back to my proposal, and it seemed like only minutes when Molly sprang up from her dog bed and woofed joyously.

"The boys are home!" needed little translation from dog-speak, and she ran from the room.

I followed and heard the thump of backpacks being thrown on the floor in the front hall and Carol's soft admonition to pick them up and carry them into the kitchen.

"Hi, guys!" I called out over Molly's whines of pleasure.

"Hey, Mom, you're here," Mike said in his measured way. He was my oldest by about fifteen minutes and a very serious person, especially for a nine-year-old.

"Yes, the new schedule means I'll be here a lot in the afternoons."

"Cool!" Sam said, his natural exuberance coming out as he threw himself around my waist. I actually staggered. They were getting so big.

"And can we have ice cream for snack?" he wheedled while still hugging me.

I looked over Sam's head to Carol, not wanting to contradict her if she had already told them what snack would be. Carol had grown up in Maine, and her parents were organic farmers. She ate an astonishingly healthy diet, and I knew it was better for the boys. The problem was ice cream sounded good to me too.

"How about those Granny Smith apples my Mom and Dad sent with vanilla yogurt and their maple syrup?" Carol countered in her soft voice.

"Well, okay," Mike said in a measured tone. "The syrup is good." My eyes met those of Sam whose face said it all.

Yeah, it was. It just wasn't ice cream.

We all trooped down the hall to the kitchen, the boys dragging their backpacks on the floor.

I had just picked up my spoon to dig in to the mound of vanilla yogurt generously topped with maple syrup when my phone rang.

I took it out of my pocket with foreboding.

It was the wedding planner.

I stepped out of the kitchen and answered.

"Hello, Kristin!" her cheery voice chirped into my ear. "I was worried as you don't seem to be getting my texts and voicemails."

I took a breath.

"Victoria, we need to talk, but not now. I'll call you tomorrow, okay?" I said in as level a tone as I could.

"Well, okay, sure, but I just wanted to check . . . ."

"Tomorrow," I interrupted and hung up.

❁ ❁ ❁

IT WAS AFTER 11 pm. I was so tired I could hardly see the screen of my computer any more. I saved the file and shut down.

I hadn't planned to work on the dissertation for so long, but Tom wasn't home yet. Kelly had called right before dinner. She wanted to spend the night at her friend Ellie's. They had some kind of joint project due tomorrow. I knew Ellie's parents, and I had insisted Kelly put them on the phone despite her "Oh, Kristin, really????" whine. The girls were indeed there, Kari, Ellie's Mom, had affirmed. Parenting is parenting, I had told Kelly a few weeks ago when she'd angrily snapped at me, "You're not my mother" as I'd told her she could not go out and meet her friend Zeke at 11 pm "for a coffee."

I'd kept my temper and had given her that line, one I had thought about in advance.

Tom had texted at just after eight. "One more surgery. Don't wait up."

But I had wanted to. I wanted to be sure he ate the dinner I had saved for him, now sitting on a microwave-safe plate in the refrigerator.

At bottom, I just wanted to see him. Our impending marriage had made me feel an intense longing for our time together that was getting stronger by the minute since our engagement.

I leaned back in my desk chair, thinking. Was this feeling, almost a craving, normal? I didn't remember it from when I'd been engaged to Marco. But then again, I had not feared losing Marco, despite his dangerous work. Did I fear losing Tom because of that shocking, earlier loss?

I just knew that I yearned for every second of time we could get together.

Then I heard his key in the lock.

My heart leapt. It actually did.

I hurried to the front hall and gave him the same kind of body slam hug Sam had given me earlier.

"Oomph," Tom said as my six foot frame surrounded him.

"I missed you," I said.

"I can feel that," he said softly into my hair.

4

Is it surprising that prisons resemble factories, schools, barracks, hospitals, which all resemble prisons?

—MICHEL FOUCAULT

I picked up my phone and looked at the weather app with apprehension. Did I want to know the temperature?

Chicago had been having another of those "polar vortex" things, and the temperatures in recent days had been alarmingly low. It seemed like a polar vortex was when the temperature right at the North Pole warms, and the frigid air there starts stumbling around. It can actually slide off the pole. In recent years, this frigid air had started tripping down Lake Michigan and over Chicago before lurching toward the unsuspecting South. The windchill could reach terrifyingly negative numbers. Wind frothed up the lake water, and it froze instantly into fans of ice.

I steeled myself. I had to check the weather. I did it every morning, in fact, before breakfast. The boys and Carol walked to the kids' school, a block away, and she went on to the School of Social Work, two blocks further. But you could get frostbite that fast. The kids' school had actually been closed for two days the previous week because it was too cold for children (and the adults) to risk coming.

I blinked. The app said it was sixteen degrees already. Must be a mistake. I refreshed the app. Still said sixteen. A heat wave.

The kids, Carol, Kelly, and Tom all got out the door. I walked Molly with the kids and Carol as far as the school and then she and I circled around the eastern part of the campus and came back.

I'd agreed to meet Jane at her office but not until mid-morning. I sat down at my desk, intending to work on the dratted dissertation. I re-read my outline and made a few desultory changes. Then I remembered I had promised the wedding planner I'd call her today.

Oh, good. A legitimate reason to procrastinate.

I picked one of the voicemails at random and hit "reply."

"Glorious Day!" rang out in my ear from Victoria's sprightly phone message. She didn't pick up. I was invited to leave a message. I hung up.

Finally I'd wasted enough time that I could get dressed and walk over to Jane's office. As University Chaplain, her office was in the cathedral-like chapel that had once dominated the campus. Nearly a century later, the campus had grown toward the west and south so now the large, stone building squatted in a corner like a crotchety, old great-aunt upset at being ignored.

As I walked along, I realized it was nice outside. I felt the sun on my back, and I tried not to worry about the wedding. I should be worrying about my dissertation, I scolded myself.

I reached the chaplain's office on autopilot and knocked.

"Come in," Jane's soft voice called from behind the massive, carved mahogany door. Jane's voice was gentle, but I'd noticed she could really project.

Jane was about fifty. She had married Rabbi Emily Gershman in 2015 when marriage equality became legal in the US. Shortly thereafter, she'd been hired as the University Chaplain, and she did a wonderful job with a position that was basically impossible. She stood up from behind her desk as I entered, and I was reminded of how tall she was. Not as tall as I, but just about. She was thin with wavy, greying hair that suited her pale skin and hazel eyes. Eyes that missed nothing. They were directed at me as she came around the desk. I squirmed inside a little. What was up?

"Hello, Kristin. Thanks for coming," she said and gestured with her long arm toward the couch and chairs set up under the window. Tom and I had sat on that couch for several visits about the wedding. I chose one of the chairs instead. Jane's teapot and two cups were already positioned on the table.

"Tea?" she asked, though the unspoken question was "or have you gone back to coffee?"

"Yes, thanks, I'll have tea," I said a little smugly. I sat down in a chair, and Jane leaned over to pour.

"I think you might like this new green tea. I find it a refreshing change from the chamomile."

Good. I hated the chamomile.

I took a sip from the cup she handed me and looked up at her. She smiled over her own cup. This brew was okay. It wasn't coffee, but it was okay.

I had become increasingly anxious when meeting with Jane about the wedding. I had not told her I was not inviting my parents. I feared she would give me soul-restoring reasons why I should, and I didn't want to have to share how my parents had no souls. I had only gotten a soul because of Marco's love. I shuddered internally.

"So, Jane. What's up?" I asked quickly.

She looked at me while taking another sip.

"Nothing with the wedding, I assure you. Don't worry so much." Clearly my anxiety was not completely hidden.

She put her cup down.

"The thing is, Kristin, I want to ask a favor," Jane said softly.

My stomach clenched. I hoped it was something I could do quickly for Jane but that wouldn't add to my overloaded schedule.

She leaned forward, and I realized Jane was a little tense about this favor, whatever it was.

"Do you know anything about the Prison MA in Professional Studies that the area seminaries run?"

I shook my head no. Prison Master's Degree?

"It started actually about twenty years ago with a professor from a school on the west side teaching one class in a men's prison in Illinois. From there, it grew with more faculty volunteering, and they began to give graduate credit through their schools."

I frowned.

"How can they give graduate credit? How many prisoners have bachelor's degrees?" I asked. "Can't be that many." Though as the words came out of my mouth, I started to feel embarrassed. What did I know about the huge numbers of people incarcerated in America's vast prison system? I only knew the US incarcerated more people per capita than any nation in the world.

Jane went on, undeterred by my ignorance.

"Well, actually, some do, and those that don't can get a bachelor's degree online from several universities. The fees for that are paid by volunteer organizations. The graduate program the seminaries run has classes in theology, interfaith studies, history, ministry, pastoral care and leadership skills. That is grant funded. Graduates that are eventually released from prison can get jobs as chaplain assistants, peer counselors and teachers. It's been nationally recognized for reducing recidivism.

"Wait, let me finish," Jane put up a hand as she saw I was about to ask a question.

"They have extended the program into a private women's prison in Indiana. That's a first, as private prisons have been reluctant in the past to let the program in. It's important the first group graduate, and, well, one of the teachers has become ill. Severe flu, I understand. Her name is Dr. Ivy Mercer. Do you know her? She teaches at the Episcopal seminary."

Again, I just shook my head no. I didn't know Ivy Mercer. I knew the school. It was not that far away. But I really meant by the head shake was "oh, hell no." I could see what was coming.

Jane pushed on despite my lack of engagement.

"Anyway, she was teaching a class that has basically the same syllabus as the class you regularly teach, the 'New Social Gospel.' I want to ask you if you could fill in for her for a week or two. These students need that credit so the program gets off to a good start."

I looked down at my hands. They were clenched in my lap. How to say no to Jane who had helped me so much?

"Look, Jane," I mumbled. "I must get this dissertation finished or I'm through here at an instructor. I just don't see that I have the time."

"Well," Jane said, seemingly undeterred. "Aren't you writing about the abuse of power? Where else is power so abused in this society as in a prison? You know, I've read a little of that philosopher you said you were using for some of the power analysis, Michel Foucault, right? Didn't he write a book on prisons as the archetype of so many other kinds of power? You'll get a unique view of that, you can use it in your dissertation, and you'll help some women who are trying to change their lives at the same time."

I looked up, thinking. What Jane was saying was true. Foucault really did think prisons were the model for how modern society dealt out power.

I realized Jane had sat back with her tea, letting me mull it over. She'd have made an excellent lawyer, and that made me think of my friend and attorney, Anna. She too knew how to bait a trap and then be quiet and let someone talk themselves into something. Or blab out the truth.

"One week?" I asked, still debating internally.

"Or two at most," Jane said, getting up and going over to her desk to get a piece of paper.

"Here's Ivy Mercer's contact information. I told her if you could do it you would call and get all the particulars from her. She did sound quite sick, I must say. This new version of the flu is quite debilitating, apparently."

Jane came back and held out the paper.

I took it. I hoped the inmates hadn't given Ivy the flu.

I folded the paper and leaned over to put it in my purse.

"Okay, Jane, I'll call her and try to help out."

Jane seemed to relax a little, but she didn't sit back down.

I didn't get up as she seemed to expect. A thought had occurred to me. Indiana was a pretty big place.

"Where in Indiana?" I asked.

"Just north of Gary," she replied.

Not that far if you took the Indiana Tollway. It cost a fortune in tolls so there was hardly ever any traffic.

"Okay," I sighed, standing up.

I STOPPED FOR A take-out slice of pizza at the pizza place near the campus. This was a guilty pleasure on a weekday as we limited pizza to Sunday night as a treat. I gobbled up my gooey slice at a stand-up table in the confines of the small, narrow pizzeria that would fit in a subway car. The air was moist, warm, and composed of about 20% oregano, 25% olive oil, and the rest garlic and tomato. I figured the calories in the air added up to nearly another slice.

I got home and ran Molly out for a short walk. Then I sat down and called the cell number Jane had given me for Ivy Mercer. She did not pick up. In fact, the phone went right to voicemail. I left a message and call back information as well as my email.

I sat back in my desk chair and thought about prisons and power. I swiveled the chair and scanned my overflowing bookcases. I thought I had some of Foucault's books here at home. Yes, there, on a high self was his *Discipline and Punish*. I stared at it for a while and then got the stepstool I used for the bookshelves that went all the way up nearly to the twelve-foot ceilings. I pulled the book out and went to the comfy armchair on the other side of the room.

It started with torture, as I recalled. Brutal, brutal descriptions. I flipped to the second chapter, "The Spectacle of the Scaffold." The spectacle. Public. Outside. Like George Floyd and many other African Americans now. Killed in public. Floyd had been tortured, his lungs gradually compressed by a police officer kneeling on his back and neck, the lack of oxygen causing his heart to stop. And it had all been caught on a cell phone camera. Foucault's idea was that the medieval forms of torture were to control the body, but the more modern forms of the prison as punishment were to control the soul. I sat back, thinking. Didn't we have both now? Networks of prisons to control the soul and public executions to control the body.

I got up and went to my computer and started to write.

MY CELL PHONE RANG AT 10 PM. I was back at my desk after the boys had gone to bed, and miles away in my mind. I answered it absently, assuming it was Tom.

"Hello?" I said.

There was a whisper.

"I can't hear you," I said, my mind still half on what I had been writing.

"Help me," the voice said, straining.

That got my attention.

"Who are you? Why do you need help?" I asked.

"Ivy," I heard from the whispering voice.

"Ivy Mercer? Are you in danger?"

"No, no sick. So sick. Just pressed wrong number."

Ivy Mercer, the person teaching the prison course. The person I had called earlier.

"Tell me your address, I will send help," I said firmly. Bad flu could lead to dehydration, even coma if not treated.

"Feel so bad," Ivy said, and then there was nothing.

There was an online directory for all the graduate seminary faculty in the Chicago area. I accessed my faculty account online and looked up her name. Good. Her home address was listed. It was not far from the university hospital.

I quickly called 911, gave them her address, and described the situation.

They assured me they would send someone right away.

Should I meet the ambulance at the hospital ER? I asked myself. Yes, I instantly concluded.

The phone rang, startling me. It was Tom.

He started to say, "finishing up," and I interrupted him, filled him in on what had just happened and said I was going to come and meet the ambulance. Ivy Mercer's faculty information had listed no spouse or partner. Tom said to page him when I arrived.

I went to the bottom of the stairs on the second floor and called up to Giles and Carol, explained briefly that a colleague had been taken to the hospital, and I was going to the emergency room to meet her.

It was only a few blocks, but I drove. It was not safe to walk around the university or hospital at night.

I entered the ER trying to tamp down my fear of this part of the hospital. I'd been injured a couple of times since working for the campus police and brought here. I tried to distract myself, focusing on the squeak of my sneakers on the linoleum. Drat. The sound made me flinch even more.

Pull it together, I told myself, and I paged Tom. He said he'd be right down. Then I squeaked my way over to the desk clerk to ask if any emergencies had been brought in, but she said no. "Quiet night."

I sat down to wait, and Tom arrived shortly. As he walked toward me, I noticed his sandy hair was too long, and his blue eyes were tired. I could count the times I'd not seen those blue eyes tired.

"Any news?" he asked. I said not.

"When did you call 911?" he asked.

I looked at my phone. "Forty-five minutes ago," I said, astonished so much time had passed.

"Too long," he said and turned to go up to the desk. I watched his tall frame bend down to speak quietly to the desk clerk. She listened and handed him a piece of paper.

"Let's step outside," Tom said, and I was aware that a couple of other people were also in the waiting area.

"The ambulance was sent from here," Tom said when we got outside. "Apparently, Ivy Mercer was dead when they got there."

5

I can't breathe.

—ERIC GARNER

Police Sergeant Harold Dabrowski arrived at my front door at about 11 pm. The ambulance crew had seemingly followed procedure and called in the police when they had found Ivy Mercer dead in her apartment. They had clearly given the police the contact information for the emergency caller.

That would have been me.

I invited the Sergeant in and, after taking one look at him, offered him hot coffee or tea and "perhaps some cookies?" His heavy uniform winter jacket hung on him he was so thin. He chose tea, and Tom went into the kitchen to make it.

"How long had you known Ms. Mercer?" he asked after he had sat down and taken out his notebook. I was glad he was seated. He looked like he might be ready to faint. His face was thin and very colorless except for two red spots high on his cheeks, I assumed from the cold.

"Dr. Mercer," I said automatically and added I didn't know her personally. Then I explained how I had come to call her on her cell phone. I was relaying the brief conversation when Tom came back with a tray and three steaming mugs of tea. He had brought cookies, I was glad to see, and I encouraged the Sergeant to "take plenty of sugar and some of those cookies."

He just chuckled a little and lifted a mug off the tray.

"Everybody tries to feed me," he commented with a smile that creased his narrow face from nose to chin. Then he blew on the tea and took a sip. "I'm just thin, he added. "And an embarrassment to my mother. She seems to take it as a critique of her cooking." Another smile. That's how the creases got there, I thought.

"Anyway," he continued, putting the mug down on the tray on the coffee table where Tom had placed it, "you were saying?"

"Well, Dr. Mercer called me back on my cell phone earlier this evening. I have the time here for you," I said and scrolled to "recent calls" on my phone and read it out.

"I was barely able to hear her at first and so she spoke a little louder. She asked for help. I think then she realized she had just connected to the most recent call she had received and gotten me. She said she felt sick. Then there was silence. I looked up her address in the online faculty directory and called 911."

"So you didn't know her?" he asked again.

"No. As I said, I was just going to substitute teach for her in a class as she was reportedly sick with flu." I then filled him in on Jane's request and gave him Jane's full name and contact information.

"Her graduate school should know her next of kin and so forth," I added and gave him the full name of the Episcopal seminary.

Sergeant Dabrowski indicated he had no more questions and after two gulps of the now cooler tea, he said good-night.

Tom and I silently climbed the stairs, both too weary and sad to talk.

I CALLED JANE AT 9 am when I thought she'd be in her office, and I gave her the bad news. Her distress came through in her tone, but she just said she would call Ivy's Dean a little later this morning giving the police time to notify her.

Then she gave me the bad news for me.

"Kristin, you'll need to finish out the rest of the class for the students and for Ivy too. I know she felt strongly about helping incarcerated women get back on their feet."

She knew just how to get to me.

"Jane, I don't even have the syllabus. It's not a piece of cake to just pick up someone else's class," I protested though even to my own ears it sounded feeble. There was no stopping Jane when she wanted something.

"I'll get it for you from the woman who administers the prison master's program," she rolled right on. "The syllabi had to be approved by the prison administrator where the courses would be taught."

Of course.

I bowed to the inevitable and told Jane I'd look for the emailed syllabus.

Oh God, I needed coffee. I did the next best thing. I called Alice and asked if we could get together at our regular coffee shop meeting place. I need to talk, I told her when she picked up.

"An hour," she said and disconnected.

The cell rang again, and I absently answered, thinking Alice had something else to add.

Victoria Layne's cheery voice rang out into my ear.

"Kristin! So glad I caught you. Are you sure about that groom's cake? Normally it's not the same as the wedding cake."

"Yes, I'm sure," I said resisting the urge to throw the phone across the room.

"Well, you see . . . ." Victoria started in.

"I have another call," I said. "Good-bye."

❀ ❀ ❀

I SAT OVER MY STEAMING cup of green tea in the fake sunny coffee shop. I'd gotten Alice the English Breakfast tea she liked, and I could see her walking briskly across the quad through the big, faux medieval windows that faced it.

She saw me immediately after she entered and marched over to the table. While she took off her hat and gloves, I could see she was checking the little label on the tea bag that I had left hanging out of my cup precisely so she'd see it.

"So, what's got you all het up?" she asked, seating herself and unbuttoning her coat.

I launched right in to my tale of woe, both the terrible and preventable death of Ivy Mercer and then my own complaints. I didn't have the time, Jane shouldn't have asked me, now I was supposed to do a class that I didn't even know yet what it was about. I could hear the petulance in my own voice, but I just couldn't seem to stop. I finished up with a complaint about the wedding planner.

I finally ran down and took a sip of the tea. Over the lid, I could see Alice's face had completely shut down. I knew that stone face of hers from the past. It meant "I do not want to talk about it," whatever it was.

"What?" I said, putting down my cup.

"Nothing," she said, and she looked at her watch.

"Alice, I know that face. It's something. Come on. What is the matter? Is it Ivy Mercer, did you know her? You know you'll tell me eventually," I said when she remained silent.

Alice took out a stick of gum from a pack she always carried now and started twirling it like she had twirled her cigarettes. But she didn't say anything. More stone face.

I took another sip of the tea and waited.

"There's prisons that have schooling?" she finally asked, the stick of gum now whirling like a propeller.

"Apparently so," I replied levelly. "I don't know a lot about it, though it seems like some prisons do. The state ones, anyway. It's apparently a big deal to get this program into a private prison."

I waited again, sipping the green tea. It had some caffeine. I could feel it or thought I could. Then I wondered if it was just a placebo effect.

"My brother's in prison in Georgia," Alice ground out through nearly clenched teeth.

I just waited. In the early days of our relationship, I would have peppered her with questions, but now I knew better. I shut up and waited, even though that was contrary to my nature.

Alice glared at me.

"What? No, 'oh Alice, so sorry, why's he in prison' blather from you?" Her face was still rigid, but I could see the smolder behind her dark eyes.

I just raised my eyebrows but continued shutting up. It wasn't me she was angry at.

"Oh, hell," she sighed, and she put her hands up into her short hair and pulled on it as she bowed her head.

"Georgia, that's where we grew up," she said into her cardboard cup. "Most of the family's still there. Mama's there. Daddy's dead now, goin' on seven years."

She lifted her head and dark, intense eyes bored into mine.

"Georgia is like one giant, private prison these days. Lots of them. These companies, they come in, they get contracts from the state, promise it'll be cheaper, and they build'em all over. My brother's in Millen, a private prison place called Jenkins Correctional Facility. It's cheaper because they don't feed'em right, they work all day, and the guards paid just shit wages. They say he was dealin' drugs. Not hardly. My brother Chauncy is a little retarded. He's a sweet, sweet boy. He wouldn't know how to do that. Those companies just needed another black body to make some money off of. Mama, she takes a bus to see him every week. I get down there when I can, write him every week. He can read," she said somewhat defiantly.

Then she sighed so deeply it sounded like it came up from the soles of her feet.

"And he can fix cars really good. He had a job and everything."

I felt my eyes well up, but I better damn not cry some white woman's tears or Alice might smack me. I took a giant sip of the tea and murmured "too hot" and put it down, shaking my head and my tears away.

Alice's mouth pursed. I hadn't fooled her.

"How much longer?" I ventured.

"Two years," she said wearily.

"I shouldn't have complained, Alice," I said quietly.

"Yeah, well. You're you, you know. So ignorant about so many things no matter how many of those books you read."

It was the truth.

6

Power is not a means; it is an end . . . The object of power is power.

—GEORGE ORWELL

I walked slowly home, lost in thought about the toxic spider web of prisons that covered the country, catching people and holding them in filaments so strong and sticky they could not escape it. The web was made of so many connecting strands: corrupt cops and prosecutors, judges and politicians, and a society that spooled out racism like a spider spooled out silk. Alice was right. It was for money, yes, certainly, but also for the power to control lives and even destroy them. I sat down at the computer with my coat still on, opened the dissertation file and just started to write.

When Molly woofed hello to the boys, I jerked in my chair. I had been sitting and writing for hours. As I sat up, I felt stiff and realized I still had my coat on. I shrugged it off on to the back of the chair and tried to pull my mind into the present. It was actually difficult.

"Mom!" Sam yelled.

That did it. I shook myself.

"Right here!" I called back. "I'll be there in a minute."

But as I moved to save the file, the words on the page seemed to want to pull me back in. I hesitated, but then I saved and closed down the computer.

The noise had moved to the kitchen, and I followed it.

When I got to the kitchen, Giles was putting a large, oven-proof casserole dish in the oven. I smelled the spices that told me it was Thiéboudienne, the national dish of Senegal. It was basically fresh fish, rice, and tomato-garlic-onion-chili puree, all served with many vegetables like pumpkin, cassava, eggplant and carrot.

I shook my head, still trying to clear it. If I hadn't smelled the preparation of Thiéboudienne over the last couple of hours, I must really have been out of it.

Giles only made that dish for special occasions, and I guessed dinner tonight qualified. Kelly had asked at breakfast this morning if she could invite her friend Zeke to dinner. Giles had nodded from the stove where he was stirring the Senegalese porridge we all loved called Bori, not pausing in the constant stir. That was essential with Bori. Otherwise, it went from delicious to landscaping rocks in about a minute. I knew that from having tried to cook Bori.

Tom had already left for the hospital, but I let him know by text.

"I guess so" was his unenthusiastic response. Kelly and Zeke had been dating now for months, and Tom had not worked it out in his mind that his little girl was serious about a guy. He should have sent a "sigh" emoji.

When we'd first been introduced to Zeke Williams, he had been a skinny, African American guy who wore wire-rimmed glasses. Now he'd grown, it seemed like a couple of inches, and broadened out. Black framed glasses, longer hair. Teenaged kid was becoming a man. I thought he was taller than I now.

Kelly had developed a crush on Giles when I'd first gotten to know Tom. Then she had started dating Zeke and to my worried mind, Zeke had seemed to resemble Giles a little. Needless worry, it turned out. Giles was still thin and wiry and still a math nerd. Zeke didn't look anything like a nerd, though he was in some ways I guessed.

Carol was in the kitchen too, plating some of her apple, raisin, walnut, and oats brownies. I went to the refrigerator and got chunky peanut butter for us to slather on the top. It helped a lot when the so-called brownies broke into bits in your mouth.

"Thanks, Mom," Mike said reaching for the peanut butter and spooning out a heaping tablespoon full. They knew how much peanut butter was required.

"Thanks, Carol," I said and glared at the boys.

"Yeah, thanks, Carol," they chorused around mouths full of the crunchy, sticky snack.

"You're welcome!" Carol said sweetly, grabbing a couple for herself and heading up the back stairs to their apartment.

Giles sat down and poured himself some juice from the pitcher on the table.

"Brownie, Giles?" I asked.

"*Non*, I think perhaps not," he said and smiled his wry smile at me. I'd never seen Giles eat one of those brownies. He finished his juice and also headed up to their apartment.

"So, tell me about your days," I said to the boys when I could free up my mouth to form words. They both started talking at once, apparently outraged at what had happened in the gym period they shared with another class. "Some kid" had been bullying another kid when teams were picked, saying he'd be picked last. The boys said they had yelled at "some kid" and were proud of it.

Why did the whole "pick teams" thing still persist, I wondered as they crunched their snack and bragged about how many balls each had kicked. I'd been tall as a kid and always athletic. I had almost always been picked first or second and remembered being proud of that. But what about the kids who got picked last all the time? I was proud of my boys for standing up against bullying.

❋ ❋ ❋

TOM AND I WERE now sitting in the living room, relaxing over a little red wine. The evening had gone very well. I should have known it couldn't last.

Dinner had been relatively relaxed. No nine-year-old fights or teenaged, emotional angst, and Kelly and Zeke had volunteered to do the dishes. Carol and Giles had taken their meal portions to their apartment as they liked to do. Both boys had gone to bed without too much hassle. They had eaten so much of Giles's fish casserole, they had quickly fallen asleep.

At dinner, the boys had peppered Zeke with questions about chess club and math team, Mike especially. Zeke had been good about it, making jokes about his math teammates and opponents he had checkmated "in about a minute." Kelly had contributed a little, but her interest in the martial arts had grown, and that's how she spent her spare time, I guessed, when Zeke was off zinging opponents with math problems solved or acing chess matches. Tom had said nothing. I thought that made Zeke a little anxious, but if so he hid it well.

Tom and I shared a few wine-flavored kisses between sips and just as things were starting to get more interesting, my cell phone rang in the study. Tom's arms tightened around me a little, and he whispered, "just ignore it." I should. I really should I told my muscles as they tensed and my brain as it switched on. It's probably the wedding coordinator, I told myself. But I couldn't relax again.

"I'll just check the display. Probably nothing," I told Tom. I got up and hustled into the study.

"Ginelli" it said on the display. Oh, no. Marco's father. I had labeled his mother "Nonna." I tensed and pressed "accept."

"Hey, kiddo, you okay?" The voice of Vince Ginelli, Marco's father, boomed out of the phone.

"Yes, yes, I'm fine, Vince," I said as I walked down the hall so Tom could hear who it was.

He nodded and did his best to stifle a sigh. He took the wine glasses and headed to the kitchen.

"So, you okay? Natalie okay?" I asked, heading back into my study.

"Yeah, yeah. We just fine, fine. Natalie visiting Vince Junior and the kids. Nothin' goin' on there, just a school play, I think."

Vince sounded odd, I thought. A little stilted. And he was not likely to have just called me up for a chat. He clearly didn't want to get right to why he'd called.

I loved Marco's parents, Vincent and Natalie Ginelli, far better than my own, and they loved me and the boys so much. The boys and some-times even I called them Nonno and Nonna, Italian for Grandpa and Grandma. I don't think I could have made it through the early years of widowhood without them. As Italian as could be, they had just exuded affection that had surrounded me and the boys like a down blanket on a bitter cold night. Natalie, despite having been born in Chicago like Vince, spoke with a pronounced Italian accent. She cooked incessantly and the pasta and sauce and rich, creamy desserts rolled out of her kitchen and filled me and the boys up with tangible, unjudgmental affection. Vince, a solid, honest Chicago cop until he had retired, made us feel safe.

I decided just to play along.

"We're fine too, Vince. The boys grow about an inch every day, it seems, and I am getting a good start on that writing project of mine." I paused, but he didn't say anything. There seemed to be someone talking in the background.

"Where are you?" I asked.

He coughed and then answered me.

"I got the bus, stayin' in a campground near Oak Park."

Vince and Natalie had a big RV that they drove around to visit all their kids and grandkids. It was very odd that she was in Wisconsin and Vince was staying in their motorhome in Oak Park, a suburb of Chicago. I felt a little prick of anxiety. Had they separated?

"Really?" I said in as noncommittal voice as I could. "Why?"

Another cough. Another pause for a whispered conversation.

"Well, you see, I gotta buddy from the force, he retired too but now does a little PI work. I asked him to look into Marco's death again. And, well, Kristin, he's got somethin'. In fact, a lot of something."

I stopped breathing.

"You okay? You there?" Vince's anxious voice came out of the cell phone that I realized I had put down on my desk. I picked it up and held it at arm's length like it was ticking.

No, no, no, no, no my mind was grinding out. Not again. Not all that pain. Not again. Vince and I had spent years trying to find who had set Marco up and who had shot him in cold blood. We'd found nothing.

"Yes," I said, still holding the phone away from me.

"Whatayousay?" I could hear Vince starting to shout. His own Italian accent got worse when he was stressed.

"Yes," I said more loudly, though I couldn't bear to actually touch the phone to my face.

"Yeah, well," Vince coughed again. "Can you come here tomorrow, hear the guy out?"

I heard the words but couldn't exactly make sense of them.

"What?" I said.

"Come to a meet. I text the address. Like middle of dah morning, okay?"

"Okay," I breathed and ended the call. I sat down in my desk chair feeling like I might fall down.

Tom appeared in the doorway, a look of profound concern on his face.

"Kristin, what happened? What's wrong? You look pale as a ghost."

Ghost was certainly the right word.

He came in and knelt next to the chair. He put his long arms around me, saying nothing else.

I didn't want to speak. I just wanted to be held. He was so tall, I could put my head on his shoulder even when he was kneeling, and I just breathed in his scent of plain Ivory soap mixed with a little sweat from operating all day.

There was a choice to be made. I knew it. I could tell the truth and there would be a marriage, a real marriage. Or I could hide that I might be looking into the murder of my first husband again.

I breathed some more. I chose marriage. I raised my head and whispered in his ear only inches away from my face.

"Vince thinks he has a line on Marco's murderer," I said slowly.

He took a shuddering breath, and then he nodded, and his arms tightened around me even more.

7

Discomfort is always a necessary part of enlightenment.

—PEARL CLEAGE

I was driving west out of Chicago along the Eisenhower Expressway, squinting through curtains of sleet. The warming weather, well, warm for Chicago, had produced this freezing rain instead of snow.

I had agreed to meet Vince and his PI contact by mid-morning, and I'd hoped by then the reverse commute folks would have reached their destinations. Instead, the traffic was crawling along given the treacherous conditions, and I was crawling along with it.

This wasn't good. My ability to focus on the road was impaired by fatigue and anxiety. I had been up before dawn, having slept very fitfully. Tom had snoozed next to me, not stirring. I envied his ability to just fall deeply asleep, stay that way and then wake up fully conscious if he got a call. I had contemplated the ceiling off and on, noting the cracks in the plaster and thinking that for Tom being able to sleep and wake on cue had probably been learned over years of sleep deprivation.

Finally, I'd gotten up and tiptoed downstairs. Molly had stuck her head out of the boys' room, and then she had followed, her nails clicking on the hardwood of the hall and stairs.

I had stood in the kitchen, wrestling with my overwhelming urge to fix a cup of regular coffee. Then I took down the container of decaf beans and poured enough into the grinder to make a single cup. Feeling like a thief, I'd shaken ten regular beans in. I'd also stuck my nose over the opening of the vacuum-packed container of regular and inhaled a couple of times.

I'd put the ground coffee into the single drip pot and poured boiling water over it. I'd let it brew for twice the time recommended and then poured it into my insulated cup. I had taken a sip and actually shivered from pleasure. Then I'd cleaned up the evidence and put everything back into the cabinet before I went to my study.

How bad was this really? I'd asked myself, but only after I'd had several big swallows. It was 95% decaf. And smokers had those patches to help them. What did coffee drinkers have? Nothing. Well, nothing but decaf. I'd gulped the rest down and resisted the urge to go back to the kitchen and fix some more.

To distract myself, I'd turned on the computer and saw that Jane had sent Dr. Ivy Mercer's syllabus for the prison class. I'd opened the file and downloaded it.

Mercer's prison class was, indeed, very similar to the class I regularly taught at the university. There were some differences though. Her class had a section about "convict leasing" in the late nineteenth and early twentieth centuries and the reformers who protested it. I had only the vaguest recollection of what that had been. I made a note of the journal articles she had assigned and then downloaded them from the University Library. I'd almost pressed print but then realized the sound might wake the family.

I kept the first article on the screen and started to read. It was a horror show.

When the federal government pulled out of the South after Reconstruction, the southern states began to effectively remake slavery. Laws were passed that carried long sentences for minor offenses and "vagrancy statutes" made it a crime to not have a job or not have proof of a job. African Americans were arrested, convicted and then, rather than being jailed, as that was more expensive, they were leased to commercial enterprises who were supposed to feed and house them. I scrolled down, reading about how these men were underfed, clothed in mere rags, and how they died in droves to be replaced by more convict-fodder. Entrepreneurs bid on convict leases, driving up the demand for more prisoners.

I sat back, thinking of W.E.B. Du Bois, the sociologist and civil rights activist whose work both Ivy and I included in our classes. Du Bois had written, "The slave went free, stood for a brief moment in the sun; then moved back again toward slavery." I had vaguely known about sharecropping in the south after slavery, but, as I sat back in my desk chair, I thought about all I didn't know, especially this choking legal system that just swooped in and captured men still reeling from having been enslaved. Didn't want to know? Was kept from knowing? Hurried over because it didn't seem important enough?

What would the women prisoners themselves think of this? I wondered. I would find out, apparently.

I'D ENTERED THE ADDRESS of the RV park into my GPS and, when I exited the highway, I'd been directed to follow a winding, secondary road past some frozen fields. I had to drive slowly as it was sleeting even harder here. The white ice forming on the tops of the dried stalks in the fields could have been masses of cotton, cotton that was picked not in freezing rain but in broiling, southern heat, first by slaves and then by convict labor. I shuddered.

The computer-generated voice interrupted that terrible vision as it instructed me to turn left, and I did. I pulled into the campground and stopped. I was so anxious I could hardly breathe. I realized I'd been obsessing about the convict labor, horrific as it was, to keep from obsessing about Marco's murder. Also horrific. But now, in the campground, I had to face it. Suppose this guy had found out something about Marco's murder? Or not found out, and it would be another gut-wrenching dead end. I took a couple of deep breaths, then drove slowly on through muddied tracks glistening with ice.

I knew from Vince's text that their RV was parked toward the end of the second row to the right past the entrance, and I saw it easily when I turned. It had brown and grey swirls on the side and a steel grey front and roof. They sometimes trailered their small Honda behind and, sure enough, as I came alongside, I saw the dark blue, little car parked alongside an unfamiliar, silver Toyota. Must be the PI. My heart skipped a couple of beats.

The door in the side opened, and Vince came down the narrow stairs, holding on to the handle bar on the folding stairs. He stayed under the awning that was unfurled on the side of the massive RV. I could see the icy droplets bouncing off the canvas.

He beckoned me to get out of the car, and I did, running the few feet to the protection of the awning.

I smiled as I came up to him. His wrinkled face was partially hidden by giant glasses I'd not seen before. I didn't know if he'd had his cataracts fixed or if this was a drugstore substitute so he could pretend to see better. I moved to hug him. He seemed rounder and shorter even than when I'd seen him last. His arms held tightly to my waist, and I felt a little tremor.

A man just slightly younger than Vince appeared in the doorway of the RV. This must be the PI. He waited until Vince stepped away from me, then he came briskly down the stairs.

He had ruddy skin, sagging jowls, a broad forehead and white hair. The hair was brushed straight back. He reminded me of someone, but I was so stressed I couldn't bring it to mind.

"Kristin, this is Yitzhak Kelly, Yitz this is my daughter-in-law, Kristin."

Yitz. Yitzhak Rabin. That's who he reminded me of. He could have stepped out of a portrait of the famous and tragically murdered Israeli leader.

His blue eyes twinkled. He saw the recognition on my face.

"Kristin, hello. Yes, I am the only Jewish/Irish cop I think in Chicago. Maybe in the world, who knows?" He stuck out a big, calloused hand, and I shook it.

His accent was pure Chicago Irish with a little of the guttural "chuh" sound of spoken Hebrew thrown in.

We all trooped into the RV, and Vince shut the door on the sleet. Inside the metal tube of the motor home, though, the ping of the frozen droplets could still be heard. I shrugged off my jacket, and Vince took it to hang in the little bathroom. I breathed in the familiar smell of garlic, olive oil and tomato sauce. Nonna must have made countless pots of sauce on the tiny stove under the narrow window. Yet the odors were stale, mixed with the smells of an older man who was not showering enough.

I wedged myself onto the bench behind the small table that was next to the little kitchen. Everything was, in fact, next to everything in the camper. Vince and Yitz sat in actual chairs at either end. Vince might be losing height, but he was gaining in girth. Yitz wasn't much smaller around the middle, and he was just a few inches shorter than I am.

There were already two open beer bottles on the little table, and they were half full. Ten in the morning, Vince, not good. Not good at all. And Natalie would kill you if she knew. But I said all that in my head.

"Getcha somethin', Kristin?" Vince asked. "I can make coffee."

I felt a little twinge of longing, but bravely said, "No thanks, Vince. I'm fine." And the last thing I needed was some caffeine. I already felt even more anxious, trapped on the bench seat between the two of them.

The two men looked at each other across the small table, and my dread increased. Here it comes.

"Yitz, you tell her," Vince said finally as the silence grew.

"Right, well, you see, Ms. Ginelli, like I know you know a lot from the earlier looks you and your father-in-law did but there's new bastards in the mix, if ye ken believe it. Two filthy lads from that El Chapo gang, the ones that been runnin' drugs from Mexico into Chicago. Well, two of these scumbags got turned and been singin' on that gang to the Feds to try to save their filthy hides from a long, long stretch in the jug."

I knew about El Chapo. Everyone in the country, maybe even the world, knew about the Mexican international drug lord Joaquín "El Chapo" Guzman. El Chapo meant "Shorty" in Spanish as Guzman was apparently quite short. He'd been caught and escaped numerous times until finally he'd been successfully imprisoned in the US. Up until then, he'd been one of the most powerful people in the world. Using tunnels and big trucks, he'd made drug trafficking into a kind of multi-national conglomerate.

"And have these 'Feds' said who murdered Marco?" I asked, too tense to wait for him to spin out an Irish/Jewish tale.

"Well, no, not exactly," Yitz said, and he shrugged his big, sagging shoulders at Vince.

Vince took up the story. I swallowed my impatience. I should remember how hard this was on Vince as well.

"We get to that. There was these big trucks, see, comin' from Mexico, lotsa vegetables and the drugs they was in the vegetables. Hell, they even brought sheep sometimes, whoda thought? Anyway, big warehouses on the west side unload the stuff, and they take and pull out the drugs, send the vegetables or whatever on. Drugs, they went in smaller vans to places for meets, transfer them around the city or start haulin' 'em north and east."

Marco had been shot in the face by the driver of a dirty van with mud on the plates. That much I knew. I tried not to show my impatience, but come on, come on, I said in my mind, wanting to hear the name of my husband's killer. Get to it.

"Well, that was no simple traffic stop. Your husband, he'd been tipped about the drugs," Yitz said, leaning toward me. I could smell the beer on his breath. It made me feel anger as well as anxiety. How dare he drink and then think he could tell this story? My rage threatened to overwhelm me. I shook with it.

Vince must have seen it. He put a hand over my clenched fist that was on the bench seat nearest him. I calmed some. Marco's murder had cut him to the quick as well. I took another breath.

Yitz coughed, gave us a second.

"So anyway, yeah," he went on. "The Feds think Marco had a snitch inside the gang, not these twin iejits. Somebody else. So that guy gave up that van that musta been loaded with the goods. The stop took place right near the Denny's parking lot that was off the highway where they would transfer it to other vans."

He paused and looked at me with heavily lashed, Irish eyes that were, God help me, twinkling at me.

"With me so far?" he asked, and he took another sip of his beer. I bit my tongue to keep from lashing out at him. With him? With him?

Vince patted my hand harder, or was he trying to hold my fist down so I didn't take a swing at this pompous jerk? I couldn't stand to keep silent any longer.

"Yes," I said through my teeth, "not only am I 'with you' but I am way and the hell down the road and back. So will the Feds try to find out who the snitch was, the rat who clearly betrayed Marco to the El Chapo organization? Is it part of their murder investigation now? And what about Carl Kaiser, Marco's partner? Has he been linked to the El Chapo gang? Was he in on it?"

I was literally panting when I finished.

Old Yitz had the grace to look a little ashamed.

"I don't know yet, he said defensively.

I snorted.

"Well," he continued, "I mean I think that Kaiser guy was just a bloody coward and didn't get out of the car. Not heard they're investigating him. But they're keepin' such a tight lid on this investigation, what I told you is all I could worm out from my contact."

I slid out of the confining bench on Vince's side and walked around the table. I couldn't stay trapped like that anymore. I placed my hands on the table in front of ole Yitz and spoke directly into his face.

"So let me get this straight. There's a federal investigation of the organized crime syndicate of the now jailed El Chapo, and a lot of it is centered in Chicago. Two guys, twins, are ratting out everybody they can think of in the organization in hopes of getting shorter sentences. You've learned that Marco had a source in the El Chapo organization who tipped him to a van full of drugs being taken to a meet. You're saying he was set up by that source and then murdered in cold blood. The driver of that van is the one Vince and I want and you don't know who that is because the Feds are 'keeping a lid on it.' Have I got that right?"

I glared at him with my ice blue, Scandinavian eyes, the eyes of generations of Viking raiders.

"Well, yes," he said. He looked at his beer bottle. I looked at it too. He didn't touch it.

"Vince," I said. "Walk me out, will you?"

I went to the tiny bathroom to retrieve my jacket and to calm my breathing. I didn't want my anger to spill over on to Vince.

I just nodded to Yitz who was still seated at the table and followed Vince down the stairs.

"Kristin," Vince said once we got down the stairs, but not facing me, "he's not a Fed, he knows what he knows from sniffin' around. We got more than we usta have."

"I know, Vince. I know. I shouldn't have lost my temper."

He turned.

"It's okay, kiddo. I know. We'd kill Marco's murderer with our bare hands if we could. I know it and you know it," Vince said with a menace in his voice I'd rarely heard.

"Well," I said, "maybe we'll get the chance." I laughed a harsh laugh, and Vince huffed a little, but we knew we weren't entirely joking.

"Listen, Vince," I went on. "Keep him going with his sources. I know you will. But I know some Feds too now. Let me poke around a little, see if I can get one of them to talk to me." Even as I said it, I was mentally scrolling through the FBI agents in Chicago I'd come to know.

"It's good. It's good. Double-team them. Good, good," Vince said, but slowly. I hated the toll this was taking on him.

"So what's with Natalie? She okay? You're here alone," I asked.

"Nothin' to worry about there, Kristin, just don't tell her about this. I told her poker week and hangin' out with the boys. I tell her about this, she'll just cry her eyes out again." He turned and gazed out at the sleet, now mostly rain.

I put my arm around his shoulders and gazed at the sodden campground landscape, saying nothing. We'd said so much before, silence said it all.

I got into my car with Vince's admonitions to "take it slow" in my ears. But I wouldn't "take it slow" with this investigation. Somebody had set my Marco up to be killed.

8

Planning my wedding was really easy and stress-free, said no bride, ever.

—ANONYMOUS

When I got back home, it was barely after noon. Molly was getting used to seeing me during the day, and she went to the front door and looked pointedly at her leash. Walking in freezing rain didn't bother her, and it didn't bother me. I had so much on my mind I barely noticed.

Wet dog and damp human settled down in the kitchen. I heated up some canned, chicken noodle soup that I kept hidden from Giles and Carol in the back of the pantry. Its glutinous, flavorless warmth was just what I needed. I wished I had some Wonder Bread.

I opened my phone to find my FBI contacts and saw there were three texts and seven (seven!) voicemails from the wedding planner. I have to deal with that I thought as I shoveled in the tasteless soup.

But first the FBI. Agent Paul Lindsay, Cybercrimes. Kamal Nadar, Counterterrorism.

I knew Lindsay best and thought I'd start there. I sent him a text asking if we could meet in the next few days. I didn't specify why.

Then I called Victoria. "Glorious Day!" she chimed, then giggled out a "Hello, Kristin!"

I gritted my teeth and asked as calmly as I could if she could come by my house later this afternoon so we could "get clear on some things."

She happily said she could, and we arranged for her to come by in an hour.

After I changed my damp clothes, I sat down in front of my computer and opened my email.

37

Jane's name caught my eye, and I opened hers first.

"The prison warden, Dr. Herbert Snyder, would like to meet with you before you begin teaching the class next week. He called me and specifically requested that. He also wants to give you a tour and a list of the students in the class. Please call him. Jane." She had left a number below the message.

More driving, I sighed inwardly, but it did make sense for him and me to meet and for me to get an orientation.

I called the number Jane had included, and a woman answered "Warden's Office" through her nose. Apparently she either had a cold or suffered from adenoids.

I gave her my name and had to spell Ginelli several times. She couldn't seem to get the hang of two ll's. I spoke more slowly, enunciating as well as I could, and I thought after a couple more tries I got her to understand why I wanted to see the warden. He asked to see me, I kept repeating. Finally, I had an appointment for tomorrow at one o'clock.

"In the afternoon," she emphasized. "Good," I replied, inwardly glad I didn't have an appointment for the middle of the night.

Since I still had some time before Victoria arrived, I googled Dr. Herbert Snyder and the name of the Indiana prison. "Doctorate in Criminology" was listed beside his name on the prison website and that was all.

I searched beyond that website and discovered that his so-called "doctorate" was an online degree from a school I'd never heard of in Arizona and that he'd also been a car salesman in Hammond, Indiana. The latter was a little iffy since I didn't have a middle name, but there was a photo from a dealership's website. If it was the same person, he was a pasty, white guy with suspiciously even-toned, brown hair and eyes set a little too close together. He pretty much looked like you would expect a Herbert from Indiana to look.

The doorbell rang, and Molly trotted into the front hall. I followed.

"Oh, a doggy!" Victoria trilled when I opened the door, and she saw Molly. She immediately crouched down and bent her head over the dog. Her long, auburn hair fell on either side of Molly's head as she started petting her. It was a little hard to see where Victoria ended and Molly began. Molly liked this from a new human, or any human really, and she wagged her tail wildly.

I just stood there and watched. Victoria's reaction to seeing a dog reminded me of the son of one of my faculty colleagues who was now nearly eight and who adored dogs. His mother, not so much. He loved playing with Molly, and he had begged for so long, his father had gotten him a teacup poodle he'd named "Hulk." Hulk and Molly played together sometimes at the local dog park. Hulk was no pushover for a five pound dog.

I looked down at Victoria and Molly and thought I should cut this enthusiastic human some slack.

Finally, she stood up.

"Oh, Kristin, sorry for neglecting you!" she said. I was a little surprised to see her dash away a tear from her eye. "I so miss my dog. I can't have a dog right now."

"Hello, Victoria. No problem. Molly loves to be petted. Won't you come in?"

I took her coat. It felt dry, so the rain must have stopped. I offered coffee or tea, and she chose tea. I ushered her into the living room, and she and Molly happily resumed the orgy of petting.

I brought in the tray and poured her a cup. Molly lay down adoringly at her feet. Victoria added lots of sugar, not surprisingly. After a couple of sips, she dug around in her big purse that was on the couch beside her and lifted out an amazingly large binder. I'd seen murder files from twenty-year-old cold cases that were smaller.

She placed this somewhat precariously on her lap.

"So! I made a list of all our outstanding issues, and we can just get right to work," she said, flipping to a page that I could see had single-spaced type covering the whole of it. She took out a pen with a little feather sticking out the end of it. She held it poised over the page.

"No, Victoria. That's not why I asked you here," I said firmly.

Her dimples disappeared as she looked up at me. Alarm crossed her face, and then she actually looked a little frightened.

She must think I'm going to fire her, I thought.

"Now, don't be alarmed, but you need to listen. I need some very specific things from you in this planning, and there are some other things I really don't need and want to stop, okay?"

I took a sip of my own tea, green again. I was getting used to it. I let her pull herself together and sipped again, then put the cup down.

She started to speak, and I held up a hand.

"Listening, remember? So here's what I need. I need three of those binders with sample attendants' dresses, fabric attached. No patterns, only solid colors, muted pastels for spring. One of them for a woman about five and a half feet tall, one for a young woman who is almost six feet tall, and one for a woman about five foot three. The dresses should be simple, just below the knee." One for Alice, my matron-of-honor, and one each for Kelly and Carol, my bridesmaids.

I saw she had flipped to a blank page and was writing. Good. There was a small frown at "just below the knee" but she gamely wrote it down.

"I want a few samples of a dress for me. This is my second wedding, and I don't want a traditional bridal gown. Just a classic dress, no frills, in ivory, cream or perhaps very pale blue. No veil." Deeper frown.

"Tom is wearing his own suit as is his best man and his attendant."

No tux for me, Tom had insisted. His brother was going to be his best man. I'd not even met him yet as he worked for Doctors Without Borders and was flying in from Africa for the event. Tom had asked Giles to be one of his groomsmen, and, to my astonishment, had asked Zeke to be the other. Kelly was over the moon about it. Typical of Tom to know she'd feel that way. But then, I thought suddenly, would a guy coming from Africa have a suit? And what about Zeke? I'd need to ask Tom and Kelly. I thought Giles had a suit, but I wasn't even sure about that.

"Oh, but men look so handsome in formal clothes," Victoria burst out, unable to hold in her dismay.

"No. Not happening," I replied. "And that should be it. You already have our preferences on all the food, wine, flowers and so forth. Really, that's it. That's all I want from here on out. What I don't want is calls and texts and emails. I have to concentrate, Victoria, and I hired you because I wanted to put this whole wedding in the hands of someone with good taste and who is trustworthy."

I was laying it on a little thick, but I needed to get her to just stop the ceaseless communication and yet feel good about that.

Victoria looked up at me, her big brown eyes swimming with tears.

"Oh, Kristin," she said in a whisper.

Tears again. For God's sake. I picked up my teacup to forestall her getting up to hug me.

Molly got it, though. She put a gentle paw on the open binder on Victoria's lap, and the emotional wedding planner bent over her.

Good. I hoped that took care of it.

It didn't. We ended up going over her notes on what I'd said twice more, but finally I got her binder into her big purse and her coat wrapped around her. After some final Molly pets she headed on down the walkway.

I shut the door behind her and realized I was exhausted. Now I wished I was the one who smoked, not Alice.

❀ ❀ ❀

It wasn't until later that night and Tom and I were sitting in bed with a little red wine each that I was able to bring him up to speed on what Vince's pet PI had said.

"El Chapo, really?" Tom had said in an astonished tone when I'd mentioned the drug cartel. His thick, sandy eyebrows shot up above his wire-rimmed glasses. "Good grief, Kristin. How awful. I do think you're right to try to get information through your own sources as well." He paused and put his wine glass on his end table. Then he turned back to me.

"You know, the other thing is, I am concerned about Vince. The last time we saw them, what was it, just a couple of months ago, his color was mottled, and I thought he was having a little trouble breathing. Does he have a good doctor?"

"Oh, Tom, I wish I knew. Every time I bring it up, he deflects. I'd have to say I don't think so, but there were some prescription pills in the bathroom of the RV as I recall. I wish I'd looked at them more carefully. I was upset and didn't think of it."

Tom patted my clenched hand that was on the coverlet.

"You'll need to drive out there again and meet with him, right? You can snoop then. But seriously, it is a good idea to get a doctor's name and what he's taking, even though technically if he doesn't give you permission you shouldn't have that information. But if you see the bottles, you can ask him about it, see if he'll tell you."

I was pretty sure Vince Junior was the one with their medical power of attorney, but the few times I'd met him, I'd thought he was kind of dim. Tom's suggestion was a good one.

"Yes. Vince might tell me at that. Thanks."

Tom and I had already changed our wills so I would take care of Kelly, and he would take care of the boys should anything happen to either of us. The Ginellis were getting too old to raise two rambunctious boys. We also had each other's medical power of attorney. I shuddered, thinking about how fragile life was in so many ways.

I took a final sip of my wine and put the wine glass on my own end table. Tom did the same, and he looked at me. What I saw in his eyes made me glad that life wasn't all tragedy and loss.

For a while Tom made me forget my worries completely.

But just before I fell asleep I thought, "I have to ask him if his brother is bringing a suit."

9

Why do prisons tend to make people think that their own rights and liberties are more secure than they would be if prisons did not exist?

— ANGELA Y. DAVIS

Another drive, this time to the east to get to the prison. No snow, sleet or rain today, just the midwestern, leaden skies that were so depressing. As I navigated the toll road, the transponder that electronically paid the fees kept lighting up like a Christmas tree. The road had almost no traffic. Unsurprising since the cost to drive it was probably just shy of a semester of college.

The urban decay of Gary, Indiana lined the highway for a short while, and then I exited and went north as the tinny GPS voice directed. I was suddenly thrust into a flat landscape with barren fields on both sides, bisected by the straight, two-lane road I was traveling. How quickly these cities gave way to farmland, I thought, remembering the approach to the RV park.

I could see a symmetrical arrangement of two-story buildings in the distance surrounded by a chain link fence topped with barbed wire. Probably the prison and not an immensely secure suburb.

As I got closer, I could see women outside. There was a range of ages and races, though it seemed like African American predominated. This "campus," as it was described on the website, had several playing fields and sure enough I could see women in tan pants and maroon sweatshirts running around playing soccer. From the way they were moving, they were likely the younger ones. Picnic tables dotted the brown, winter grass as well, and those were occupied mostly with older women talking. Without the barbed wire, it could be a rural, community college campus.

I approached what a sign indicated was the main gate. It had a small guardhouse inside the gate. This was obviously the visitor entrance. A beefy, white guy came out and unlocked a door in a much larger, sliding gate. "What's your business here?" the guard asked in a high-pitched voice as I rolled down my window. It really startled me. From his muscular physique, I guess I had expected a deep voice.

Steroids, I thought, though what I said was "I have an appointment with the warden."

"Driver's license," he trilled and went back through the gate to the guard house, I assumed to check I had an appointment.

He had been wearing a patch with "CGA" in gold thread on it. That stood for Corrections Group of America, I knew, having researched the conglomerate this morning. CGA built prisons in bulk, moving into states to get contracts, then throwing up the buildings like so many Amazon warehouses, only these had guardhouses and walls that were trimmed with barbed wire. Given the trajectory of both companies, I wondered when prisoners would start to just be confined in the giant "fulfillment" centers, a kind of updated convict leasing program.

I was deep into these grim thoughts about our country when the larger gate opened and the guard came out of his little house, gesturing me to drive through. When it closed behind my car with a large and what seemed, under the circumstances, to be a very ominous clank, he returned my license and just waved me on. Why didn't he have a name badge, I wondered.

Up ahead, I saw a similarly garbed guard who looked a lot like beefy, white guy #1. He'd exited a door in a building directly ahead, and he was pointing me toward a parking lot to my left. He followed me on foot. The lot was nearly empty.

"Keys?" he asked, also with a high voice, holding out his hand. Beefy, white guys #1 and #2 must work out together, I thought as I silently got out of the car, took the car fob off of my keychain and handed it over.

"Follow me," he squeaked. No greeting, no "Welcome to our happy prison" chitchat. Also no name badge on him. I was beginning to get a sense of what the anonymity and routinization of this system did, and these were just the guards.

I followed beefy, white guy #2 to the door from which he'd exited. He took out a large card that was connected by a chain to his belt. He waved it at a scanner by the door frame and the door clicked. He entered, and I followed.

A fluorescent-lit corridor was painted beige and smelled of Lysol. It led to a steel, sliding door ahead of us. To the left was a window behind which sat an enormous, white woman with red hair so processed it sprang out from her head like she'd just had an electric shock.

"Credzzzshalls," she said through a round, slotted device. It hissed with static breaking up the word. Apparently she meant "credentials." A drawer below banged open.

I put my driver's license on the tray, and it banged shut.

"Pick zzz up zzz you exit," she said, the device hissing again. I just nodded. Something in the atmosphere was working on me, suppressing my own desire to speak to these people or even make eye contact.

Beefy, white guy #2 used his card on another scanner to open the door, and we went down a corridor that had many closed doors with slots in the center for cards to be slid in to indicate the occupant and what the office did. Many looked quite new. Lots of turnover? I asked myself, trying to engage my surroundings despite the atmosphere.

We arrived at the end and beefy, white guy #2 pressed a buzzer. The door had "Warden" painted on it and on the wall next to it was another of the electronic, two-way speaking devices.

"Ginelli for the warden," he said into the circle. I hated to think what it sounded like to whoever was on the other side of the door.

But no hissing returned. Instead, there was a clack of the electronic lock disengaging, and a woman in her fifties with iron-gray hair in a bun and a uniform that hung on her thin frame opened it.

"Come in," she said and turned away immediately. I recognized her by her adenoids. The warden's secretary.

The warden's secretary went right to the door opposite the entrance, knocked discretely and entered. The door shut with a pneumatic hiss behind her. Left alone, I took the initiative and sat down in one of the molded, plastic, orange chairs. Even doing that felt like a tiny bit of rebellion.

Then I stood back up, too restless to stay seated. There was a window and I could see out the thick glass that more winter grass fields extended throughout the so-called campus. In the exact center was a red brick church that could have been transported from New England and placed there by devout Martians. Now that's interesting, I thought, my mental processes starting to engage again. The whole entry and its forced suppression of feeling was fading a little. I moved closer to the window. I contemplated the chapel, wondering if religious observance was compulsory. Private prison, I mused. Could be.

The door to the warden's office hissed open, and the secretary emerged.

"You may go in," she said. Her high, nasal voice echoed the pneumatic hiss.

I entered, and the door whooshed shut behind me.

Warden Herbert Snyder did not rise from his desk, or even actually look up from whatever papers were in front of him, but merely indicated the vacant chair in front of it with a desultory wave of his hand.

He was the car salesman. I was not surprised.

❀ ❀ ❀

FIVE MINUTES HAD PASSED, and Warden Snyder was still flipping through a folder in front of him. I decided to disengage in kind, and I took my cell phone out of my purse and started reading my email. There was no cell phone reception, I noted, but I had a backlog of emails to look at. I always did.

Warden Snyder harumphed, and I looked up. He had the nerve to look offended by my looking at my phone.

"So, Mrs. Ginesky," he said in his flat, midwestern voice, "you have volunteered to teach Miss Mercer's class?" He had acquired horn-rimmed glasses since his car dealership photo. I wondered if they were fake, designed to make him look smarter. It wasn't working.

"Ms. Ginelli and Dr. Mercer," I corrected him in as calm a voice as I could manage.

"What?" he asked, puzzled.

"My name is Ms. Ginelli," I said slowly, "and Ivy Mercer had a PhD, hence, Dr. Mercer, and yes, I volunteered to teach the remainder of her class."

He blinked and then nodded, returning his gaze to what I assumed was the resume I'd had to submit yesterday.

"Are you a Christian, Mrs. Ginelli?" he asked, looking intently at me through the glasses that I noted were smudged.

"Ms. Ginelli. I teach Philosophy and Religion, Mr. Snyder. That's in my resume that I believe you have there."

"Dr. Snyder," he corrected huffily.

"Oh, really?" I asked. "Where did you do your doctoral work?" I looked around the walls of the office as though expecting to see a framed diploma from Harvard or Yale.

"I will ask the questions here, young lady," he said, his pale, doughy cheeks reddening from rising irritation.

Good. I thought. I had deflected him from asking about what I believed. That would have taken hours. But car salesman Snyder seemed to be getting very upset.

"You egg-head types need to wake up," he said, wagging a pudgy finger at me. "There's a great awakening happening, and all you idiots are missing it, missing it totally!"

"Great Awakening? You mean Johnathan Edwards and that nineteenth century movement?" I asked, genuinely puzzled.

"Just look it up," he said sharply, and then drew back in his chair. His face curiously shut down then, the heightened color draining away and his eyes losing their focus for a second.

After about a minute during which I sat and watched him, riveted by this odd display, he seemed to come back to himself, and he looked down at the folder, sighed, and then extracted a typed list.

"Here's a list of your so-called students," he said, handing over the paper. "Their names, offenses, sentences, time served, educational level and religion. Not all are Christians, I'm sorry to say."

I took the paper and glanced at it. So-called students? It seemed the warden was not exactly behind this educational initiative. And not all Christians? Good grief.

"And here's an approved class reading list and topics for you," he said as he picked up another piece of paper and waved it a little. "That Mercer woman had too much about race and prisons and such things and that's all over now. No point in raking that up, making prisoners jumpy and whatever."

He finished waving the paper and handed it across his desk. I took it, and I could see he'd used a black marker to draw a line through W.E.B. Du Bois's "The Souls of Black Folk," as well as that of Michelle Alexander and her book "The New Jim Crow." He'd left the white reformers like Rauschenbusch alone.

He squinted little piggy little eyes at me through the smudged lenses of his glasses, and I could see he was itching for me to object, probably so he could cancel the class.

I calmly folded the paper in two and placed it on my lap with the class list. I said nothing and that clearly got under his skin. The red mottling was back, rising up the rolls of fat on his neck.

To myself I was thinking of ways I could just alter my lectures to summarize key elements of the reading that the students would not get.

"Well," he finally harumphed when I continued to say nothing. Then he went on. "I'll have someone show you your classroom. You'll need to be a half hour early each time so you can be processed and escorted to where you'll teach."

I just nodded, seemingly further disconcerting him. This was a very odd guy. No wonder he was no longer selling cars. He seemed incapable of regular human interaction.

He pressed a buzzer on his desk and the adenoidal secretary came right in.

"Is Corrections Officer Jackson here?" he asked her.

"Yes, sir," she replied.

"You may go," he said to me, looking down at the file. He did not say good-bye. Neither did I.

As I exited his office, I wondered to myself why he didn't ask me about my time on the Chicago police force. I had included it in my resume. Curiouser and curiouser.

❖ ❖ ❖

THE CORRECTIONS OFFICER WAS an African American woman of about forty. Unlike the intake woman or the two beefy, white guys, she was trim, about five and a half feet tall, and she seemed friendly. She actually introduced herself to me.

"Corrections Officer Quisha Jackson," she said, holding out her hand to shake mine.

"Kristin Ginelli," I said warmly. Ordinary human contact had started to feel precious to me.

"So, you're goin' to take over Ivy's class?" she asked when she'd let us out of the main building, and we started walking side by side on a path that bisected the complex toward what she called "Building C." She'd informed me that's where the library and the classroom were located.

"Yes, I am taking over the class," I said and turned to look at her, surprised both by the conversational tone and her use of Ivy Mercer's first name.

She nodded, responding to my look.

"We found we both got some family live in the same town down to the south tip of Indiana, almost Kentucky. She was a good person, Ivy," Officer Jackson said in a low tone. "Good person."

"I didn't know her," I replied, "but I know it was a tragedy for her to just die so young."

Jackson looked away and did not reply.

We were about to skirt the chapel, so I asked her about its uses.

"Well, used to be just for some preachers who came by, but inmates they could go or not go, depending. Now, well," she paused and actually looked around to see if we were within earshot of anyone, "the warden he preaches on Sunday and everybody got to come. And I mean everybody." She shook her head as we kept walking.

Just then, in the distance, three other uniformed guards, all men, appeared from behind a smaller building on the right, and they stood in a circle, talking. Two of them glanced over at Officer Jackson and me. Those two seemed to indicate our presence to the third, and he looked at us as well.

"How long have you been here?" I asked.

"What?" she asked, seeming distracted.

"I asked how long you have worked here," I repeated in a low tone. Perhaps sharing such details was not allowed.

"Since the first two buildings built, eight years ago," Officer Jackson replied in almost a whisper.

"Long time," I commented neutrally. "And the warden?"

"Two years," she said softly, but with a tone of finality. I thought she was regretting letting me know something about herself.

"This here is Building C," she said in a louder voice and pointing. Since there was a giant letter C on the front, it wasn't much of a reveal. "Building C is the best building, has the library, classroom and toward the back, there's an exercise room. Only model prisoners placed in here. One false move, and they out. Everybody wants C." She took out a keycard like beefy, white guy #2 had, scanned it, and opened the door.

It was so clean. That was my first impression. And there was more color. The walls were beige and the floor was made of shiny, three-foot-square, vinyl tiles in a marble pattern, but the doorways were trimmed in blue and as we walked into a large, central room with round tables and chairs, I noticed the chair seats matched the trim. Pleasant. It was two-stories high with a central staircase. Cells lined the first and second levels. All the doors were open, I was interested to see, and women milled around. They wore the tan pants I had seen on the soccer players with white T-shirts and running shoes. Except for the bars on the cells, it could have been the courtyard of a mall, especially since the women here seemed older.

As we walked in, all eyes swiveled to me and Officer Jackson and conversation stopped.

She paused and made eye-contact with another officer, a middle-aged Hispanic guy standing mid-way through the room toward the wall. Both nodded.

"Ladies," Officer Jackson called out in a carrying voice that echoed in the large space. "This here is Professor Ginelli. She gonna take Dr. Mercer's place with that class. She'll be here once a week until that gets finished up."

"Hello," I said and nodded at the room.

No one replied.

"Classroom this way," said Officer Jackson and turned to the right. I could hear the buzz of conversation start right up, louder than before, as she led the way.

The classroom seemed to also double as a crafts room since there were some stacks of folded fabric squares on a credenza along the far wall. Another credenza held books, mostly contemporary novels as far as I could see. A whiteboard was screwed into the third wall. A dozen chairs were scattered around an oblong, plastic, fake wood, veneer table.

"How are people liking having these classes so far?" I asked Officer Jackson who had stayed by the open door as I walked around the room.

"Okay, I guess," she offered in a stiff way. Where had the friendliness gone? I asked myself.

"I guess I will find out," I said as I came back to her and the door.

"That you will," she replied in the same stiff way.

We exited the building and started back down the walkway toward the chapel.

"Would you stop for a minute, Officer Jackson?" I asked.

She stopped so abruptly she staggered a little.

"What?" she asked, a little alarm in her voice. Her lips were pursed, and she was frowning. She seemed increasingly stressed.

"I'd just like to get oriented to the whole complex, if that's okay?" I asked in as neutral tone as I could manage. From what I'd seen, the buildings were arranged in a semi-circle where C was in the center. The administration building where I'd entered was at the opposite end. The chapel was in the middle.

She blew out a breath she'd apparently been holding in and nodded.

I pointed to the left. "So is that one E and so forth back around the circle?" There were a total of five other buildings.

"No. Not exactly," she said curtly. "A is that one to the left, and then yes, it is B, C, D, E, but then that's the medical building," and she pointed to a smaller structure farther outside the circle where the three officers had come out and talked. I didn't see them now. The building backed up nearly to the fence that surrounded the whole prison, and there was a small ramp behind. I could just see the corner of a medical van parked there.

Made sense. I'd read there were 1200 women housed here. A population that size would have many medical issues big and small.

"Thanks," I said and made to walk on. Officer Jackson, however, was staring at the medical building. A gurney was being taken out of the van by two of the guards. Then they started to push it up the ramp. I stopped to watch it as well.

"I hope no one is seriously ill," I contributed, still looking at the gurney. Then I abruptly turned back, and I thought I'd caught her off guard. Her eyes were squinting, her lips were pursed and her cheeks sucked in. She looked like she was going to throw up. Then she saw me looking her way, and she turned and stalked away calling over her shoulder, "Hurry up!"

Officer Jackson took me back through the administration building to the door where I'd entered. I thanked her, but she merely turned and walked away. I retrieved my driver's license from the woman whose hair stood on end and beefy, white guy #2 walked me to my car and gave me back my fob.

Beefy, white guy #1 opened the gate for me after checking in my trunk and in the backseat.

I drove slowly down the two-lane road thinking about this prison and what it would feel like to spend years there. As I approached the highway, I pulled into a McDonald's drive-through and got a cup of black coffee, regular. McDonald's coffee is so weak it doesn't even count, I thought. I'd had a French friend visit a few years ago. I'd picked him up at the airport, and he had come out through security carrying a McDonald's cardboard cup.

"*C'est du thé, pas du café*," he had remarked to me in some outrage, holding the cup out. Not coffee, tea, he was complaining.

I had taken the offending cup and sniffed it.

"That's McDonald's coffee," I'd said, handing it back.

"*Mais, non*," he'd replied and tossed the cup into the trash. Not coffee to a French guy. And, not coffee to me either, I rationalized. Just really dark tea.

I parked and drank the hot, brown water, and I pondered what had just happened at the prison.

10

I just like to have words that describe things correctly. Now to me, 'black feminist' does not do that. I need a word that is organic, that really comes out of the culture, that really expresses the spirit that we see in black women. And it's just . . . womanish.

—ALICE WALKER

I was walking west, toward the university campus. It was only five in the afternoon, but the sun was already setting behind the faux medieval building where the Department of Philosophy and Religion was located. I get it, I thought, gazing at the giant metaphor for the sunset of academic life. The sun is definitely setting on academia.

Still, I had a faculty search committee meeting that I was attending by my own choice. I wanted to push my preferred candidate, and I wasn't going to be shy about that. I had literally shed blood for us to get back two full-time positions. This hire would fill the second one.

When I'd been hired, the department had been being systematically deprived of teaching positions. We'd lose full-time faculty one way or another, and the position would become part-time or worse, adjunct. Through power manipulation that would have made Machiavelli envious, I had managed to get back two of the full-time positions we had lost. That mainly had been due to the incompetence and corruption of our former department chair, now deceased. I had exposed his machinations and to keep me quiet, I'd gotten the university powers-that-be to give us back almost all our previous full-time faculty quota. But there had been years of erosion.

I still found it perversely humorous that the former department chair's field had been in ethics, since he had seemed to have no ethics at all. Come to think of it, I mused as I walked, that whole episode might be worthy of some oblique reference in my analysis of power in the dissertation.

I was a little early for the meeting as I had an appointment with our current department chair, Dr. Adelaide Winters, Professor of Women and Religion. I counted Adelaide as a friend as well as a colleague, but she was one tough cookie when it came to standards in her department. I was there to report on my dissertation progress. Fortunately, I had some.

I trudged up the steep flights of stairs to the third floor. No one who cared about personal safety took the elevator, and I headed down the corridor toward the large office at the end. All the office doors were closed, and it seemed very quiet. That would change when the meeting started.

I knocked, and Adelaide's gravel voice called "Come in!" I opened the door and saw her seated behind her desk across the room, her gray, frizzled hair lit up with a blue and green halo from the last of the sun's rays coming through the stained glass window above her.

She had just celebrated her 60th birthday. She'd shut down any idea of a celebration for that and gone away for the weekend. I hadn't seen her in more than a month.

"Hello, Kristin," she said wryly, aware I was assessing her as I crossed the room. She'd had a health scare last semester, but there was good color in her face that I didn't think was just the light from the stained glass.

"Come on, I'm fine. Let's sit," she said walking briskly around her desk toward a couch and chairs arrangement she had fixed up against one wall. I saw a carafe on the table. The ugly demon of caffeine temptation rose up in me, and I tried to squelch it.

"Hello, Adelaide," I said, forcing my gaze away from the carafe. She had lost a few pounds, I saw, and was moving easily.

I took a seat.

"Tea?" she asked, watching my face, and then she laughed her deep laugh that I liked so much.

"Lord, look at you. Well, you're not the only one who is trying to give up caffeine," she said and poured out two mugs. I could smell it. Drat. Chamomile. "Doc says I have to quit that kind of stimulant. Raises my blood pressure or some damn thing."

I picked up the mug she pushed toward me and took a sip. Ick.

"So, how's the writing coming?" she asked after her own first swallow. Adelaide did not engage in chit chat.

"Actually, really well now," I said, leaning forward. I described the narrowed focus I had on power given the prison teaching. She frowned at that, but I pre-empted what I thought might be a lecture on "don't get distracted" and launched into a description of my first visit.

"The deadening of feeling was deliberate, Adelaide. I'm sure of it. I think it is an aspect of power and control I had not previously considered. I teach my first class next week, and I'll see how that is or is not affecting the students."

I remembered the warden's contemptuous "so-called students" remark and repeated it to Adelaide.

"Really?" she commented, leaning forward, her hands holding her steaming mug.

"Yes. And he is quite an odd duck. I looked him up before heading out there, and he has an online degree from a for-profit school but calls himself 'Doctor.' He was a car salesman before doing this prison work. First, he asked me if I were a Christian. I got around that, then he turned all hostile to universities and then he brought up the Great Awakening and told me to 'look it up' and so forth. He was increasingly agitated while saying that, and then he just quit and hustled me out the door for a tour."

"Oh, my stars," Adelaide exclaimed in a horrified voice. "Say that again. Just tell me word for word." She put down her tea, picked up an iPad that was on the coffee table between us and started typing while I spoke.

I repeated as well as I could what the warden had said, but I was getting concerned about how agitated she was becoming. And she was gazing at the screen of the device, not at me, her eyes fixed on what she had apparently found online, and she had a red flush on her cheeks.

"Look," she said, passing over the iPad that had a website open on it. "He's one of those QAnon conspiracy nutcases. Those are their codewords to test whether someone else is a 'believer.' You've heard of it, right?"

"Well, yes, sort of. I mean it's a fringe element, right?"

"Kristin, don't be naïve. The fringe has moved to the center," Adelaide said in a harsh voice.

I took the pad. The website was one of those new sort of "news" sites, and the headline was "How to Spot if Someone is a QAnon Conspiracist."

I scanned the article and sure enough these conspiracists had infiltrated deeply into white, Christian evangelical churches. So "are you a Christian?" might make sense as a question. And they did use terms like "great awakening" and "look it up" and so forth when challenged. I read on, and my stomach turned over. Apparently 17% of Americans now believed that "Satan-worshipping elites" were running a child sex ring. There was mention of cannibalism and the usual "running our country behind the scenes" kind of screeds.

"I had thought this was just a wacko thing, Adelaide. I mean this is Hillary Clinton and 'Pizzagate', right?"

"Yes, but as you see, incredible as it seems, 'wacko', as you call it, is spreading." She put the iPad down on the coffee table like it hurt to hold it. "It gives these people a sense of control in a world that is radically changing. The success of the Black Lives Matter demonstrations, human rights legislation that protects LGBTQI people and the increasingly non-white US population as well as threats from disease and climate change have all combined to literally, I think, make a group of people substitute this kind of conspiracy theory for reality."

She tapped a finger on the iPad.

"And you're telling me the warden of a prison is apparently part of this conspiracy. It makes sense, in a messed up way. White males who crave authoritarianism are the most drawn to it."

She fixed me with her eyes.

"This is dangerous, Kristin."

I sat and thought for a couple of minutes.

"Yes, Adelaide, but apparently this is what the abuse of power looks like today, right?"

"I should have known," she said, sitting back with a sigh. "Far from putting you off, this is becoming an investigation-slash-dissertation for you."

"Don't worry so much. I'll read up on this and take care. I'll be fine."

"Oh, if I had a nickel for every time you've said that to me," she snorted. "And drink your damned tea."

❀ ❀ ❀

I HAD ESCAPED MOST of the tea drinking by telling Adelaide I had to go check my mail, and I'd return her mug later. She'd nodded, but I hadn't fooled her. I dumped the tea out my window after checking there was no one entering our building who could get showered by herb tea.

After dispensing with the tea, I sat down in my half of a divided office and turned on the computer. Our downsized department still had too few single offices, but currently I was not sharing. That would change when the new colleague arrived.

Our newest hire, Dr. Aduba Abubakar, who was Associate Professor of African Diaspora and Islamic Studies, had shared with me for a short time and then moved to a larger, single office down the hall. That large office had been occupied for decades by the Professor of Judaism, Hercules Abraham, who had graciously ceded it to him as he now only taught one class. Since he was over eighty, that was a lot. Rabbi Emily Gershman, Jane's wife, also taught a class in "Contemporary Jewish Thought" that was very popular.

I typed "QAnon" into my browser. Dozens of articles popped up. I read several, and it became clearer that this was the emergence of a new religion. It had all the hallmarks: prophecy of a coming end times, a savior figure (the former president), and "secret knowledge" that only the elect had.

I sat back in my chair. This is a new version of the Millerites, I realized. I taught about that movement in my "Religion in America" class. At another time of great upheaval in the country, the first half of the 19th century, Baptist Minister William Miller predicted the world would come to an end on March 21, 1844. That clearly didn't happen and Miller's prediction became known as the "Great Disappointment." Then another Millerite preacher bumped the date forward to October 22, 1844. The Second Coming didn't happen then either.

That didn't stop them. As I knew from teaching about the Millerites and the Second Day Adventists who sort of adopted it, it is very hard to give up an energizing conspiracy that gives you permission to do and say pretty much anything. Far from admitting they were wrong, the leaders of the Millerite conspiracy just decided that the event had happened, only in heaven.

I made a few notes and put them in my "Religion in America" file. I'd certainly add that to the class. Then I looked up and realized our meeting was about to start. I locked up my office, though it was pointless as all the doors opened with the same key, and headed down to the big seminar room we used for meetings.

Aduba was sitting at the head of the table as he chaired the search committee, and he glanced up and said a warm "Hello" when I entered. We'd become friends last year in a time of terrible turmoil on campus, and our sons had had frequent playdates. He had come to us from his home in Nigeria via a time at Oxford. He had close-cropped black hair and a well-trimmed black beard and mustache. I noticed a few gray hairs in his beard that I'd not seen before. Teaching here had probably done that to him. But his dark, copper-colored skin was still unlined and his go-to stress move of a muscle clenching in his cheek was absent as he looked down through his horn-rimmed glasses at a file in front of him.

Aduba was tall and broad-shouldered so even seated he towered over the man sitting next to him, Donald Willie.

Donald was Associate Professor of Psychology of Religion. He sat in his usual spot to the left of whomever was chairing a meeting. I thought he had kind of a "left hand of God" thing going on, but my field was not psychology, so perhaps he just liked to face the door. He was a weedy, little, white guy, but from what had happened last year with white supremacists on campus, he was increasingly figuring out that some white guys could be dangerous. I still did not have a lot of respect for him. He was one of those people who couldn't seem to care about something harmful unless it was actually happening to them. But still, I no longer insulted him every chance I got. I wondered if it would be productive to ask Donald about QAnon. You had to wade through a lot of Jungian word salad to get at what Donald thought, but it might be worth it.

Right then, I just smiled a greeting at both Aduba and Donald and headed for a chair.

The door opened behind me, and I heard a soft, French-accented voice. Oh, good, Hercules had decided to attend. He was talking to Adelaide about "a small gathering only, *et bien*, and when one is as young as you . . . " Hercules had been upset Adelaide had not wanted a birthday celebration. He must still be trying to bring it off. I turned and greeted them.

Adelaide just patted him on the back but did not reply. Smart. Hercules was as compassionate a person as I'd ever met, a refugee from the Holocaust, but he was also extremely stubborn. He'd come back to a topic again and again. I didn't think it was senility, it was strategy.

They both sat down.

Aduba had a stack of file folders in front of him, and he handed them out. We'd already decided the new hire would be in Ethics, the field of the former, deceased chair. I had agreed with that, even though I still felt a little chill about what that guy had done.

We had whittled the long list of possible candidates down to three, and those resumes were in the folders that Aduba now handed around the table.

Three of us had agreed to present one candidate each, then we would rank them and invite them to come to campus, give an address to the college, and go through interviews. Standard procedures. I had volunteered to present Nia Zendaya Turner, a Womanist ethicist who had both a BA and a JD from Harvard and a PhD from Claremont. I had emailed Aduba I wanted to go last. It was a negotiation tactic. Speak last and people remember better. I didn't tell him the latter.

Aduba called on Donald who opened the folder and started extolling the merits of Dr. Nigel Wilson, Kings Church, Oxford whose field was "Moral Philosophy."

"First, we need to have an international presence on this faculty," Donald said, apparently oblivious to the fact that he was sitting between Aduba Abubakar from Nigeria and Hercules Abraham from France.

"Another international presence, you mean, Donald?" Adelaide interrupted, her lips pursed and her eyes narrowed. It was a good thing for Donald she was across the wide table from him, I thought.

"What?" he said, looking up, and then it seemed to dawn on him that he had insulted both the most senior and respected member of our department and the internationally recognized scholar chairing the meeting.

"Yes, yes, certainly, that's what I meant," he burbled. Then he droned on a while, but I paid no attention.

Aduba's deep voice saying, "Thank you, Dr. Willie," woke me up a little, and he called on Adelaide. She was presenting Dr. Sandra Ellen Parker, an environmental ethicist who had trained both at the well-recognized environmental studies program at the University of Colorado, and then at Vanderbilt. Since we were all going to freeze and fry alternatively in the not too distant future, I thought her work very important as well. Adelaide made a great case for her work.

My turn.

"Dr. Turner has two books to her credit," I began since the other candidates only had one each and publication still ruled our diminished academic lives.

"She has edited a widely used reader called *Womanist Ethics*, and just recently published *Survive to Prevail: Womanist Ethics and the Politics of Death* that won the Harvard Distinguished Book Award. She is constantly in demand as a speaker both for colleges and universities, and she occasionally is interviewed on television news for her views of the current crises this country faces." I went on covering some of those events, and then made a strong pitch for "the person we need right now."

Aduba opened the meeting for discussion, and we argued for two hours. Donald insisted that "Womanism is a made-up word" and that there wasn't that much interest in the environment. Hercules countered him quite sharply on that, saying that he would like for his great-grandchildren to be able to breathe in the future. I thought he might even get out the photos of his great-grandchildren as he often did, but he stuck to arguing for Parker.

Aduba pointed out that Womanism was a global field now and that we would garner great interest for the department by hiring such a well-known, national figure.

"Given the times, hiring an African American will make much sense," he argued. Adelaide nodded, I thought also seeing the advantages to her department of national recognition.

"Well, I mean, the African part, you can handle that, right?" Donald commented, speaking to Aduba.

Aduba's large shoulders rotated so that he completely faced Donald, a grim expression on his face.

Donald immediately realized he'd stepped in it.

"Well, no, I mean, not really, of course, just that you know . . . " He trailed off and looked down at his folders.

Finally we all just ran out of steam, and Aduba called for a vote. We ranked them Turner, Parker, Wilson, as I'd known we would several hours earlier.

Exhausted, I trudged home in the dark with the remaining university toilers.

I opened the front door and heard sobbing coming from the front living room.

I dropped everything in the hall and dashed into the room.

Victoria Layne was sitting on the sofa, crying. Her face wasn't just red, she had the beginning of a bruise on her cheek, and she was cradling her left arm. She had a blanket around her, and Kelly was sitting next to her, an arm cradling her shoulders. Tom was sitting in an armchair facing them, holding his stethoscope and looking very concerned. Giles sat in the other armchair, a grim expression on his face.

Carol and the boys were mercifully not there.

"What?" I asked the room.

1 1

When women are disobedient, they disrespect the power hierarchy.
That means they are no longer sacred and, therefore,
violence against them has a "just cause."

—SUSAN THISTLETHWAITE

Victoria raised her drowned eyes to me and then dropped them to
her lap.

"I'm sorry, Kristin. I just had nowhere else to go," she whispered.

I crossed over to the couch and sat on her other side, opposite Kelly.
I could see Tom's and Giles's faces more clearly from here. Tom had his
concerned doctor face on. Giles had masked his face, but I knew violence
of any kind was very disturbing to him, given what I suspected he had
been through in Senegal.

"You are in the right place," I said quietly and met Tom's eyes. He
looked at Kelly.

"Kel, you want to tell Kristin what has happened up to now?"

Kelly sat up straight and looked at me over Victoria who was bent
over, still crying a little, but who seemed mostly to be shivering.

"So the doorbell rang, and it was Victoria. She had no coat or shoes
on, and I could see she was really cold and had been hit in the face."
I could see from Kelly's narrowed eyes that she was furious about that,
but she was keeping it out of her voice so as not to further traumatize
Victoria. I gave her a slight nod.

"I brought her in to the living room here," she went on still keeping
her voice matter-of-fact, "and I put an afghan over her shoulders. Then I

went to get Giles and Carol. Then Dad came home." Kelly gave Victoria a gentle hug with the arm that was behind her shoulders.

"You're safe now, Victoria," she said quietly.

"Thank you, Kelly," Victoria whispered, and Kelly just nodded, her brown eyes serious as they looked at me.

I thought she had acted very maturely. It was clear she was so much Tom's daughter. Compassionate and calm.

"Yes, Kel-ly came to us," Giles picked up the story on cue, "and whispered there was a problem. Carol took the boys upstairs to our apartment for frozen pizza," he grimaced at that admission. "I called you on your cell, Kristin, but it did not pick up."

Oh, no. I had silenced my phone for the meeting and forgotten to turn it back on. I glanced at my bag sitting out in the hall but stayed put.

"And I came here to see," Giles continued, "and then Doctor Tom arrives."

"My last surgery was cancelled, and I got home early," Tom said, picking up the thread, "and I saw that Victoria here was not feeling well." He nodded at her, and she smiled a tremulous smile.

"I asked her if she wanted to go the emergency room, which is still my recommendation by the way, and she refused. So I did a little check with her permission to look for shock and to see how bad her injuries were. Her face and arm are bruised, but I don't think there are broken bones. She had no shoes, and her socks were not much protection from the cold and the pavement, so I had her soak her feet in warm water and now they are wrapped. I did recommend she keep drinking that hot tea with lots of sugar." He looked pointedly at the big mug in front of Victoria on the coffee table. Kelly picked it up and helped Victoria get hold of it with one hand.

Victoria seemed to have calmed some with this round-robin recitation of what had happened, and she took a good swallow of the warm, sweet liquid.

"I am so sorry to be so much trouble," she said, putting the mug back down.

"It's no trouble, Victoria," I said. "I'd like to hear what brought you here and how you got injured. Perhaps, Kelly and Giles, you could leave Victoria with Tom and me while she tells her story?"

"Sure," Kelly said. "Giles and I heard what happened already." She stood up slowly, clearly trying not to jar Victoria and spoke to her.

"That Trevor guy is a jerk, Victoria," Kelly said sternly.

"Yes, indeed very much so. *Cochon*," Giles concurred, and they left.

A jerk in English and a pig in French. Seemed to be a good assessment to me of whoever had done this to a young woman.

Victoria lifted her chin and turned a little to face me.

"Trevor, well, he's my boyfriend, or maybe, was my boyfriend. He lost his job, and he's been staying at my apartment. He has been bugging me to charge you more for the wedding planning, Kristin. I explained over and over that it was a contract for a set fee, and you'd paid a retainer up front. He made me give him that money, and he kept pushing me to call you and text you, and he said that then I could tell you I had to increase the fee because I was doing all this extra work."

Victoria seemed to shrink a little into the back of the sofa. I picked up the mug and handed it to her so she would take another drink. She took a sip and put it down again. Her face, except the cheek where there was already a darkening bruise, was turning red from embarrassment. She started to talk faster and faster, like she wanted to get the words out of her while she could.

"So I did, but you didn't want that, and why would you? I told that to Trevor right before dinner tonight, and he got so mad. He slapped me, and I fell against the table. That's how I hurt my arm. He pushed me out the front door and closed and locked it behind me. I had no coat, no shoes, no purse, no cell phone, no keys, no money, no nothing. I called for him to let me back in, but he just yelled bad names at me and didn't open the door.

"I only live three miles from you, Kristin, and I walk a lot. I thought if I walked fast I could make it. I know you have been a Chicago policewoman, and I thought you would know what I should do."

She put her arms around herself and rocked back and forth.

I put my arm around her back like Kelly had done and looked over at Tom. What now? his expression said.

"Well," I said lightly, "Kelly and Giles are right. Trevor is a jerk and a pig. I need to ask you what you want right now, Victoria. Trevor has assaulted you and taken your property. You could file a police complaint against him."

I felt her physically seem to get smaller.

"Oh, no, no, no. I couldn't do that," she said closing her eyes and shaking her head.

I'd expected that. Pretty typical for abused women not to want to file a report.

"I just want him to go away. I want my stuff, and I don't want to be afraid like I have been. I just want it to end."

"I'm sure you do," I said calmly.

I picked up the mug of tea and handed it to her to drink some more while I thought.

"Here's what I propose," I said, taking my arm from behind her and sitting so now I was facing her.

"Give me your address, and I will go to your apartment. I will get your purse, keys, phone and all the rest, get Trevor to leave and get the locks changed. You can stay here for a couple of days in our guest room while you heal."

Victoria stared at me with those big, brown, Bambi eyes. No wonder Trevor had pegged her as an easy mark.

"He won't do that. He won't leave," she said jerkily.

"Oh, he will, Victoria, you let me worry about that."

Mentally I was already making a list. I'd need to call Vince's old friend Victor, the locksmith, and get my voice activated recorder, my stun gun and my Taser.

"Well, if you think you can talk him into that, it would be great," she said letting out a breath. "And could you bring my laptop computer?" she asked hesitantly. "He might try to sell it or something."

"I think I can get him out of your house, and I'll definitely get the computer," I said, but now I was watching Tom's face. His eyebrows were nearly in his hair.

"So, Victoria, can you walk?" I asked, looking back at her. She still had white, fluffy towels wrapped around her feet.

"I think so, and Kelly brought me these fuzzy slippers of hers." She actually giggled a little as she leaned down and picked up two big, Fozzie Bear slippers. Given that Kelly was probably a foot taller than Victoria, I thought they would work with her swollen feet.

"Okay, good," I said. She pulled off the towels and started to fold them.

"No, just give those to me," I said and took them into the downstairs powder room.

When I got back, she had the slippers on, and Tom had a hand under her good arm. We went down the hall to the kitchen. Giles was there, stirring a pot on the stove. It smelled like Italian wedding soup. Mama Ginelli had given him the recipe, I knew.

"So, Giles, I'm going out for a little while. Victoria will stay here. She'll stay the night in the guest room."

"Yes, that is fine. And Vic-tor-ia, this is good soup," Giles said over his shoulder. "I will serve in a few minutes. Carol and the boys can come down. The boys will eat this too, not just that cardboard pizza," he said, his voice very firm.

"Oh, thank you," Victoria said, and she took a seat at the kitchen table.

Tom and I walked back down the central hall.

"I need to get some things from the safe in the bedroom closet," I told him.

"I'm coming with you," he said in a voice I knew meant he had made up his mind.

I turned at the stairs and looked up at him.

"You want a piece of Trevor too, I take it?" I said, only half joking.

Tom didn't laugh.

"I want to be there," he said.

Before we left, I called Victor, the retired locksmith. He answered in his Russian-accented voice and assured me he could "fix the little lady up." I gave him the address and a time he should be there. He'd been an informant for Vince when Vince had been a detective, and after Victor got out of prison, Vince had helped him get started in the legitimate locksmith business. At least, I hoped it was legitimate, and anyway, he was mostly retired.

❖ ❖ ❖

VICTORIA'S APARTMENT WAS THE TOP half of a two-story, row house, a typical Chicago design. We parked a little ways down the street. I didn't want to alert ole Trevor. We climbed the wooden stairs that could use a coat of paint.

Before I knocked on the door, however, I turned on my voice-activated recorder. It was clipped to the top of my large tote bag that also held my Taser and stun gun within easy reach. I pushed the on button for the stun gun, and it hummed.

I knocked timidly at the door.

"Trevor," I called in a very high, frightened voice. "Let me in now?" I wasn't that good a mimic, but Trevor would hear what he wanted to hear.

"About damn time," he said gruffly and jerked the door open.

"Where the hell . . . .." and then it seemed to dawn on him Tom and I were not his fragile girlfriend.

"Get the f . . . ."

He was interrupted mid-swear as I slammed the door with my shoulder, and it banged fully open.

"Hello, Trevor," I said for the recorder. "You are Trevor Maddox, right?"

"Yeah, and why you want to know that, bitch?" Trevor said in a very unwelcoming voice. Tom stepped up behind me. Between the two of us, we had about two feet in height on Trevor, but he was no lightweight. From the size of his shoulders, I assumed he worked out. What else did he have to do since he didn't have a job?

"I'm Kristin Ginelli, the woman you wanted Victoria Layne to charge more for our wedding planning than the contract stated, right? How much more do you need?" I spoke conversationally, hoping he'd admit he'd pushed her to get more money.

His blue eyes lit up at the word "need."

"Yeah, well, I mean it's a lot of work, and you're rich. I checked. You're really rich. You can afford it, and well, about five more large ones would do it."

Trevor wasn't bright, that was clear.

"So you hit Victoria to make her up the price? Is that right? And then you threw her out of this apartment, which is hers, by the way, with no coat, no shoes, no purse, no cell phone and caused her to nearly freeze?"

"I don't know what that bitch told you, but she had it coming to her, and yeah she was giving me crap about some contract. You need to pay more, that's a fact. And well then she stormed out."

"Right. So you wanted to defraud me on a legal contract, you committed assault and forced an injured young woman out into the freezing cold with no coat or shoes or a way to get help, is that right?"

"Can't prove a damn thing. I told ya, that little chickie had it coming and, anyway, she won't say a thing against me, so that's that."

"True, Trevor, true," I said, keeping a level tone. "But I have everything you've admitted on tape, and my lawyer will make your life a living hell in court when I sue you. I don't need Victoria to say a thing."

"The hell you say!" he burst out, and he grabbed for my tote that was still on my shoulder. The stun gun was on the top, already set to the lowest setting. I just reached in and pressed the button a second before Trevor stuck his hand in.

"Christ! Ouch! What you got there? You're crazy!" he yelled, pulling his hand back and shaking it from the little shock I'd given him.

I felt Tom move up closer behind me, but per my request in the car as we drove over, he didn't intervene.

In any case, stupidly violent Trevor was almost no challenge.

As Trevor lunged for my tote again, I stepped back, reached in and got the Taser. I flipped the switch to on and held it pointing at his genitals. My Taser says "Taser" on the side. Apparently Trevor could read. He stopped abruptly and threw his hands over the target area.

"Okay, Trev, this is how this is going to go," I said, keeping the Taser pointed at him. "You're going to give me Victoria's keys, her purse and her phone, and your wallet."

"Why my wallet?" he yelled, outraged, but still staring at the orange Taser in my hand.

"Because you stole from her, you miserable excuse for a human being. I'll leave you a little cash, but the rest is surely money she earned. Whatever you haven't spent yet. We also need to check for her credit cards because I bet they're now in your wallet."

He gingerly removed one protective hand and pulled his wallet out from his back pocket and threw it on the floor. What a juvenile, I thought.

"Pick it up and hand it to me," I said calmly, not moving the Taser.

"Shit, okay, right," he said. His pale face was mottled with rage that I supposed he was used to discharging with his fists.

He bent slowly, and I could actually see when he decided to try to take the Taser from me in the way his back muscles tensed up.

I took another step back just as he lunged up. I kicked him in the crotch, and he fell to his knees, moaning.

"Try that again, and I will let you feel this," I said, moving the Taser up and down slightly.

Still on his knees, he picked up the wallet from the floor and handed it up to me. Then he scooted back and got up leaning on the chair that was pulled out from the table.

I handed the wallet over my shoulder to Tom.

"Get your stuff," I said, gesturing with the Taser. I could see there was a laptop open on the table. Trev had been using Victoria's computer. I knew it was hers as the cover was decorated with applique flowers and little hearts. Her purse was open on a chair next to the one where Trevor was sitting and panting. He really was a wimp. I hadn't kicked him that hard.

"I took Victoria's credit cards out of his wallet." Tom said from behind me. "He's got just short of 500 dollars in here."

"Leave him fifty," I said. He'd need shelter for the night, and I wasn't willing to do to him what he'd done to Victoria by shoving her out into the freezing night with nothing. I'd put the cash back in her wallet before I'd give it to her tonight, however.

Trevor made a big show of getting up slowly from the chair and hobbling into the bedroom. I just watched him through the open door. He was muttering obscenities, and he started shoving some shirts and a pair of pants that had been on the floor into a large backpack. I watched him as he came close to what must be Victoria's little jewelry box on the of the dresser.

He glanced back to see if I were looking.

"No, no, no, Trevor. Not yours," I said like I was talking to Molly.

"You . . . ." he muttered. I chose not to hear what he was calling me.

"Victoria's purse has her cell phone and a key ring," Tom said. I knew he'd gone over to the table to check that. It was like working a crime scene with an efficient partner.

"Get your coat and get out," I said to Trevor who was standing in the bedroom clearly scanning it for anything he could slip out and sell.

More muttered curse words accompanied his grabbing a worn, plaid, woolen jacket off of a chair. He shrugged it on and pulled a strap of the backpack over one shoulder.

"Happy now?" he said, spitting the words out.

"No, not quite. You will not come back here. You will not contact Victoria. She will change her cell number and her email address. New locks will be installed tonight and her car re-keyed. If you come anywhere near her, I will take this tape to the police, and I will also start a civil suit against you. I will sue you for so much money, you will always live in poverty. Get it?"

"You rich bitches think you can do anything to anybody, don't you?" he countered, but I could see the calculation in his eyes. He got it.

"Get it?" I repeated. "Say yes, Trevor, and you can go."

"Yeah, I get it, but what you don't get is there's lots of needy girls like Vicki, and I can just get another one."

I didn't reply to that. I knew he was right.

I just gestured to the door with the Taser. I watched him go down the stairs and saw a beat-up, maroon Chevy Malibu pull up. Victor the locksmith was right on time.

❁ ❁ ❁

I DROVE VICTORIA'S PINK and silver MINI Cooper back to the house, and Tom drove my car. I doubted Tom could have driven the MINI with his long legs, and I was a very tight fit. We met up at the garage behind the house, and I was able to move a pile of toys on the left side so I could fit her tiny car in. I parked it, and it looked like a toy itself.

We went in the back door and entered the kitchen. Victoria and Kelly were sitting at the kitchen table over two empty plates of Carol's cobbler.

They both stood up when Tom and I came in, Victoria a little slowly.

"What happened?" she asked in a shaky voice.

"Yeah," Kelly chimed in. "Did you have to kick his butt?" Kelly and I both studied Tae Kwon Do, and she knew I could have done that.

"No, it wasn't necessary," I said, and it wasn't really a lie. It wasn't his butt I had kicked. Tom placed Victoria's computer on the kitchen table, and I put her purse on top of it and handed her the new keys to her apartment and her car.

"Really?" she said joyfully. "How?"

"I can be really persuasive, Victoria, let's leave it at that. I did tell Trevor if he did try to contact you again, I would sue him, and I think he got the message."

"Oh," she said. I watched her face. For a moment, I could see that even then she might have taken him back if he'd said the right words. I thought after she moved back to her place I'd suggest a good domestic violence counselor I knew to her. But the odds of her following up on that were very slim. And the odds on her telling me if Trevor got in touch again were also pretty slim.

I sighed.

They hook them by holding out the promise of love, I thought. And I briefly wondered if she'd go back to him even so, or find another Trevor. She would without counseling, of that I was certain.

"Well, hey, that's terrific," Kelly responded, and she high-fived both her father and me. I silently wished Kelly would continue to have the self-confidence she had built in these last couple of years. And with a black belt, I thought wryly, she could fight back.

Victoria looked completely spent.

"Come on," I said to her. "I'll give you a couple of Tylenol, and you will feel so much better in the morning."

I carried Victoria's laptop up to the guest room for her. Tom brought the small suitcase of her clothes and toiletries I'd packed after the new lock on her apartment door had been installed. Kelly brought the purse.

We set her things on the bed in the guest room. I came back with the Tylenol and a glass of water.

"It will be better in the morning, Victoria," I said.

She just nodded wearily, and I closed the door.

❋ ❋ ❋

As I WALKED DOWN the long, central hall to our bedroom, I wondered what Tom had thought of the whole evening. He had done exactly as I had asked, but it was the first time he'd seen the cop version of me in action.

I shut the bedroom door behind me. He was sitting on the bed, and he got up and came over to me. He started unbuttoning my blouse.

"I don't know what it says about me, or you, but that was the sexiest thing I have ever seen," he said in a low, husky voice.

I undid the buttons on his shirt as a reply.

12

The nature of the criminal justice system has changed. It is no longer
primarily concerned with the prevention and punishment of crime,
but rather with the management and control of the dispossessed.

—MICHELLE ALEXANDER

Victoria had been with us for four days, and now she was packing
up to leave.

Her natural exuberance had slowly returned. I thought Molly had
helped a lot with that. Victoria had regained the use of her arm enough
to work on her wedding business online while sitting at the kitchen table.
But she had flatly refused to change her cell phone number and her email
address.

"My clients need that information!" she had protested when I had
brought it up for the third time sitting across from her at the table. Since
she had admitted I was her only client, I doubted it.

"And if Trevor wants to contact me, he just has to go to my website
anyway!" she had said firmly, but her head was bent over Molly's head
that was on her lap when she said it.

I pushed over a piece of paper with the name and contact information of the best domestic violence counselor I knew.

"At least make an appointment to see Jacqueline," I said encouragingly.

"I'm fine now, Kristin," she had said, but she did take the paper and
put it in her pocket.

Finally she was ready to leave. I tried to give her another advance on
the wedding planning contract, but I got another "I'm fine, Kristin" so I
gave up on that. I had noticed her carrying quite a few sealed containers

of food out to her car. Giles had cooked what looked like a couple of weeks of food. He knew what she was up against, and he knew how to provide help she would accept.

I walked her out to her tiny car and encouraged her to "call and text frequently." God help me.

I walked slowly back to the house. I still had a lot of work to do to prepare for the first class at the prison. It was tomorrow, and I was still vacillating on how to approach it.

❈ ❈ ❈

It's a class, I told myself as I drove east on the dreary, expensive highway toward the prison. Approach it like any other class. Except it would be behind prison walls.

I could see the circle of buildings with the brick, New England style church in the center across the winter-scoured fields. The church seemed more ominous to me this time, knowing what I did about the warden with his fake doctorate and his QAnon delusional beliefs. I wondered about the compulsory chapel. I suspected he used that for indoctrination.

The same beefy, white guy #1 came out of the gatehouse when I pulled up to the tall, razor-wire topped, chain-link fence gate. We went through the same procedure. Then metal scraped and whined as the gate slid open, and I drove in. I took back my credentials. He waved me on and went back into the little house. Beefy, white guy #2 came out of what I now knew was the administration building to escort me to parking and take my key fob. #1 and #2 actually looked a lot alike, I realized this time, not just in their body habitus and their likely steroid-induced, high-pitched voices, but their faces. I wondered if they were actually brothers, or even twins, like the twins ratting out the El Chapo gang.

That made me remember I had an appointment later in the week with Paul Lindsay of the FBI. I'd let Vince know that yesterday, and I'd told him I would come out to see him at the RV park before the weekend. He'd sounded old and dispirited on the phone. Old Yitz had nothing more, he'd said in a monotone.

As I followed beefy, white guy #2, I realized I was pulling back from where I was, already retreating from the reality of the prison. I tried to focus. I would need to be totally present to the women in the class. They deserved no less.

But it was astonishingly hard. Beige walls, clanking doors, the hiss of the speaker on the window of the woman with the electrocuted hair, all of the suppressive atmosphere rolled in like a brain fog.

You had to actually use mental energy to resist it, I realized.

"I need to search your bag," beefy, white guy #2 said. I had brought a shoulder bag big enough for my class notes, copies of the syllabus and the list of students, and a bottle of water that attached to the outside in a sleeve. Beefy, white guy #2 actually tested the cap to see if it was an unopened bottle. It was.

Officer Quisha Jackson met me and beefy, white guy #2 right outside the door that led from the administration building to the rest of the so-called "campus."

"Ginelli, over to you," he said with his high-pitched voice.

Officer Jackson said, "Acknowledged." Beefy, white guy #2 departed.

I saw she looked thinner, and the skin of her face sagged a little. It had not been that long ago since I'd seen her. I wondered if she'd had the flu that Ivy had. Then I wondered whether I could catch it. I'd had a flu shot at the beginning of the winter, but didn't they wear off?

The brain fog was encroaching. I tried to shake it off.

"Hello, Officer Jackson," I said.

She just nodded and turned toward Building C.

"How are you?" I risked asking, though she was giving off every sign of not wanting to talk. She was not looking at me, her shoulders were tense, and she started walking very fast, trying to stay ahead of me. Walking too fast didn't work as my legs were probably twice as long as hers. I easily kept up with her.

"Fine," she said flatly, still not looking at me. But then she went on.

"I see you have an unopened bottle of water. Good. Don't drink or eat anything from inside this campus. Nothing."

"Okay," I said, but I thought about beefy, white guy #2's fingers touching the cap. Good thing I had some antiseptic wipes in my bag.

❖ ❖ ❖

As I CROSSED THE MAIN room of "C," following Officer Jackson who was still setting quite a pace, the room quieted as before, but I thought I detected a slight lowering of tension. Women looked up, and a couple even nodded.

I hustled after Officer Jackson into the smaller room off of the library. The craft materials had been put away. She continued to ignore me and just took a seat in the far left corner, crossing her arms over her chest. She was so rigid and her face was so deliberately devoid of expression, I thought she looked like she belonged with the statues on Easter Island.

I put my bag on the table and started taking out my notes and two class lists: the one with just the names I had made for myself, and the one the warden's office had sent with all the additional detail on backgrounds, offenses, time left to serve, religious affiliations if any and reason for being in the program. I had done my own research on each of the names. The warden had left a lot out about these women.

I planned to get the class used to a seminar method by having each woman introduce herself to me by name and describe her religious affiliation if she chose to say. Then I planned to ask what she had liked best about Dr. Mercer's class.

"Will you be staying for the whole class?" I asked conversationally of Officer Jackson. She had been looking down at her phone, and she visibly jumped.

"We'll see," she replied, not looking up.

Her presence in the room would alter the teaching dynamics substantially, I thought, and not for the better if she stayed the whole time.

The class didn't start for another fifteen minutes, so I took the time to write my name on the board behind me along with the three questions I had for them. I had brought my own marker, having noticed there had not been any when I last visited the room.

Behind me I heard footsteps, and the women started to file in. I should have realized they would be escorted to the class and not just show up on their own. Another regimented aspect of this place where bodies were moved around like those large, outdoor chess sets.

I counted eight women, and that matched the list I had been given. The guard who had escorted them nodded to Officer Jackson and departed.

"Please sit down," I said when it dawned on me they were still standing behind their chairs. Eight chairs were pulled out, metal legs screeching on the composite tile floor.

"Hello, my name is Kristin Ginelli, and I am taking over Dr. Ivy Mercer's class."

A hand shot up.

"Yes?" I said, nodding at the fortyish, white woman who seemed to have a question.

"She dead?" she asked in a gruff voice.

"Yes, she died," I said quietly.

"Why?" the woman continued, her faded blue eyes locked on mine.

"That's enough, Wiley," Officer Jackson said sharply.

"No, it's fine, Officer Jackson. I'll answer the question," I said firmly. I'd never get anywhere with this class if Jackson could dictate what I could or could not say.

Officer Jackson sat back in her chair. Her face took on a grim look, but she said nothing further.

"Dr. Mercer had the flu, and she collapsed in her apartment. She died before the paramedics could reach her. My understanding is that it was ruled a death by natural causes."

Several pairs of eyes were boring into me as I said this. It wasn't just grief. It looked more like cynicism. These were people who were likely to assume they were being lied to, I thought. And I guessed they weren't often wrong.

"Anyway, you can see I have written my name on the board behind me and some questions I have for you. Please tell me your name, what religion you are if you are religious, and what you liked best about Dr. Mercer's class."

There were some nods, but most just sat there and looked at me.

I turned to the woman seated directly to my right with a heart-shaped face and an eye patch.

"Would you please start?"

"*Certainement*, I am Fabiola Aime. I am from Haiti, and I am Christian, *n'est pas*, but also we Haitians, we know the Vodou for honoring the ancestors and for healing the people. The white man, he says the Vodou is witchcraft, but it is very spiritual."

A distinct snort was heard down the table. Fabiola gave a side-eye glance at that, but she went on.

"But when you have suffered as I have, you know you need the Jesus and Papa Legba."

She stopped and squinted at the board.

"What else do you want?"

"What did you like about Dr. Mercer's class?" I replied.

"Ah, *oui*. I liked hearing about Harriet Tubman, called Moses. Very fine woman. Many slaves escape."

I knew from reading the information from the prison that Fabiola was in prison for assault, but in looking her up on the Internet, I had found the "assault" was on a man who was guarding her at a brothel in Indiana. She had been sex-trafficked from Haiti at fourteen and been passed around in suburban brothels in Indiana until her escape at seventeen. She'd lost an eye in the fight with the man imprisoning her. Still, she had been convicted of assault.

"*Merci*," I said, smiling at her. "Next," I said nodding at the tall, broad-shouldered, African American woman sitting adjacent to Fabiola.

"I'm Nakeisha X, and I am a proud Muslim. We Muslim women will be leading mosques soon. I know it. Dr. Mercer, she said a lot about Muslims in America long, long ago. Them white idiots think we just come here yesterday."

I'd learned Nakeisha X's legal name was Emma Johnson. That was on the warden's list. What wasn't there was that her father was a Baptist preacher, and she'd been removed from her father's home and put in foster care when he was arrested for sexual abuse of his two daughters. She had aged out of the foster care system at eighteen and was arrested for passing bad checks at nineteen.

"*Shukran*," I said to her in Arabic, my hands together in the traditional "thank you" used in Islam that I'd learned that from Aduba.

The next woman was white, in her mid-twenties with sharp features and so thin her collar bones stuck out through the thin cloth of her T-shirt.

I smiled at her and nodded.

"Sarah Slotkin," she said with little inflection in her voice. "Lapsed Jew, but what Jew wouldn't be after the twentieth century, right? And, what? What did I like? Well, I liked that they tried to stop kids from having to work in coal mines at the age of six, that's for sure."

Sarah had been her college distributor for Vicodin and Oxycontin. Seeing her obvious anorexia and low affect, I thought she might have also been self-medicating for depression.

"Thanks, Sarah. Next," I said nodding at the older, Hispanic woman next to her who seemed to be praying the rosary. She was looking at the beads, not at me.

"Hey, Maria, quit prayin' and pay attention," Nakeisha barked.

"*Que?*" Maria said, clearly startled by the loud voice.

"Would you tell me your name, your religion, and what you liked in this class so far, please?"

"Oh, *si*. Maria Hernandez. *Católica*," she paused. "And other, what is?"

"In the class Dr. Ivy taught, what did you like?"

"All. I liked all," Maria said looking down at her beads.

Mariana Hernandez was forty and no stranger to prison. She had a long list of offenses and several imprisonments primarily for shoplifting, though also pickpocketing, especially wallets and cell phones, and credit card fraud. She had three children living with her mother.

Looking at her, I wondered if the distraction were an act or if she did have trouble focusing. Well, I had trouble focusing after about fifteen minutes inside, I thought.

Another African American woman sat next to Maria. She was very thin and trembling a little. Anxiety, I wondered, or something else?

"Shanice, Shanice Harrison. I'm saved. I was saved by the blood of Christ. It was a miracle. I'm Church of God in Christ, of course. I started going with my boyfriend and one Sunday morning I felt like I was filled with light, and I just went up to the altar and confessed."

"You mean that great boyfriend who got you to take the phone calls for his drug business and got you slammed inside? That boyfriend?" asked a fortyish white woman with a lot of piercings across the table.

"It's a woman's duty to submit to the man," Shanice said, glaring.

I held up a hand as the woman with the piercings started to open her mouth.

"And what did you like so far, Shanice?" I asked firmly.

"Oh, the sermons they preached," Shanice breathed. "Following Jesus is the only government program we need."

Not quite what the Social Gospel reformers preached, but I let it go.

I called on the woman with the piercings next.

"Wiley," she said brusquely. "J.C. Wiley. I'm a Wiccan. I started a coven here in the prison, but those guards," and she glared at Jackson, "they give me all kinds of shit about it. Spy on us."

"That's enough, Wiley," said Jackson, and now I was the one glaring at her. She and I were going to have a talk after class.

Wiley ignored her, turned toward the board and squinted.

"What did I like? Well I liked that Jane Adams. Man she took some shit for pushin' back against war. But got a peace prize, didn't she? That showed'em."

Wiley was also in prison for "assault" but had claimed it was self-defense against rape. It had been in the middle of a robbery, however, as I'd discovered on my own.

I gestured to the older, Hispanic woman next to J.C. She was short with a lined face and piercing dark eyes. I also noticed she had a slight facial tic.

"Isobel Rivera," she said with very little Hispanic accent. "Not Catholic any more. Those priests, they no good, you know? You know what happens to little boys with them?" she asked the table.

There were a couple of "yeahs" and one "hell yeah" from the class.

"And I like that Moses woman too. She didn't stand for that slavery shit, she run, and she take others with her." She nodded firmly. "There's places to run to, you get it? People help you on the way. Hard though, runnin' through woods. Now," and she turned and smirked at Officer Jackson, "if ole Moses woman had had a car, well then, good help close by."

"That's enough, Rivera," Officer Jackson said, though she didn't put much energy into it.

I knew Isobel Rivera had been arrested for driving a shipment of cocaine from Chicago through Indiana. I wondered if she'd been one of El Chapo's mules.

The final student had long, glossy black hair and a pronounced Slavic profile. I knew from the material on her she was forty-five, but she looked younger and almost chic, even in the prison T-shirt and pants. She had been a human trafficker, bringing young women from Russia to brothels in the U.S.

I nodded at her, hoping I could keep my revulsion from showing on my face.

"Anastasia Popov," she said with a slight Russian accent. "Russian Orthodox, at least some of the time," she said in kind of purr.

"What I like?" she said, also squinting at the board. "I like how Amerika is so many immigrants. I am immigrant. I fit right in," and she gave a musical laugh.

I became aware of the body language of most of the other women around the table. They were turning their heads or even their bodies away from Anastasia, not looking at her. There was a palpable revulsion visible. She noticed it and seemed to sneer at it.

Once Anastasia finished speaking, Officer Jackson got up and left the room. Shoulders relaxed all around the table. Good. I wasn't the only one who seemed to feel her absence made the room larger.

I then got out the syllabus. I had extra copies, but all the women had theirs and the books for the remaining weeks of the class. There were several copies of both the Du Bois and Alexander books. Apparently the warden had been too lazy to realize that the books had already been ordered and distributed. I dutifully mentioned that the warden didn't want them to read those.

"Too late," J.C. remarked snidely, and the others nodded except for Anastasia.

I wondered why Anastasia was actually in the class.

I opened my notes and began the lecture.

❊ ❊ ❊

"Officer Jackson," I said as we walked back toward the main administration building. "I would like you to remain outside the classroom when I am teaching. Your presence distracts from the educational context."

I thought I'd use that kind of useless "education-speak" like "educational context" that seemed to go over in authoritarian situations.

She stopped walking, brought her head up sharply and looked me full in the face.

"Who the hell do you think you are?" she asked angrily.

"A teacher," I said firmly. "And I mean what I say."

13

It is said that no one truly knows a nation until one has been inside its jails.

—NELSON MANDELA

T hunder rumbled and shards of ice hit my face as I hurried over to the university campus to meet Alice for a non-coffee, non-smoking get-together. Thunder sleet. Was that even a thing? Apparently it was in early spring in Chicago. I pulled the giant hood of my "best sub-zero parka" further over my face and struggled on. Good thing my coat was all black. If the hood had been white, I might look like one of those "Handmaiden" women.

I stood just inside the warm, fake sunny coffee shop for a moment while the rivulets of melting sleet dripped off my waterproof coat. Then I walked over to the table by the window where I could see Alice sitting, her own damp coat hanging on an extra chair she'd placed in front of the heaters that ran along the wall under the windows. I snagged another extra chair as I walked up and hung mine up next to hers.

"Hey," I said. "Get you anything else?" She already had a cardboard cup in front of her with a tea bag label hanging out.

She slowly raised her head, a distinctly morose look on her face, and just shook her head.

"Okay, I'll be right back." As I waited for my green tea, I wondered if she was so down from the lousy weather, nicotine withdrawal or something else.

"You okay?" I asked as I sat down.

"Nah. Gutierrez. Think maybe he's fixin' to leave. Then who are we gonna get next? Gutierrez is good, sharp. Mel and me, we're worried. Just a feeling. A bad feeling. He won't say, but there's talk. Who knows?"

She was talking about Captain Alfonzo Gutierrez, the head of the campus police. That would be bad if he left. I could see his wrinkled, mustached face in my mind's eye as his back eyes would bore into me. He took nothing off of anybody.

"That'd be awful," I said, taking a sip of the hot tea. We'd already had an investigation of a previous head of campus security who had been involved with a drug dealer. Drugs were such a scourge, I thought, trying not to let my mind go to whether there might or might not be a lead on who killed Marco. Too much pain. I pushed it back where I kept it, not locked but wrapped up so the shards of loss wouldn't constantly tear at me inside.

"You cryin'?" Alice asked abruptly, her brown eyes narrowing at me. "What's with that?"

"No, no, just the bitter cold," I lied, dabbing at my eyes with my napkin. Not so wrapped up as I pretended to myself.

Alice just snorted.

"So, that's my bad news, what's yours?" she said as she took out one of her packs of gum from her pocket, selected a foil-wrapped stick of gum and twirled it. She was getting so good at that.

"Well, I just taught my first class at that women's prison. There's a lot going on there, a lot I don't get."

"You think?" Alice said, narrowing her eyes at me.

"Yeah, yeah. I know, but one thing I do get is that the women in the class, they've been through a lot in their lives. For most of them, though, I think there's no point to their being locked up except to make money for Corrections Group of America. And the place, it's like a factory for suppressing emotion. Even the colors of the walls seem to be designed to shut people down. It shuts me down unless I fight it."

"That so bad?" Alice asked as her brown eyes narrowed. "You and all, you think about stuff a mile a minute, try to get what's goin' on, but what if you were locked up like that all the time? Shut down your brain. That's not such a bad thing then, is it?"

I just stared at her. It occurred to me that if I were locked up like that I would likely go insane. Wouldn't being shut down be preferable?

"I wonder though, Alice," I said finally. "Are they shut down or is all that they are feeling being stored up inside, so when they get out, what happens? Does it start to come out? I know for the ones I think are there for no good reason, they've got to feel a lot of anger, a kind of deep down, smoldering anger. I don't think that goes away."

"No. No. I done think so either." She paused. "My brother now, he behaves so good, he's got a job now, makin' electronic parts or something like that. Assembling them. He likes it. Mama says he's so much better now that he has that job. But he's, you know, simple. Thinkin' is not his thing," she said with a wry smile.

"Well, there's another thing," I said. "The warden is really peculiar. He has a fake doctorate and was a car salesman, but he's bought in to that QAnon conspiracy stuff big time. He asked me questions like he was trying to find out if I bought it too," I said slowly, remembering.

"The what?" Alice asked, frowning.

"It's called QAnon. Yeah, I didn't know much about it either. Adelaide said it's growing. I looked it up and sure enough there's people who believe that Democrats, liberals, people like that are kidnapping children and abusing them and then there's the idea that the former president was trying to save them, and that's why he was forced out. And there's stuff about cannibalism and dates when miraculous political changes will happen like that guy getting to be president again."

"That moron who painted his face orange, wore a wig and was always sayin' racists are like not such bad people? Who'd want him back?" Alice asked angrily.

"Well, they do. They say he's a savior, and a whole bunch of white Christians have bought into it, apparently. And you know, some of them are violent about it, like the ones who attacked the Capitol Building."

"Savior? Savior? They believe this nonsense?" Alice had drawn back in her chair as I was speaking and her facial muscles had frozen in shock.

"Well, those Christians, apparently, you know the white, conservative, racist ones. A lot of racist rhetoric from these people, like you said," I replied slowly, concerned she was holding her breath she was so still.

Alice blew out the breath she was holding, gave one giant snort and leaned forward, her fists on the table.

"Well that's not Christians," she snapped. "That's crap. And you say the warden of this place believes this garbage?" She pointed her stick of gum at me.

"Yes, well, he said their favorite code words, so I think so."

"Dangerous fool," she said. "Of course you wouldn't just get to teach in an ordinary type prison. No, you have to go where the place is run by a nutcase. Suppose he finds out what kind of a liberal type you are and that you are like one of the people they say are runnin' this whatever kidnapping ring? What then?"

"Well, I hadn't quite thought of it that way, Alice, but, you know, people know I am going there and when. What's he going to do to me?"

Alice shook her finger at me. I didn't know people actually did that any more.

"You listen up. There's a lot could happen to you in that place. A lot. And it'd be an 'accident' and all."

I drank some tea and thought about what she was saying. Then I thought I'd better not tell Alice the last teacher of this prison class had died.

"Don't worry so much. If I don't come back when I should, come get me, okay?" I said with a forced chuckle.

Alice snorted so hard the tag on her tea bag fluttered up.

"Don't do me like that, Kristin," she said. "You listen."

"Okay, Alice," I said seriously.

We finished our tea in silence. I didn't think it was such a good idea to tell Alice my plan for the rest of the day was to meet downtown with the FBI.

❀ ❀ ❀

LAKE SHORE DRIVE GLISTENED with the thin layer of ice the sleet storm had deposited there. It was a treacherous road at the best of times as it was a main, north/south artery into the city that ran along the lake. The speed limit was supposed to be forty miles an hour and people routinely drove above sixty. I already had seen two cars that had simply slid off the side of the road on to the narrow stretch of park that led down to the lake. A little further and the drivers might have gotten to the frozen expanse of water.

My Subaru and I chugged along in the slow lane. I was heading for my afternoon meeting with Agent Paul Lindsay, head of the Chicago FBI Cybercrimes Division. When I'd met him in the fall, he had described his work as crimes committed through or with computers. I knew he might not be directly plugged in to the El Chapo investigation, but I had found him efficient and trustworthy. That counted for a lot in my book when dealing with Feds. He said he was going to ask Kamal Nadar to join us. I'd also met him before. I'd thought he was in counterterrorism, but I'd take Paul's word for who needed to be at the meeting.

There was a large parking garage opposite the building where the Chicago FBI offices were located. I pulled in and a took a ticket from the machine. It felt like applying for a small loan. An hour could end up costing me up to fifty dollars. As I searched for a spot, I thought of my lawyer friend, Anna. She just took a limo service everywhere claiming it was cheaper than having a car and parking in the city.

I dashed across the street, but still managed to get quite wet. The sleet had turned to a driving rain. I felt my coat dripping on to the marble floor of the lobby while I gave my license to the security guard and was checked in against a list of approved visitors. By the time the elderly guard had finished scanning, looking at a list, calling to the FBI offices and printing my name badge and card with bar code to get me through the barriers and up the elevators, there was a spreading pool of water around my feet.

I had to check in again in a foyer inside the FBI offices, and this included a fingerprint scan. I didn't blame them for all the security. With what had happened in recent years in our country, the FBI itself had become a major target.

One good thing was I'd been able to leave my coat in a closet off the foyer shown to me by the agent sent to escort me to the meeting. My shoes still squelched as I walked beside him, though he seemed not to notice. He ushered me in to a conference room and said, "The agents will be right with you."

On a credenza along the wall, several insulated carafes stood invitingly. They had little chains and labels around their necks. Not one said "Tea." I went over like I was being pulled by one of those sci-fi tractor beams in the Star Trek movies the kids loved. I filled an insulated cup with "Decaf" and then put in one pump of "Coffee." I totally deserved it, I thought, as I put on the fitted lid.

I'd taken only one sip before Agents Lindsay and Nadar arrived.

"Hello, Kristin," Lindsay said as he sat down. "Nice to see you again."

He was a tall, broad-shouldered, African American man who spoke very slowly and deliberately.

Agent Nadar nodded in a cordial way. I thought he was Arab American, and he seemed to be a man of very few words, event for an FBI agent.

Both agents wore "I'm an FBI Agent" suits, perhaps the same ones I'd seen them in the last time.

"Hello," I said, and my voice sounded thin to me. "Thank you for meeting with me."

"Your help has been invaluable to the Bureau," Agent Nadar said in his deep voice. He looked at me steadily with his large, dark eyes. I noticed his long, dark lashes almost brushed the inside of his glasses. This was like being at the prison, I realized. I was retreating from the situation by focusing on extraneous details.

Lindsay just nodded at that and then said, "Agent Nadar, I wonder if you'd just like to take it from here. This is really your area."

"Thank you, Agent Lindsay," Nadar said, and he turned toward me again, his eyes almost boring into me.

Focus, I told myself. Focus.

"Ms. Ginelli, I have been seconded to the very large task force that is working the El Chapo investigation from many different angles. And, as the El Chapo gang is being broken up, they are branching out into new areas like human trafficking. And worse. Word is it's very nasty."

What was worse than human trafficking? Well, murder I supposed. But murder wasn't new for them, was it?

Agent Nadar cleared his throat. He'd seen my mind was wandering. Not good. He went on.

"We are now reasonably certain your husband, Detective Marco Ginelli, was set up by the man who was his confidential informant, Santiago Lopez. Lopez was killed by a rival member of the gang, we believe, so this is conjecture. He was trying to save his own skin by fingering your husband as there apparently were rumors that he had met with Detective Ginelli. We have narrowed down the possible murderers of your husband to two people."

I felt the blood drain from my face, and I even swayed a little. Close. So close. After all this time.

"Ms. Ginelli," I vaguely heard Agent Lindsay say. "Ms. Ginelli. Are you okay?"

Odd. I could hear my own breathing. It was so loud it was drowning out Lindsay's words.

"Here, drink your drink," Agent Lindsay said over the roar of my breath. "Go on, drink some."

I felt the cardboard cup put in my hand, and I felt the plastic lid against my lips. I swallowed some obediently.

My vision cleared, and I saw the concerned faces of the two agents. Lindsay was on his feet, leaning on the table to look directly in my face.

"Better now?" he asked in a soft voice.

"Yes," I said. At least I could hear him.

"Good. Finish that drink now," he said, and he resumed his seat.

I took some more swallows of the cooling liquid, looking at them over the top of the cup. I put it down and faced them both.

Two actual suspects in Marco's murder. The thought penetrated the haze.

"Who are they? Have they been arrested? Are they in custody?" I asked, all in a rush.

"Not yet," Agent Nadar said firmly, "and I cannot tell you their names or it will compromise the investigation. I can tell you there is an operation to locate an electronic facial scan of each. As I know you know, the police dash-cam of the patrol car your husband and his partner were driving got only a partial of the driver as that person shot from inside the van. But technology has improved tremendously since then, and we have been able to refine that image and combine it with a partial from the van's side mirror. It will then have to be matched to an actual facial scan of the suspects as that is more precise."

Progress. Actual progress. I felt limp, as though my bones had suddenly been removed. I sat back in the chair and tried to breathe as deeply and evenly as I could. I could feel the hard metal frame of the chair through the thin padding. I smelled the disinfectant that had been used to clean the room. A whiff of stale coffee and human sweat floated up my nostrils.

I opened my eyes. The two agents were looking at me with concern.

"Thank you," I said, sitting up straighter in the chair. "After all these years, to know there is actual hope of finding my husband's killer, it's a lot to take in. But really, thank you."

"We will be in touch," Agent Kamal said calmly and rose, preparing to leave.

"When will this operation take place?" I asked him.

"You know we cannot tell you that, but you will be informed when it is over."

I exhaled. Of course.

"Do you want to sit here for a few moments?" Agent Lindsay asked kindly.

Did I?

No. I knew there was a coffee shop downstairs that Alice and I had gone to when we'd come to this office before.

"Thank you, but no. I'll be going," I said and retrieved my giant parka as I passed the coat closet on my way out of the FBI offices.

I took the elevator down to the main lobby and turned in the direction of the coffee shop like I was on autopilot. My mind cycled through what the agents had said. Two real suspects in Marco's murder. And what was worse than human trafficking? I wondered.

14

To the real question, How does it feel to be a problem?
I answer seldom a word."

—W. E. B. DU BOIS

"I want to talk this afternoon about W. E. B. Du Bois," I said to the class after Officer Jackson had stepped out of the room. I could still see her through the rectangular glass and mesh window in the door of the little classroom. She was sitting on a chair and looking at her phone, but when she looked up, she would have a clear view of the classroom behind the door. But she couldn't hear us. I hoped. It was now or maybe never to get to the brilliant American civil rights activist, leader, Pan-Africanist, sociologist, and educator.

I knew from Ivy Mercer's syllabus that she had assigned Du Bois's classic work, *The Souls of Black Folk*, before she had taken ill. I had seen copies of his book in the materials students had brought to class. The warden had apparently thought just eliminating the book from the syllabus would make the actual books disappear or perhaps burn to a crisp, fried by the Jewish space lasers the wacky and prejudiced QAnon conspiracists contended had caused the California wildfires. I had done some more research into QAnon views. It was so off the wall, it actually still stunned me that someone that held such views could run a prison, or be in Congress and yet, both were the case.

On the walk over from the administration building, Officer Jackson had told me Shanice Harrison was sick. I remembered Shanice. She was the whip-thin, African American woman who had converted to the Church of God in Christ and whose boyfriend had involved her in his drug business. I hoped she didn't have that flu that seemed to be going around. Women living together in such close quarters would certainly pass germs around quickly.

As Jackson practically race walked toward building C, I started focusing on how I was going to get her out of the room long enough to get in the key points Du Bois had made. I wanted to present enough of his insights on American racism to have them connect it to their incarceration. These women, all of them, were deemed a problem to American society. And whatever else they could become after they left prison, they would always be an "other" as an ex-con. Could I help them break through the deadening of consciousness that the prison constructed, a deadening I had felt myself, and then have that give them insight into their own situation and how it connected to the layers of prejudice in American society?

I was going to try.

As it turned out, Jackson had made it easy for me after the students had filed in.

"I'll be right outside," she had said, glaring not only at the inmates, but at me.

I took attendance as it was a chance to say each of their names aloud and look them in the eye. Or, I tried. They were very subdued today and most, with the exception of J. C. and Anastasia, just nodded and did not make eye contact when I said their names.

"How many of you have already read the book Dr. Mercer assigned, W.E.B. Du Bois's 'The Souls of Black Folk'"? I had asked as soon as the door shut behind Jackson.

Nakeisha's hand shot up, and then Fabiola raised hers. Five more hands moved up, even Maria's though Isobel's did not. Instead, she made eye contact with me and then said, "Sure."

It seemed the incarcerated did their reading, unlike many undergraduates.

Even so, I gave a short lecture on Du Bois and his astonishing life and work. Then I picked up my own copy of the book.

"Let me read out one short passage, and then I'd like you to let me know what Du Bois means by 'the prison house' for himself and how that is the same or different from this prison house." I made a circle with my hand, encompassing the walls that surrounded us right at that moment.

"Why did God make me an outcast and a stranger in mine own house?" I read. "The 'shades of the prison-house' closed round about us all: walls strait and stubborn to the whitest, but relentlessly narrow, tall, and unscalable to sons of night who must plod darkly against the stone, or steadily, half hopelessly watch the streak of blue above."

"Allah did not do that, that is for damn certain," Nakeisha burst out. "That is the white man's doing, no doubt about it." She sat back, her face a map of suppressed pain.

"Why do you think Du Bois brings God into it, then?" I asked. "He knows what you say is true. You know that from reading the book and from my lecture. So, why?" I asked levelly.

"How should I know?" she shot back.

"You could have an opinion," I countered mildly.

"Pass," Nakeisha said sullenly.

"That's fine," I said. "Anyone else?"

"Yeah, well, people should try to live in the prison house of antisemitism," Sarah said, nearly hissing the words. "My mother's parents were in a concentration camp and nearly starved to death but they survived. My father's family, well, they escaped Germany but not the hate. My parents are so messed up, they can't even look up out of their own pain and see any blue. That's a real prison."

She clenched her thin hands together so hard all the blood seemed to drain from them.

"So we're supposed to think God did that? Well, maybe," she went on, fixing me with her pale, icy blue eyes that were rimmed with red, like a rabbit's, and she went on, her voice gaining strength.

"Teacher, you ever read that guy Elie Wiesel? He was in a concentration camp, and he made it his business to tell people what that was like. And he didn't let God off the hook for it. His book, *The Trial of God*, says it all. No wonder so many of us Jews are really basically atheists. Who can stand a God like that? A concentration camp makes this place look like a country club." And she waved her hand around in a circle, perhaps parodying my earlier gesture.

Then she grasped her hands together again, and the hand-wringing became more violent. It had to be incredibly painful, but she pressed on.

"How could Du Bois stand God?" she asked defiantly.

I remembered Sarah had gone to an elite college and had done well until she'd been arrested as a campus drug dealer. I also thought what she had just revealed might explain her anorexia.

"Complicated question, Sarah," I said slowly as she kept accusing eyes on me.

"Remember Du Bois was a sociologist," I replied levelly, "so he wanted to understand and describe. He especially examined the role of the Black church in sustaining and uplifting the Black community. For himself, he seems to me to have been functionally atheist, but he could see religion clearly in its role in oppression and its possibilities for liberation."

She frowned, leaning back in her chair. At least she'd stopped punishing her emaciated hands.

"Du Bois showed how white religion was used to help whites justify their murderous oppression of Blacks," I continued, "but he also suggested that Black community members were the true children of God. And he is credited with being a source for the Black liberation theology of the 1960's, imagining a Black God, a Black Christ and, get this ladies, a Black female God."

Fabiola sat up straight in her chair like she had received an electric shock. I had been aware of her increasing tension, as I was of the affect of the rest of the class. Nakeisha and J.C. had been paying close attention. Maria was doing the rosary again. Isobel and Anastasia both looked bored. How much of an act were those two putting on? Even Maria's doing the rosary struck me as possibly an act. But Fabiola was entranced.

"A Black woman God?" Fabiola said in a reverent whisper. "We have this in Vodou. Like the Ezili Banda, protector of women. Haitian women, we need protection, that is for certain."

"Well, hell," J.C. said, narrowing her eyes at me. "Du Bois said that stuff? I mean what guy says stuff like that? You sure?"

"Yes, I'm sure," I said.

"Well, I can tell you this for sure," J.C. went on, a defiant tone in her voice. "Patriarchy is a prison. It's a prison for all women, and it is a double prison here, a prison within a prison." She snorted. "They love it, those guards," and she jerked her head toward the door where Officer Jackson was sitting outside. "Our bodies are what they've got. They know they can do anything. Anything. Like a body farm."

Nakeisha broke in, her voice rising as she looked accusingly around the table.

"Well, you all have managed to paper over the racism Du Bois is actually writing about, now haven't you? Slavery, lynching, Jim Crow, burning crosses, you name it. That's what he's talkin' about. That's the prison. That's the prison that makes this prison," she nearly shouted, and she made a hand gesture around the room that was another mocking parody of what I had done. And now wished I hadn't.

I looked at the group, assessing. I hadn't given them a break in the last class, but I thought we all needed it. I wanted to let the temperature drop some.

"Thank you, Nakeisha, for that insight. Let's take a break," I said. "Officer Jackson can escort you to the rest room if you need it, and I saw there is a water cooler out in the hall. Let's say fifteen minutes." I closed my file on the table and reached for my own water bottle in my bag on the floor, and for my antiseptic wipes.

There was the usual scraping of chairs and everybody except Fabiola and Anastasia got up. Then Anastasia stood up and walked over to the bookcase on the far wall, turning her back on us and acting fascinated by its contents.

Fabiola leaned over toward me.

"Miss Ginella," she whispered urgently, "Shanice maybe she go get the special treatment. You know special treatment? Is it good to do this?"

"I do not know what you are talking about, Fabiola," I said softly, leaning toward her.

"Well, us prisoners, n'est pas, I think we can give a piece of us, of our bodies, you know, like, what is word, le rein? And then we can get out of the prison quickly. You know this? Is good idea, non? People say."

I knew le rein was the French word for kidney. What was she talking about? Give a kidney and get out of prison? What the heck?

I must have looked horrified because Fabiola sat back and looked away from me with her good eye toward Anastasia who was still appearing to be riveted on the books. It occurred to me that perhaps Officer Jackson didn't need to stay in the room if she had a spy all lined up.

"You think this is what Shanice has done?" I whispered, my eyes also on Anastasia's back.

"Sais pas," Fabiola said repressively, now looking down at her lap. "Don't know."

"Okay," I said very softly. "But I'd think twice about doing something like that, Fabiola."

I sat back, cleaned my water bottle, snapped the cap off and took a big drink.

I wondered if J.C. had been warning the others about their bodies with her comment on Du Bois and women's bodies in prison, specifically this prison. A farm? But then, I pondered as I took another drink, she'd said "people say." Prisons had to be huge incubators of gossip that spun way away from reality. Not that far from conspiracy theories, really.

Just then, the door opened, and the rest of the class trooped in. Officer Jackson accompanied them. She took a chair in the corner, took out her phone and made it clear she was staying.

I slipped out my notes on Walter Rauschenbusch, the early twentieth century Baptist preacher who'd started his ministry in Hell's Kitchen in New York City and who decided, basically, Jesus condemned the conditions that held his flock in abject poverty. He went on to write a book on that, *Christianity and the Social Crisis*, and helped found what was called the "Social Gospel."

I lectured on Rauschenbusch for a while, asked if there were any questions. No hands went up, and no one made eye contact.

I thought they were emotionally exhausted. I knew I was.

I dismissed the class.

Officer Jackson walked silently beside me as we headed back across the so-called campus. She normally had very erect posture, but now she was walking with her head down and her shoulders slumped until the medical building came into sight on our right. She turned her head that way, and I looked too. There was another ambulance, and another gurney was being rolled up the ramp. She looked away quickly and sped up to nearly a run for the administration building.

Was Shanice giving a kidney and getting a reduced sentence? Or did she simply have a kidney infection and was being taken for treatment?

I couldn't wait to get home and ask Tom. I seriously doubted kidney donation could be a "get out of jail free" card. And if that was actually happening, it couldn't be legal, could it?

※ ※ ※

"WAIT, RUN THAT BY me again," Tom said putting down his glass of wine on the library coffee table. We had retreated there again after the kids were in bed for quiet catching up and a glass of wine.

This topic did not qualify as "quiet," I knew. But I had gone over and over what Fabiola had whispered to me, Shanice's absence from class, and the reaction of Officer Jackson to another ambulance and gurney at the medical building. It was just so odd, I couldn't dismiss it.

"Well, what this woman, Fabiola, said was," and I tried to reproduce her exact wording, "'I think we can give a piece of our bodies,' and she used the French word for kidney, and went on to say 'then we can get out of the prison quickly.' Fabiola asked me if I knew about it and if it was a good idea. I told her that I didn't know about it but I didn't think it was a good idea." I paused, took a sip of wine and then turned toward him. "And there was this student, Shanice Harrison, missing from class and then an ambulance and a gurney heading up to the medical building. When Officer Jackson saw that she got very tense and nearly ran from the sight." I paused, remembering, including what I thought might be J.C.'s warning to the class. A farm?

"So, Tom, can that be true? Who would approve such a thing?" I asked, and I could hear the fear in my own voice.

Tom leaned forward, his serious doctor face in place.

"Some states have actually debated an organ and tissue donation program for prisoners, Kristin. That much is true. The sticking point has been getting a reduced sentence in return. It's inherently coercive. The transplant community has done very well with the American public perception of living organ donation by insisting it be free of coercion."

I nodded as he took a sip of his wine, and then he went on.

"And really, it's not such a great idea for the recipients either. People in prison are not the healthiest population, and they can carry many diseases. And in any case, doing something like that would be a violation of Federal Law. In 1984, Congress passed the National Organ Transplant Act, and that makes it a federal crime to transfer any human organ for what I think they called 'valuable consideration' and to use it in transplant. A reduced prison sentence would be a valuable consideration, that is certain."

"I suppose she could have misunderstood something she heard," I said slowly. "English is not her first language."

"You could ask that warden, I suppose," Tom said, consideringly. "I mean, why are there so many women being taken out on gurneys? That's disturbing in itself. I very much doubt it is a donation for early release program as that is illegal, however. That doesn't mean there aren't very unhealthy conditions in the prison."

Ask the wacky warden? I thought.

"I don't know, Tom. He's so odd." I sat back into the circle of his arm and took a sip of wine.

I need to talk to Alice, I thought.

15

The other night I ate at a real nice family restaurant.
Every table had an argument going.

—GEORGE CARLIN

"Why are you so damn crazy?" Alice asked, glaring at me over her cooling tea. Even our insulated cups wouldn't keep our tea warm for long as we were sitting at one of the outside tables next to the fake sunny coffee shop.

It was one of those weird Chicago days where the sun came out, there was a light wind from the west, and the temperature rose. Most days, even much later in the spring than this, the wind blew over the giant ice cube we laughingly called a lake and flash froze those close to it. It wasn't exactly warm outside even now, but we both preferred it outside, though for different reasons.

I had just finished bringing Alice up to speed on the class, Fabiola's question, Officer Jackson's tension around the medical building and what Tom had said.

"Just crazy in general," I asked, "or did you have some specific comment on what I just said?"

"You think you're oh so cute, right?" she asked, but she couldn't sustain the glare, and I saw the quirk of a smile try to escape.

"I am cute, Alice. Everyone knows it. But seriously, what do you think?" I asked in a more subdued tone. I took a sip of my own cooling tea while I watched her over the lid.

"Well, I think your Tom is right, for one thing. Too many women leaving on gurneys. What's up with that? I mean prisons are not the healthiest places, and flu and such spread like wildfire. My brother, he gets one cold after another, even in summer."

She paused, selected a stick of gum from her ever-present pack, and twirled it.

"Could be that idiot warden is slacking on the cleaning and such," she finally went on. "And maybe overcrowding the place, puttin' three inmates in cells that should have two. Or worse. You said Mercer got flu and Jesus help her, died. Maybe that."

She paused and gave me the patented glare she used on the students that stopped them in their tracks.

"You've got kids. You're gettin' married. You wanna risk that?"

"I've had a flu shot, Alice," I said seriously.

Her snort could have powered a small sailboat out on the lake.

❀ ❀ ❀

I WALKED HOME, my brain full of what Alice had said. She was likely right, as usual. And the "give a kidney" thing was likely a prison rumor. It had to be that rumors spread exactly like germs in a prison. Could be germs and rumors together, I thought.

It was still early. Molly greeted me with less surprise these days and just got her own leash for a quick walk. When we came back, I sat down at my computer and thought about bodies and prisons. J.C.'s comment about the prison being "a farm" certainly brought Orwell's classic, *Animal Farm* to mind, but what seemed far more relevant now was "Womanism," the field of religion and philosophy invented by Black women scholars. I had been reading more widely in it, and with the prison teaching, the insights were ever more central.

The construction of the Black woman's body as Other, a dangerous Other that inspires fear and violence especially by white males in authority, was fundamental. It ran through not only the scholarly literature, but also through the Black Lives Matter protests of the serial violence against Black women's bodies in white supremacist policing. The #SayHerName campaign drew attention to that crisis, as with Breonna Taylor, shot and killed in her own apartment by police who had broken in with a no-knock warrant.

But, as I started to write, I began with Anjanette Young, the Black woman social worker who was in her own home when Chicago police burst through the door and handcuffed her. She had been naked and despite telling them forty-three times they had the wrong apartment, they continued to search. Fully two minutes passed before she had been covered with a blanket, and even then it had continued to slide down.

Prisons within prisons, prisons so powerfully constructed by racist societies that people were surrounded by them even when going innocently about their own business in their own homes. The police leaving her naked while they searched the wrong apartment said so much about the role of Black women's bodies in the abuse of power. The articles and books I had read connected up that violence with the violence directed at Asian and Pacific Island American women, Latinx women and the scores of missing and murdered indigenous women. So many connections.

I wrote so furiously I nearly jumped from my chair when my cell phone rang. I looked at the screen. It was Vince Ginelli. I remembered I was supposed to drive out to the RV park today to see him before he left tomorrow.

"Vince!" I said, after I pressed "Accept."

"Hello, kiddo," he said, but he was so subdued I could hardly hear him.

"Looking forward to seeing you today, Vince," I said, sneaking a look at my desk clock. It was already nearly noon.

"Yeah, well, I was callin' to see when you planned to get here. And you want some lunch? I got some bologna, some bread." He continued to speak in a monotone, very unlike himself.

"I was just about to leave, so I'll be there in about half an hour. I'll bring a few things too," I said, wanting to avoid the likely stale bread and dried out bologna.

"Good," Vince said and just disconnected.

No, not good, I said to myself as I hustled into the kitchen to see what I could bring.

Molly followed, and I gave her a dog biscuit. It was probably tastier than Vince's bologna. I opened the freezer and took out a container of the Italian wedding soup. Vince would love it.

❊ ❊ ❊

I DROVE WEST ON THE HIGHWAY. Along the horizon, I could see a large cloud bank. It was so big and darkly ominous it reminded me of those alien space ships in the movie "Independence Day." The further west I drove, the more the thick, gloomy cloud covered the sun, and the sky leached out almost all light.

Just as I turned into the RV park, pings of hail hit the roof of my car. I approached the RV and saw there was only one car pulled up under the awning. Apparently, Yitz was not here. I took the other protected space, got the container of soup and the loaf of Carol's nut bread I had grabbed from our pantry and dashed up the stairs.

Vince opened the door before I could knock.

He silently took the soup and bread from my hands, and I shrugged off my coat. Even in the dim light of the RV, I could see he was drawn and even pale. All the time I had known him, he'd had a ruddy complexion. Too ruddy at times, I'd thought. As he turned back to me, I thought he looked diminished.

"Hi, Vince," I said, trying to avoid being falsely cheerful. I moved toward him and gave him my customary hug. He even felt smaller. He leaned in to me and gave me a pat on the back.

"Good to see you, kiddo," he said, and then he moved to the little table.

"I brought Italian wedding soup, the recipe Nonna gave Giles," I said. He just nodded, and I turned to the stove, lit it, and went to put the nearly defrosted soup in a pan. The pan showed food still crusted on it. I washed it thoroughly, put the soup in it, and turned the little stove on low. Then I took a seat at the table.

"How is she, Nonna I mean?" I asked, trying to get a rise out of him.

"Oh, tired, you know. Those kids they run her ragged. She wants me come get her, says I shouldn't have come here alone."

"Well, that's probably true. It will be better when you two are together again."

He nodded.

I heard the soup start to simmer, and I went over, got two bowls, some plates for the bread, and utensils. Those looked a little scummy, like they'd just been rinsed and not washed. In fact, the whole interior of the RV looked dusty and smelled like garbage and unwashed clothes. No Nonna, no cleaning, I thought.

I quickly washed bowls, plates and utensils in the sink and dried them with a paper towel. I didn't like the look of the cloth kitchen towel either. I carried everything over to the table and went back to look in the little refrigerator. There were two cokes in there, and I grabbed them. The rest of the small interior was filled with beer.

We both ate silently for a couple of minutes. Vince actually looked better with the hot soup inside him. He had gotten some color back in his cheeks.

"So, Kristin," he said after he'd chewed a bit of bread. With Carol's bread, it took some chewing to get through it, though it was delicious.

"You said on the phone the FBI guys had somethin'? I ain't heard from Yitz since you was here. And he doesn't answer his calls. I don't know what's goin' on there," Vince said, a trace of anger in his voice. I wondered what he'd paid Yitz up front.

"Well, I think it's promising," I said, going back over what both Lindsay and Nadar had said.

"Of course, they said lots of those 'we can't tell you that' lines, but what I did get clear is they have two real suspects, and the net is closing around them. The greater enhancement of the photo from the police vehicle, you know, new technology, has given them that solid lead."

Even as I said the words, they seemed to come from a distance. Could it be? After so long?

I looked up, and Vince's face looked almost hollowed out. His skin was pulled taut with tension. I thought I could actually see his skull, and I looked away.

"Well, that's a hell of lot more than we got from Yitz," he said. "I don't know what's with that guy. I know he don't like phones or email or any such. Always worried can get tapped. But he shoulda come here then."

We finished our soup and bread in silence.

I took the dishes over and, as I washed them and the pan thoroughly in the sink, I realized I did not want to leave Vince here in this dusty, smelly, metal tube. He'd clearly not been eating right, and I bet he'd not been sleeping. I silently put away the dishes and then turned to him. He hadn't moved from his spot at the table.

"Listen, Vince," I said. "Drive back with me to the house. The boys really miss you, and you can sleep in your regular room. I'll drive you back tomorrow morning, and you can get on the road in plenty of time."

"Nah. Nah. Too much drivin' for you," he said, his voice so low I could hardly hear him.

"It's not, and besides, the boys are not the only ones who miss you," I said. I was shocked to see a little tear appear in his eyes. I didn't turn my face. I let him see I had a tear on my cheek.

"Okay, then," he said gruffly.

"Great. So I'll use your bathroom, you can throw a few things together, and we can get going."

I was remembering Tom's suggestion I look at the bottles in the bathroom. But they were gone. Had he put them away or had the prescriptions run out, and he hadn't refilled them?

WE GOT BACK JUST before the boys got home from school. They were ecstatic to see Vince, and they pulled him into the TV room to show off their new video game. I peeked in after half an hour, and Vince was asleep on the couch, Molly was stretched out next to him, her head on his stomach, and the boys were stacking cubes that fell from the sky.

Giles merely said "is no trouble" when I'd mentioned I'd invited Vince for dinner. "I have all for lasagna already."

Then Kelly came into the kitchen looking at her phone as she did. Why teenagers did not constantly fall over while walking and looking at their screens was a mystery to me.

"I saw Nonno's here," she said, looking up. "He's staying for dinner?"

"Yes," I said, about to start setting the table.

"Can I invite Victoria?" she asked me. "She and I have been texting and, well, she's really lonely and so can she come?"

"Well, okay," I said after glancing at Giles who nodded. I could see "two trays" practically written across his forehead.

"Is a kind thought, Kel-ly," he said softly. She blushed under his regard.

"Yeah, well, okay, then I'll tell her," and Kelly hurried from the room.

Speaking of texting, I thought I'd better give Tom a heads up. I went to get my own phone. As I typed in a message that Nonno and Victoria would both be here for dinner and that it was lasagna, his favorite, I thought of Yitz and his suspicion of hacking. He was likely right.

* * *

"CANNOT."

"Can too."

The boys arrived in the dining room at a run, and they were arguing furiously.

"Hey, guys, knock it off. No arguments at dinner, you know that!"

"We're not arguing, we're talkin' about science!" Mike, my lawyerly son, argued in their defense.

"We learned about black holes from this totally cool guy who came to class, and he said . . . " Sam started to say.

"Just hold it, okay?" I said firmly. "We'll talk about that over dinner, just let's get everybody in here."

We were routinely using the big dining room table now. There were too many of us most of the time to fit around the small, kitchen table. I'd asked Giles and Carol if they'd like to eat with us or take their portion of the lasagna to their apartment. They said they'd join us. They liked Nonno too, and I know both of them realized he was having a hard time now. And I thought they liked Victoria.

As everyone trooped in and took places around the table, I thought again how we needed to gut the back of the house and make a big combination kitchen and family room there. I had briefly considered it for this spring and then told myself I was insane. Dissertation and wedding planning did not fit with tearing out one third of the first floor of the house.

Victoria had arrived a few minutes before, and she and Kelly started talking rapidly about some movie, and they headed for the kitchen. I realized with a start Victoria was not that much older than Kelly.

I never tried to manage where people sat at meals. I considered it rather like a class. They'd sort themselves into their preferred discussion groups.

Carol and Giles came in with the two lasagna pans and placed them on trivets on the credenza. Kelly followed carrying the salad, and Victoria had a pitcher of juice in one hand and water in the other. Tom followed them, I was surprised to see. I hadn't heard him come in. He was carrying a bottle of red wine and a corkscrew that he put down on the table.

There was a brief scrum at the credenza but finally everyone got food. The boys sat next to Nonno, one on each side. Kelly and Victoria sat next to each other, still talking, now about certain actors I thought. I took a spot next to Tom at one end of the table and Carol and Giles sat together at the other end.

Silence fell upon the table as the lasagna took hold. I swallowed some gooey mouthfuls and sighed. It was delicious. Another of Nonna's recipes she'd passed on to Giles.

I looked over at the boys who had shoveled in about half of their meal already. I thought some talking might be a good idea at this point.

"Okay, guys, so what did you learn about black holes?" I asked.

"So like see, when a star explodes it like falls into itself . . . " Sam began.

"Supernova," Mike interrupted. "It becomes a supernova."

"Yeah, right," Sam said. "So it like becomes small and pulls everything in, and it just grows and grows, and it can eat up like whole galaxies. Nothin' can escape!" he finished triumphantly.

"Can so, if it doesn't cross the boundary, it can escape!" Mike said loudly.

"The event horizon," Victoria said, smiling.

The whole table looked at her.

"Science major," she said.

Everyone was silent for a second, absorbing that.

"And, indeed, some energy that crosses the event horizon can then leak out, even so," Giles contributed.

"No way!" Sam said.

"This has been measured," Giles said quietly. "The Atacama Large Millimeter Array, a big group of 66 radio telescopes in the Atacama Desert in the north of the Latin American country of Chile, has measured the radiation of this." Giles paused, looking down at the boys puzzled faces as they were trying to take in what he said.

"So, yes. The black hole eats and then, *eh bien*, it drools!" he said with a smile.

The whole table laughed at that.

"You learned that from your studying math?" Mike said curiously.

"Yes," Giles replied, still smiling. "There is so much that is interesting in mathematics."

I looked at Mike's face, and I could see he was seeing Giles and his study of math in a new way. Mike absorbed information like a black hole, I thought.

"So the black hole drools like this?" Sam said, letting a little spit come out of the side of his mouth.

"Sam!" I said sharply. "You know that's not dinner table manners."

"Yeah, okay Mom, whatever," Sam said, and he wiped his mouth.

"Good one, buddy," Vince whispered to him.

16

The creed which accepts as the foundation of morals, Utility,
or the Greatest-Happiness Principle, holds that actions are right
in proportion as they tend to promote happiness, wrong as they
tend to produce the reverse of happiness.

—JOHN STUART MILL, *UTILITARIANISM*

As the sun was rising behind us, I drove Vince out to his RV, cautioning him about driving the big vehicle alone back to Wisconsin. Then I got out my sunglasses and drove back to Chicago into the rising sun. The piercing rays slowed traffic. I crept along, basically on autopilot anyway, thinking about Father John Ryan for the next class at the prison.

Ryan was a Catholic priest and economist who had come up with a moral and economic argument for what he called a "living wage." Ryan's work had greatly influenced the Roosevelt administration.

I was so deep into an inner debate with myself about how to present Ryan's work that I jerked the wheel when my cell phone rang. It was Vince. Cars going only thirty miles an hour still honked at me for that. I pressed the "accept" button on the hands free device.

"Yes, Vince," I said.

"Yitz is dead," he said in a flat voice. "Shot in the back. Buddy from the force called me. Been dead maybe three, four days. Found in a dump site, south side."

"Hold on, Vince. I'm getting off the highway," I said. There was an exit coming up, and I put on my blinker. I pulled into the lot of a Subway and shut off the engine.

"Okay, I'm parked," I said. "Did your contact know anything else at this point?"

"Nah. Just that."

"Listen, Vince. I'm not that far. I can come back."

"Don't do that," he said sharply. "Don't. I won't be here."

"But . . . " I started but he interrupted almost angrily.

"Lemme finish, will ya? I'm leavin' the bus here, gonna take the car and go get Natalie. She'll nag me to death if I don't. We'll come back here. I can't leave."

I was silent for a minute, thinking about what he was saying.

"Hey, you there? I gotta get goin' you know?" His voice was rough with suppressed emotion.

"Yeah, okay," I said slowly. There was no stopping him in this mood anyway, I realized.

"Well, yeah then." He paused. "We got to get these murdering bastards, Kristin. We gotta get them."

"I know, Vince," I said grimly. "I know."

❀ ❀ ❀

I DIDN'T EVEN REMEMBER the rest of the drive home. Vince's words rolled around in my mind, over and over, but I couldn't make much sense of what had happened. One thing that was getting clearer is that the remnants of the former El Chapo gang were active in the Chicago area, likely even in adjoining states. Unless Yitz had been murdered by someone else he had royally ticked off that wasn't connected to the gang activities, I thought. The trouble was I didn't know anything about him, really.

Somehow I arrived home safely. I sat down at my computer, though I thought writing was likely out of the question. Still, I turned it on, and a calendar reminder popped up on the screen.

Oh no.

"Today. Dr. Nigel Wilson lecture. 5:00 p.m. Myerson 102." Of all days to have this. And I couldn't skip it. Adelaide would have my head on a platter.

I groaned aloud, and Molly sat up from where she had been sleeping at my feet and put a paw on my knee.

"Oh, Molly. Warmed over John Stuart Mill's 'Utilitarianism' with a side of contemporary British elitism disguised as virtue." Molly lay back down and went to sleep immediately. She had the right idea. I had almost dozed off when I'd read the title he'd submitted for the lecture, "Super-erogation Across Normative Domains." Wow, that would pack them in. "Supererogation" was an obscure, academic term that just meant going beyond what was strictly necessary in moral terms. Like helping an elderly grandmother across the street and then going a little further, like walking her to her destination. Myerson 102 was a small lecture hall on the first floor of our building. I didn't think it was small enough.

I remembered the first public lecture by my colleague Dr. Aduba Abubakar, "The African Roots of America." The whole campus had been in an uproar. It had made quite a statement. I doubted that would be true for Dr. Wilson's lecture.

I gazed mindlessly out the window for a few minutes, and then it dawned on me that the sun was still out. I went upstairs, changed into my running clothes and came back down.

Molly started dancing around in the front hall, her leash in her mouth. She knew those clothes. And we'd not had a real run in almost two weeks.

We bounded out of the house and headed for the lake.

As it turned out, I should have looked back to the west. We ran for three miles in the sunshine and then turned. I almost gasped at the ugly, greenish streaks with dangerous dark towers moving toward us. We sprinted for home, but didn't quite make it. Freezing rain in the face can really hurt.

❊ ❊ ❊

I HAD HURRIED OVER to the campus. The rain had stopped mid-way over, but it was still bitterly cold and overcast. As I entered the small auditorium, I saw it was completely empty, and I had my choice of seats. Well, I thought as I put my still-damp coat on the back of my chair, a guy from England won't be put off by a little rain and cold. I'd never been in England when it hadn't rained and been cold.

The rest of my faculty colleagues trickled in. Aduba took the chair next to me and nodded. I wondered if he was remembering when he'd had to wear a bulletproof vest to speak safely in public. That would not be necessary here.

Adelaide arrived along with Hercules. They were in deep conversation and moved down toward the front seats facing the lectern.

Donald came in, escorting the lecturer. Wilson was a tall, thin, pale-faced man with thinning, light brown hair and a stoop. He wore a baggy, tweed jacket with suede elbow patches, a wrinkled shirt and tie, and baggy, brown pants. He looked like every member of college I had met when I'd done a short stint at Oxford. There must be a large closet somewhere at Oxford that contained dozens of those jackets and pants.

Wilson towered over Donald who was speaking up at him earnestly. He ushered Wilson up to a chair next to the lectern and took the adjacent one.

We all waited.

The back door opened, and the sparce audience turned at the sound. An elderly man with white hair and a cane came in. He was shaking rain off an umbrella which he placed in a stand by the door. Hercules rose and walked up the aisle to greet him and escort him down to a chair at the front. I thought the white-haired man was an emeritus professor of philosophy, but I was not certain.

Silence fell. No one else came.

Finally, Donald cleared his throat and introduced the speaker.

Dr. Wilson rose. If he was distressed by the lack of attendance, he did not show it. He took out a sheaf of papers from an inside jacket pocket, smoothed them out on the lectern and began to read. In a monotone.

"How ought we to live? How do we solve the moral dilemmas we face in life? What is right to do, and what is wrong? These are the kind of questions that moral philosophers seek to answer."

I took out my phone, silenced it and then opened a notes app. I started to type some questions of my own. The first was, "Who killed Yitz and why? Why had he been found on the south side?"

I had a solid list of questions by the time Wilson droned to a halt an hour later. There were no questions from the audience.

The faculty and our guest trooped upstairs to our conference room. Some appetizers with assorted beverages would be laid out. With our increasingly spare budget, this was all we could afford. In the past, we'd have gone to a nice restaurant.

I took a glass of sherry and a little cheese. Giles would save me some dinner, I was certain, and besides the appetizers looked quite unappetizing.

When I sat down, I took my phone out of my pocket and turned off the mute. The phone started buzzing like a swarm of bees had taken up residence inside it. I glanced down at the screen.

Six messages from Natalie Ginelli in the last twenty minutes.

I gasped and stood up.

Adelaide turned toward me, a look of concern on her face.

"Something wrong, Kristin?" she asked.

"I think so, Adelaide. I need to answer this."

I grabbed my coat and purse. I doubted I would be coming back. I was terrified Vince had had a car accident on the way to Wisconsin.

I just pressed "reply" without listening to the messages.

"Kris-tin-a," Nonna's voice came on. "Oh, thank the saints. Kris-tin-a, we back here at the you know, place you park camper, and Vince, he no look so good."

"How does he look, Nonna?" I asked, as calmly as I could.

"His face, all like a bag one side. And he no talk right."

Stroke.

"Have you called an ambulance?" I asked.

"No, no. Call you," she said shakily.

"No, Natalie, hang up and call 911. Tell them it is an emergency. You think your husband is having a stroke."

"Stoke?" she asked, dazed.

"Never mind. I'll call them. I can give them the address. Then I will call you back."

I hung up. Moments counted with stroke. Vince needed treatment right away.

"911 Operator," the crisp, professional voice said in my ear.

I gave the operator the address and the location of their RV in the compound. I stressed it was an elderly man with heart troubles exhibiting signs of stroke. I gave her my cell phone number.

"We will send an ambulance right away," she said and hung up.

I called Natalie back.

"They're coming, Natalie. Call me back when they get there and let me know what hospital they will be taking him to, okay?"

No reply.

"Natalie!" I said, louder, afraid she was having medical difficulties now too.

"Yes. Yes. I call."

I called Tom.

He picked up on the first ring.

I quickly filled him in on what was happening.

"I'm actually walking home," Tom said. "Meet me at the house, and we can go out to the Oak Park hospital. It's the nearest to that campground, I think. It's a university affiliate."

"Okay, okay," I said hurriedly and hung up.

"Kristin, is there a problem?" Adelaide asked, stepping out of the seminar room and seeing my face.

"It's Vince," I said, shrugging into my coat. "He's being taken to the hospital. I need to go."

"Oh, certainly," she said. "Let me know, will you?" Her round face was creased with concern.

"Of course," I said, and I sprinted for the stairs. Vince must have driven the hour and a half to Wisconsin, grabbed Natalie and driven right back. He had to stop thinking he was invincible, I thought angrily.

I had gone two blocks when my cell rang. Natalie.

"Kris-tin-a," she said in a shaky voice. "They here. Vince in the ambulance now. I going with him."

"Where, Nonna?" I said urgently.

I heard her quavering voice asking someone.

A male voice answered, "Oak Park Hospital, ma'am."

"He says Oak Park. You know this place?"

"Yes, Nonna. We do. Tom and I will come. Meet you there."

I heard her start to cry, and the same voice said, "Now, now, ma'am, your husband will be fine. You come this way." And then the line went dead.

I broke into a run.

17

Illness is the night side of life . . .

—SUSAN SONTAG

I drove west again. Tom sat in the passenger seat, called the Oak Park Hospital operator and asked to page Dr. Ameer.

"He's an excellent vascular neurologist," he said while he was on hold. "We actually trained together for a while."

It was after eight at night, but Tom fully expected this doctor to still be at the hospital, and it turned out he was.

"Yes, Anal. Hello, it's Tom Grayson. Thanks. Yes. But I called because the father-in-law of my fiancé is being taken by ambulance to your ER. His name is Vincent Ginelli. Late sixties I think, and I suspect a heart condition." He paused, listening. "Right. Right. Partial paralysis of the face and slurred speech have been described to me." Another pause. "Actually, I'm on my way there with my fiancé. Should be about fifteen more minutes." Pause. "Thank you so much. See you shortly."

"Good," Tom said. "He'll head to the ER and try to see Vince right away." Tom settled back in his seat to look at his email.

I tried to focus on my driving, but I kept thinking about how violent acts produce wave after wave of harm, often for many years. The ripples of pain and loss from Marco's murder kept spreading out like a rock thrown into a pool with an oil slick on the surface, the ugly stain spreading out further and further. The paved highway became that pool in my mind's eye, and I imagined the dead fish that had suffocated, their corpses littering the expanse of the road in front of me.

I shook my head to clear it. I was fairly conversant with my own subconscious, and I thought that grim image meant I thought Vince was going to die.

I managed to get off at the correct exit, largely because Tom was pointing at it, and I followed the big H signs toward the hospital. It was very close to the highway. In fact, in a few more minutes we were there. I tried again to shake off the miserable image of oil and death as I headed for the public parking.

We hurried over to the emergency room entrance and went in. Tom spotted what must be Dr. Ameer. He was a tall, slim, Indian American man who had to bend over a little to talk to the tiny, Italian American woman who was standing in front of him wringing a handkerchief in her hands the way women had done laundry for centuries.

Nonna.

"*Grazie Dio*," she said when she saw us. "Kris-tin-a, Doctor Tom, you come."

Tom didn't hesitate. He walked quickly over to her, leaned over and folded her in his long arms. He could easily talk to Dr. Ameer over her head as she was barely as tall as his waist.

I teared up. I couldn't help it. That direct compassion and focus on healing said everything about why I had fallen in love with Tom. I went and stood next to them, just lightly putting my hand on Nonna's shoulder.

"He's already had an injection of tPA," Dr. Ameer was saying. "We think we're within the three hour window of onset, so that's a good indicator he may be able to make a full recovery."

I heard full recovery, and I patted Nonna. Tom bent his head and spoke softly to her.

"Natalie, that means they gave Vince something to break up the blood clots that were likely causing his symptoms. This is very good."

"*Grazie Dio*," she said again without lifting her head. I silently said the same.

"He's awake, actually. I'll check and see how soon you can see him," said Dr. Ameer. He looked at me and Nonna. "And, Tom, there's another thing I've been meaning to ask you," he went on. "Could we step down the hall a moment?"

Tom smoothly moved Nonna over to me, and I led her to one of the molded plastic chairs in the waiting area. She was not quite steady on her feet, and it crossed my mind to take her pulse so I could tell Tom. I put one arm over her shoulders and held her wrist in my other hand. As best

I could tell, it was 150. Too high, I thought, but she'd been through a lot. I'd check again in a few minutes.

It occurred to me she might be better for some fluids and a little sugar.

"Nonna, you want some tea to drink? I saw a vending machine down the hall a little ways."

"I get my rosary," she said and reached for her purse that she still had clutched under her arm.

"Good idea," I said. "I'll get us some tea."

The vending machine had tea and a choice for "extra sugar." I loaded Nonna's up and tested the temperature with my own lips. It was warm, not hot. On impulse, I got two candy bars with chocolate and peanuts from the next vending machine. Not a perfect meal, but I'd bet Vince had not stopped for them to eat on this flying trip.

I carried the covered cup and the candy to her. She had her purse on her lap, but she was motionless. I removed the purse and put the insulated cup in one of her hands. Her grip seemed lax, so I did not let go. I merely put the cup to her lips and bit by bit got her to drink it down. She shook her head no at the candy.

❋ ❋ ❋

DR. AMEER CAME OUT of Vince's room. Tom, Natalie and I were waiting just outside the door in the Intensive Care Unit.

"He is doing much better," he told Natalie. "We'll keep him here in the ICU to monitor him overnight, but if he continues to improve we'll move him to a bed in the neurology wing tomorrow. I think he'll need to stay here at the hospital for at least two days after that, and then he can go to a rehabilitation center. He's not happy about all that," he said to her, his dark eyes concerned, I thought as much for her as for Vince and then he added, "You can go in, but just stay for a minute. He needs to rest."

He opened the door, and I hardly recognized the old man propped up in the bed with wires attached to him. I had often thought of Vince as having the face of the Buddha, whether smiling or sad. Now, he looked like Bailor, the Celtic god of the underworld whose angry gaze could kill. Vince's face was locked in fury, his brow furrowed, his black eyes narrowed and his mouth in a grim line that tilted down on one side. He drooled in his effort to form words. Since I thought it was a streak of profanity, it was just as well it was incoherent.

Natalie trembled as she stood just inside the door, and I put my arm around her.

Tom and Dr. Ameer moved off to one side, still conferring.

I walked Natalie up to the bed. Vince glared at her, I thought with recognition.

"*Caro, come stai?*" she asked in Italian, trying to pat his hand. Her "darling" only sputtered with rage he could not express, and his hand moved jerkily.

"You're going to be fine, Vince," I said slowly and then gently nudged Natalie away from the bedside.

"Come, Nonna, come. We must let him sleep," I said softly. She was crying, and her round shoulders shook a little. I led her out of the room, and Tom followed.

We took the elevator down to the ground level. Natalie was dabbing her eyes, but had stopped crying. I stood with her at the entrance while Tom got the car. I got in the backseat with her.

Tom drove in silence for a while and let her collect herself.

"Natalie," he finally said over his shoulder. "Vince seems so angry because he is frustrated. This is perfectly normal. In fact, it is a good thing because it shows he knows what is happening."

"In fact," and he chuckled a little, "he knows, and he doesn't like it at all."

"No, no. No like any time be sick," Natalie said sitting up a little straighter, her voice a little stronger, reassured by Tom's matter-of-fact description. "He just keep going, no stop."

"Well, he has to stop now for a little while and get well. He is really angry about that, but he'll get over it. There is an excellent rehabilitation center right next to the university hospital. In two to three days, the doctor thinks, Vince can be transferred there, and he will get some therapy. Then he can leave and just come back a couple of times a week."

While Tom was speaking, I realized we would have Vince and Natalie with us for a while. I started thinking about that. The stairs might be a problem. I wondered if I should consider fixing up a small, downstairs parlor as a bedroom. The powder room was right next to it. I knew I was focusing on practicalities to avoid thinking of that strange, angry man. Tom's explanation had helped me as well as Natalie, but not entirely.

"Kristin?" Tom's voice startled me.

"Yes, sorry, what?"

"I actually need to go back to the hospital for about an hour. Could I drop you and Natalie at the house?" he asked.

"Yes, certainly," I said automatically. In a few more minutes, he pulled up in front of the house. He helped Natalie get out, and took my hands in his before I could even scoot over and follow. He stroked my hands gently for a few seconds and then helped me out as well.

❋ ❋ ❋

WHEN NATALIE AND I came in, Molly came down from upstairs where I guessed she had been sleeping with the boys. I looked at my watch. It was nearly midnight. I steered Natalie to the kitchen as I could see there was a light on there. I found Kelly in the kitchen, her phone in front of her, but she was just sitting there.

"How is Nonno?" Kelly asked anxiously, simultaneously getting up and coming over to hug Nonna. "Dad texted me from the hospital." Of course he had.

"Nonno's recovering," I said calmly. "Angry as a hornet at being kept there, in fact."

"Is true," Nonna said from the circle of Kelly's arms.

I realized Nonna was not just being hugged by Kelly, it seemed like Kelly was holding her up. She must be exhausted.

"I will take you up to your room, Nonna," I said. "I'll bring you a little soup, and you should rest. It has been a very hard day."

"Si," she said, and she turned a face to me that was gray with fatigue. As Kelly let go of her, she staggered a little, and we looked at each other over her head. I took one arm and Kelly took the other. We mostly carried her upstairs and placed her on the bed against the pillows.

"I'll heat the soup," Kelly said and left. Fortunately, Nonna's house-dress buttoned up the front. She had already fallen asleep, but I was able to pull it off without waking her.

I covered her with a spare blanket, hung up her dress and tiptoed out.

While I ate the soup Kelly had heated up, I told her what the doctor had said about Vince and his prospects for recovery.

She made us some chamomile tea, and I drank it without shuddering. Far worse things had happened today.

Kelly said goodnight, and I stayed in the kitchen, waiting for Tom.

Tom's love was sustaining me these days, but I realized that now I was alone in searching for Marco's murderer. The FBI were investigating, it was true, but they were not exactly my partners on the case. Not like Vince had been.

Vince looking so furious and yet so helpless had shaken me, I realized. Part of me had counted on him for years. And right now, he wasn't there. Intellectually, I knew it was as Tom said, he was frustrated beyond bearing at the effects of the stroke. But he wasn't Vince.

I put my head in my hands and sobbed.

18

When Black women stand up—as they did during the Montgomery Bus
Boycott—as they did during the Black liberation era,
earth-shaking changes occur.

—ANGELA Y. DAVIS

I woke to the sound of laughter. It sounded like there was a party going
on downstairs. That couldn't be right, I thought groggily.

I'd finally fallen into bed and into a sleep coma at about one in the
morning. Tom had not come home that I'd realized, but I glanced over
and saw his side of the bed was rumpled and his pillow bunched the way
he liked it. He'd come and gone, and I'd not even waked up.

The noise from downstairs was getting louder, and it seemed like
it was women's voices with some kid whoops thrown in. I got up and
pulled on a sweatshirt and leggings. The sweatshirt fabric felt heavy on
my tired body. I finger-combed my hair and went down the back stairs
to the kitchen.

Kelly, Carol, Nonna, Victoria, Sam and Mike were gathered around
the kitchen table with a thick notebook open in front of them. Pieces of
fabric were scattered around on the table surface as well.

Victoria noticed me first. Her Bambi eyes lit up.

"Kristin, hi! I brought the book for the dresses and the sample fab-
rics too," she practically sang.

"Oh, good," I managed, and I went to fix myself some decaf coffee
with a few caffeinated beans sprinkled in. Perhaps more than a few this
morning.

As it brewed, I walked over to the table.

"Kelly, you'd look good in this one," Mike was saying as he pointed at a classic sheath-style, formal dress. "In the green, I think, to go with your eyes."

"Why, thank you, Mike," Kelly said, clearly flattered.

I thought for a moment I was hallucinating. Wasn't it two minutes ago that the boys called her "Kelly smelly"? I met Carol's eyes over the top of Mike's head, and she was smiling at me.

Oh, no. I thought. Not that. Not this soon.

I went back to the counter to pour the coffee and get a grip.

"Not this one!" I heard Sam chortle. "You'd look like a big, pink cup-cake in that."

"Si, no that one," Nonna said. "Is no good, Sam, you right."

There was the sound of a page turning. I walked back to see.

"What about the same dress for the attendants, but in different colors?" Carol asked Victoria.

"That could work," Victoria said, "especially in a classic style. "We could have the dress colors represented in the flowers to tie it together."

Victoria turned to me.

"And Kristin, I brought the same book and some fabric for your friend Alice. Do you want to take it to her or shall I?"

"I'll do it, thanks," I said. Some prep work with Alice would be nec-essary, especially if Carol and Kelly as bridesmaids liked the sheath. I thought Alice would hate it. As matron-of-honor, though, she could wear a different dress than the others. I looked over and pondered the two other dresses now displayed on the pages of the open notebook.

"What do we wear?" Mike asked suddenly, turning toward me.

"A suit like Tom's and Nonno's," I said, thinking fast.

Nonna's back was to me, but I heard a little sniff. I patted her arm.

Vince would recover, I said firmly to myself. He had to.

"Come on, boys, time to walk to school," Carol said to Sam and Mike. That broke up the party. They gave the obligatory groans and then trooped out with her.

"Natalie, I'll shower and take you out to Oak Park to see Vince," I said to her.

"Oak Park?" Victoria said. "I can drive you, Mrs. Ginelli. That's where my next appointment is."

"*Grazie*," Natalie said softly. "Not so much trouble for Kristin. Is good."

❊ ❊ ❊

A WHOLE MORNING TO work, I thought as the house emptied out. I took a quick shower and settled down at my desk.

I had been having second thoughts about devoting a whole class to Father John Ryan. I wanted to go with the interests of the class to engage them, and I didn't think just Father Ryan would do that. Mention a living wage, something they would identify with, I thought, and then move on to the early years of the Civil Rights movement. Highlighting the women leaders who had done so much of the actual movement work would keep them participating. At least I hoped it would.

Ella Baker would make a smooth transition from W.E.B. Du Bois, as she had advised and supported him, along with Dr. King and Rosa Parks. Fabiola would like hearing about Ella Baker's Swahili nickname, "*Fundi*." It meant a person who teaches craft to the next generation. Then, of course, the incomparables, Fannie Lou Hamer and Dorothy Height. Some of the older students might remember President Bill Clinton giving Dorothy Height the Presidential Medal of Freedom in 1994.

I typed out the notes. That would work to get me to Rosa Parks. The power of movements such as these women had helped to create was a countervailing force to the institutionalized power of prisons. They had all put their bodies on the line, literally, to push back against the power of white supremacy that was dealing death all through the South. And not just the South.

As I worked on the class, I realized I was feeling an increasing urgency. I was fairly certain Anastasia was a spy for Officer Jackson. She had likely repeated what I had said, and what others had said, both in the class and the break. I thought I was on increasingly thin ice in getting to teach the prison class, and I wanted to make every minute count.

I closed my class notes file and opened the one on the dissertation. I began a new chapter on "Power as Subversion." This would work, I thought as I typed furiously. What was that guy's name that Giles liked so much for his nonviolence work? I drew a blank. I googled "nonviolence" and there he was. First entry. "Gene Sharp." I saw that his primer on the subject, "How Nonviolent Struggle Works," was available for download for free as a PDF. Excellent.

I was startled when I heard the front door opening and Molly's greeting. I went to stand up and my right foot was asleep. I'd been sitting in the same position for nearly four hours, I realized. I hopped and wiggled my foot as I made my way toward the front hall.

It was Victoria and Natalie. Victoria was supporting Natalie under one arm. I took the other and wordlessly we made our way upstairs to her room. Victoria left the room once we had Natalie sitting on the bed. She looked gray with fatigue, and the muscles of her face were clenched as though keeping thoughts and words prisoner in her head.

"Come on, Natalie, lay down now," I said softly as I fluffed a few pillows at the head of the bed.

Her muscles gave way like she was deflating. I supported her, and she lay back, clearly spent.

"He no is Vince, Kristin. He not my Vince," she said in a quavering voice.

I should have gone with her, I thought, as I picked up each leg and placed it on the bed.

"He's still there, Nonna. Inside," I said in as reassuring a voice as I could muster.

"*A Dio,*" she breathed and closed her eyes.

I'd come up later with some lunch for her.

Victoria was sitting at the kitchen table, her phone in front of her, but she wasn't looking at it, she was looking at Molly who had a paw on her lap.

"Victoria," I said. "Are you okay? I take it the visit did not go well?"

"No, I don't think it did," Victoria said softly, starting to pet Molly. "I walked Mrs. Ginelli in, and then I went to meet my client. I'd given her my cell phone number and after about two hours she called. She just said, 'please come.' I'd finished and was getting some gas, so I did. She looked like a zombie, really, just hollowed out inside. She didn't speak on the way back."

Normally cheerful Victoria had been shaken by Natalie.

"I never should have imposed on you that way, Victoria," I said.

"No, it's okay, really. You've done so much for me," she said softly. "And," she continued, "here's the notebook for your friend Alice." She pointed to a second binder like the one everyone had been looking at this morning.

"Thanks," I said. "Do you want some lunch?"

She glanced at her watch.

"No, I don't have time. I have a Pilates class."

We said goodbye, Molly got another pet, and she was off. I didn't entirely believe in that Pilates class.

I grabbed a protein bar and went back to my desk, thinking I could also listen for Natalie upstairs. I opened my dissertation file and despite my worries about Natalie, I got back into the analysis pretty quickly. This was coming together. It really was all about the body and who got to control which bodies, and how.

So much for listening. I realized with a start there was a rattle of pans. Nonna was in the kitchen.

As I walked in, I saw a pot of sauce was already simmering on the back of the stove. How long had she been in here, I wondered? The countertops were covered with the remains of onion, garlic and fresh tomatoes. Several spice jars were open. The pasta machine stood to one side, ready to go.

"Nonna, did you eat anything yourself?" I asked, seeing what she had already accomplished.

"Some bread, some cheese, is enough," she said, not turning from where she was stirring the sauce. I saw some bread crumbs in Molly's bowl and decided they had shared the bread and cheese.

"Okay," I said mildly. "I think I'll walk over to campus for a while, give Alice her wedding sample book."

A wave of the wooden spoon indicated she had heard. Cooking was Nonna's therapy of choice.

❀ ❀ ❀

ALICE ANSWERED HER CELL and said she could meet at two o'clock. We didn't really need to specify where any more. I wrestled the big notebook into my backpack and headed to campus.

It was one of those "let's pretend there's spring in Chicago" kind of days where there is sun, the temperature is mild, and puffy clouds float along in the sky. Daffodils start to poke their heads up. I always want to yell at them, "Go back, go back. You're going to get killed with an ice storm in a day or two!"

I headed for my office first, thinking to throw away paper mail and print the PDF of Sharpe's work. My home printer was slow, and it balked at larger projects.

"Kristin!" I heard from behind me. I turned. It was Adelaide. She had abandoned her warm cape and had a woven shawl over her shoulders.

Without the usual gale force winds, it draped nicely over her regular, flowing dress. As I stopped and waited for her, I realized the shawl was the one I'd given her when she'd been in the hospital in the fall.

"Hi," I said as she came closer.

"Hello. Good to see you. How is Mr. Ginelli?"

How was he? I thought. Good question.

"He's in a hospital in Oak Park, but I hope he'll be moved to the rehabilitation center here by the university. That could be soon. It was a stroke, but I think they got to him in time."

"Oh, good," Adelaide said warmly. She waited a whole two seconds and then said, "So, you need to answer your email. I haven't gotten your evaluation of Wilson."

I sighed inwardly.

"Okay," I replied as we started walking. We were nearly at Myerson. "I will find several ways to say, 'that was awful and we should never hire him.'"

Adelaide chuckled as we ascended the stairs towards our offices.

"That lecture was awful, wasn't it?" she said. I noticed she was breathing normally as she ascended the stairs next to me. She really was doing better. She could talk and climb stairs.

"Utilitarianism, can you believe it?" she went on. "With all that's going on in the world, these elite white men still try to set themselves up as the arbiters of universal values."

I nodded my agreement, and we each peeled off to our respective offices. I dutifully filled out the evaluation form while the printer hummed away across the hall.

I emphasized the "lack of interest on the part of students and the whole university community" several times. Our department necks were constantly on the chopping block, and we only were saved by the interest we could generate in the university community at large. Wilson had generated no interest. That should kill the hire for certain.

❈ ❈ ❈

ALICE WAS SILENTLY LEAFING through the notebook. I had clipped the fabric swatches together at my office, realizing the wind was picking up, and they'd scatter all over the quad as we met outside. The twenty minutes of spring was about to come to an end.

I took a drink of my decaf coffee. I had definitely given up the herb tea. Over the lid, I watched her turn the pages, but as usual she gave nothing away.

"Decaf still has caffeine," she remarked, not raising her head from the book.

"French roast decaf has the least," I countered, having researched that in preparation for just this moment.

"Hunh," she replied.

"This one's not too bad," she said suddenly, pointing her ever-present stick of gum at a page.

It was the sheath.

"It's okay," I said, biding my time. I took a giant drink of the decaf coffee to keep even a hint of relief from appearing on my face.

"This one looks like a giant, pink cupcake," she said chuckling.

Perhaps my boys had a future in the wedding planner business.

19

The political investment of the body is bound up, in accordance with
complex reciprocal relations, with its economic use . . .

—MICHEL FOUCAULT

O ur lives had calmed down considerably. On Friday afternoon,
Vince had been moved by ambulance to the rehabilitation center
next to the university hospital. He had been so exhausted by the transfer
he had slept through the afternoon and evening.

Saturday was much better. Tom had stopped by the rehab center on
his way to morning rounds and had called me, saying Vince was awake,
able to speak a little and far more calm. He thought seeing the boys would
be helpful for Vince, for Natalie and for them.

Natalie and I walked over with Sam and Mike in the late morning. I'd checked with Vince's floor nurse first, and she had indicated that
would be a good time. They could bring Vince to the family visiting area
in a wheelchair.

The kids were subdued on the walk over. They had each brought a
Lego construction they thought Vince would like to see, and they carried
them very carefully. It concerned me to see how tense they both were.

I needn't have worried. The visit went very well. We checked in and
did not have to wait too long in the family visiting area until Vince was
wheeled in. I'd told the boys he'd be in a wheelchair so there would be no
surprises there. They hesitated a moment and then he had used his left
had to wave them over. They rushed to him, surrounded the chair, one on
each side, and started explaining their Lego creations. Natalie beamed at
the sight, and Vince met her eyes briefly. He winked with the eye on the

side of his face that had not been affected by the stroke. Then he turned his attention to the complicated space ships the boys had made from their Legos, and he managed to say, "What this?" and "What this?" several times.

After about twenty minutes, though, he showed signs of fatigue, and I cut it short. The boys hugged him and kissed his cheeks. I ushered them out so Natalie could have a second alone with him.

"*Cara*," I heard him say as we walked away.

❀ ❀ ❀

MONDAY FOUND ME DRIVING east on the expensive toll road toward the prison. My mind went from the revised lesson plan to the actual fact of these women who were effectively warehoused for profit. Over and over again, slavery kept getting reinvented in new forms, but the basic pattern of controlling certain bodies for profit remained. I wondered what the women Civil Rights activists I planned to talk about today would have said if they could have seen this future. "Get on with it," I imagined them saying. I knew one outcome of this experience for me was going to be far more activism on the cancerous spread of for-profit prisons.

I slowed down by habit as I went through the open road tolling, and the car skidded slightly. The morning's rain was turning to sleet and icing the road. I gingerly took the exit and drove slowly through the fields that were glistening white again. Along the roadside, wildflowers that had dared to leave their safe earth were getting pounded back to the ground.

Beefy, white guy #1 showed no sign of recognizing me as I once again identified myself at the gate. Beefy, white guy #2 was not in evidence, however. Instead, someone I could only call skinny, white guy #1 slouched out of the administration building and pointed me toward the approved parking. The sleet had turned to tiny bits of hail, and I could see the little, frozen balls were hitting the rubberized, black slicker he wore and bouncing off. Time for my own slicker. I parked, popped the trunk and dashed around to grab it. This seemed to alarm skinny, white guy #1 as he ran to the back of my car while I was putting the slicker on. He peered into the trunk and when he seemed to get his fill of the empty space, I closed it. I got my backpack out of the front seat and locked the car and handed him the fob. We sloshed through the slick puddles that had formed on the uneven, cracked concrete of the visitor parking lot and hustled into the administration building.

Skinny, white guy #1 abandoned me at the reception window without ever having said a word. I gave my license to the electrocuted-hair guard. Officer Jackson was waiting inside the exterior door, and she did the honors of searching my bag. Despite my cheery "good morning," she just frowned at me.

"Let's go," was her only comment when she'd finished searching, and we exited into the yard.

Despite the brief hail that had now turned back to rain, some women were still outdoors, huddled by the buildings, most of them smoking.

Jackson hurried along, but I easily kept up with her. When building "C" was in sight, she hissed out, "Isobel Rivera is sick. She will not be in your class." I have noticed it is very hard to hiss sibilants, and she sounded like a sputtering teakettle. I got the gist of it, however. She then put on even more speed, trying to get away from me. I easily caught up with her. I almost reached out for her shoulder to slow her down, but stopped at the last minute. The written instructions I'd been given had warned me never to touch a guard or an inmate. Still, I spoke loudly, nearly in her ear.

"Just wait a minute. Sick with what?"

"None of your business," she snapped out without turning her head, and we entered the building. She strode in silence to the little classroom, snapped on the lights and departed to collect the remaining class members.

Jackson came back, leading the students, and after they'd filed in, she'd shut the door and taken her seat outside the door in the library. The class slowly took their accustomed seats. If I'd thought they'd been subdued during the previous class, this week they seemed rigid in their posture and in their faces with the exception of Anastasia. I watched each one in turn. It wasn't difficult. We were down to six students.

Anastasia was the only one who made eye contact with me, and I thought she looked like a cat that had eaten a bird and wasn't even trying to hide it. Fabiola looked particularly grim, her good eye turned away from me and her shoulders hunched. J.C. and Nakeisha looked angry, but it seemed almost put on. They had the kind of angry face you'd make if you were going to go into a Tae Kwon Do sparring match with someone who outweighed you by a hundred pounds. Pure fake intimidation.

Overall, I thought they were very close to being terrified and trying to hide it in various ways, with the obvious exception of Anastasia. Though, I wondered, was her attitude put on as well?

I went through the motions of calling roll, saying their names, greeting them. I got just a minimal nod or a "hey" when I called a name.

I started with Father John Ryan and the living wage argument.

"About damn time somebody realized that," Sarah said derisively.

"Catholic priest? No way," J.C. snorted. "They don't take time off from raping little kids."

And that was it. They sat in silence, avoiding looking at me. Enough of Ryan, then. I went on to Hamer, Height and then Parks. There seemed to be a spark of interest, especially about some of Fannie Lou Hamer's more famous statements like "Nobody's free until everybody's free." There were a couple of "amens" and "now that's about right," but Nakeisha wasn't having it.

"Everybody never goin' to be free. You gotta get that. You gotta get that or you go crazy," she said fiercely, turning her face toward me for the first time.

I lectured on, giving the histories of these incredible women but I was unable to spark any other reactions except some nods when I got to Rosa Parks. They knew who she was, but that's all I could conclude.

Before I ended the class, I asked in a general way if anyone knew how Isobel was feeling. "I heard she was sick," I said casually. "Do you know from what?"

"None of your business," Anastasia snapped, her black eyes boring into me. Exactly what Officer Jackson had said.

I just glared at her and then started to gather up my papers and put them in my backpack. When Anastasia's back was turned as she was walking around the table, Fabiola pushed a small slip of paper under the last pile of my notes. I pretended not to notice. When Anastasia had left the room, I slid the small piece of paper with the stack of notes covering it into my bag.

Officer Jackson and I slogged across the campus in silence. I noticed that another ambulance was parked right outside the medical building. Jackson did not turn her head to look, but from the sudden shift in tension in her body, I knew that she had seen.

It had stopped raining, and I put my slicker back in the trunk. I retrieved my fob and waited until skinny, white guy #1 was walking away. I put my backpack on the seat next to me, quickly unzipping the top. As I turned the wheel, I felt inside to get the little piece of paper Fabiola had slipped me, and I stuffed it down my shirt. Then I drove slowly with one hand toward the gate while my other hand zipped the backpack back up.

Beefy, white guy #1 normally looked inside the backpack before he let me go, and today was no exception. He took it from the passenger side to his little hut and gave it a thorough examination. Then he brought it back and dropped it on the seat. The gate opened, and I pulled out slowly despite the fact that I wanted to floor it.

I drove down the road that led to that prison entrance and after I was out of sight of the guardhouse, I turned right instead of left toward the highway. I pulled on to a narrow road that seemed to run completely around the prison complex. White pine trees were lined up between the fence of the prison and the road. They had clearly been planted close together, probably when the prison was built, to shield it from sight. They looked like a long line of Christmas trees ready for sale, but, as I pulled over next to them, I knew Santa wouldn't be welcome in this place. He'd likely be searched and the presents confiscated.

The fat, long-needled trees did make an effective shield for my car, however, and after stopping I took the folded note out from my shirt.

"Help us," Fabiola had written.

I sat there and thought. There were too many flags now to ignore, perhaps even starting with Ivy's death. Shanice had been "sick" and not come back. Now Isobel was "sick" and another ambulance was waiting. Fabiola's note could be interpreted a lot of ways, but the atmosphere of tension bordering on suppressed panic in the class in general was alarming.

I decided to drive around to the other side of the prison close to where the ambulances came and went from the medical building. I hoped the line of white pine trees went that far. I could pull over in their cover, wait for the ambulance to leave and then follow it.

Where were these women being taken and why?

I drove slowly around the fence. The enclosure was more an oval than a circle, but roughly if the public entrance was at six, then driving clockwise I estimated the medical entrance was at three. The thick line of trees did continue, and I pulled over again as close as I could to their screening limbs. I didn't dare go further as I'd be exposed, even with the tree line. But I could see the diagonal road that led away from the medical building.

I didn't have long to wait. In about a quarter of an hour, the ambulance appeared. It was leaving. I waited until it had started down the diagonal road and then I followed.

There were no lights or sirens. The long, white and red vehicle moved slowly and silently down the narrow road that bisected more fields with short, brown stalks sticking up. Lots of corn was grown around here, apparently.

Up ahead, the ambulance blinker indicated a right-hand turn. It disappeared into a very narrow dirt road, likely just used for farming equipment. There were two metal frame sheds on the right, and then the ambulance backed up into a dirt area in front of a cinder block building approximately the size of a three-car garage. A double-door opened in the cinder block building and beefy, white guy #2 came out. The ambulance driver, someone I didn't recognize, turned off the engine and got out to open the back doors of the vehicle. Beefy, white guy #2 got out of the passenger side. Together they lifted a rolling gurney out and extended the legs. Someone was strapped to the gurney, covered in a dark blue blanket. Beefy, white guy #2 held an intravenous bag up with one hand. A tube ran down from it and disappeared under the blanket. The blanket was pulled way up, but did not completely cover the head of the person on the gurney. I got a glimpse of what I thought was black hair.

Isobel?

They went inside the building for no more than ten minutes and then they both came back wheeling an empty gurney. They collapsed it and shoved it in the back of the ambulance. Beefy, white guy #2 locked the door behind them, they both got in the vehicle, and the driver started the engine.

I realized if they came back the way they'd come, they'd see me. I'd left my engine running, and I quickly pulled off the road and around behind the first metal shed that was covering a green, rusting tractor. I shut off my engine.

In another few minutes, I heard them drive away, back the way they'd come. If I hadn't moved the car, they'd have seen me.

I got out of my car and walked behind the second shed. It was empty except for a smattering of tools hung on the walls. I peered around the corner, and I could see the front of the cinder block building with its double door again. There were no cars parked around that building that I could see. What was this building for and why had someone been dropped off here and just left? Likely even left alone? I stood there, thinking. There were no windows on this side of the cinder block building. Perhaps there were some at the back.

I had to get a look inside.

20

You must always remember that the sociology, the history, the economics,
the graphs, the charts, the regressions all land, with great violence,
upon the body."

—TA-NEHISI COATES

I ran to the back of the cinderblock building, and there were two alumi-
num, frame windows about six feet off the ground. The one on the left
was actually open a couple of inches. But they were too high for a quick
look. I kept going and circled the whole building. There was what looked
like a large, air conditioning condenser on the far side. It was humming
away even though the outside temperature was probably in the low 40's.
Perhaps it was a combination unit, I thought briefly, and it provided heat
as well. There were no other windows. Just those two at the back.

I came around to the back again and gazed up at the window that
was partially open. How to get up there, I wondered. I turned and looked
around for something to stand on in the weed-choked field behind me.
Then I looked over toward the sheds and realized I could drive my car
over and stand on it. Tension is making me stupid, I thought, as I ran
back over to my car and drove it up beneath the window that was partly
open.

I climbed up on the roof of the car and looked in the window. A
battered, metal desk, some shelves with cartons, and a filing cabinet were
visible. Not much. I scrambled down and moved the car underneath the
other window. I climbed up and looked in. I drew in my breath sharply.

The lights in the room were not on, but from what I could see in
the gloom, there was what looked like a fully-equipped operating room.

Holy Moly. What were these people doing? And where was Isobel, if the blanket covered body on the gurney was she? Or someone else?

I moved the car back under the window that was partly open. I tucked my purse under the seat of the car, but put my cell phone and car fob in my pocket. I climbed up again. The metal of the window frame was scratched and bent in places. I took off my jacket and used it to protect my hands as I tried to slide the window open. It screeched in protest. I stopped, listened, and waited. Nothing happened. The building really must be empty. Well, empty except for the person who'd been brought in and left there.

I pulled as hard as I could, and the window slid all the way across the frame, opening one side. I stuck my head in the window and saw a stained, lumpy couch directly below. Okay. This could work. I spread my jacket out over the bottom of the scratched, bent frame, grabbed the top, did a stomach crunch and swung my legs through. I let go and landed on the couch. It had no springs at all, I thought, as I landed painfully on my butt.

I had not made a stealthy entrance, but the door of the little office remained shut and there was no sound outside it. I pressed my ear against the flimsy wood-paneling and still could hear nothing. I turned the door-knob and pushed the door open about six inches. When I peered out, I could see the double door at the front of the building. Those opened into a kind of reception area, except it had only a few, battered folding chairs and a card table. I stepped into the hall and shut the office door quietly behind me.

The layout was simple. There were rooms at the back and this space at the front. The room adjacent to the office was the operating room. I thought there must be a third room, and I quickly saw I was right. There was a third door. I hurried down to it and saw it had a keypad with a blinking red light. I tried the door, and it was locked.

Then I felt a blinding pain in my head and gravity pulling me toward the floor. And I knew no more.

❀ ❀ ❀

SOMEONE WAS GROANING. I lifted my head to listen, and a pain so sharp it felt like my head was being cut in two caused me to groan. I realized I was the one who'd been groaning. I put my head back down and felt a freezing cold, smooth surface on my cheek. I took some deep breaths and risked opening my eyes. I saw a white wall. I couldn't make sense of it. Despite the pain, I lifted my head again intending to sit up, but my arms would not move. I felt a jolt of fear like an electric shock. I jerked my shoulders, and that set off another blazing pain in my head. I waited until the pain subsided and tested my arms. I realized my hands were tied behind my back. I tried to move my legs. They were tied too.

I did some deep breathing to still the panic so I could think. I'd been hit on the head and tied up. I was on a glacially cold floor. I took stock of my body. I was lying on my side. After about a minute, I thought I could roll onto my back and see more of the room.

I drew my bound legs up and heaved with my shoulder. I was able to get onto to my back. The fluorescent light in the ceiling stabbed at my eyes, and I felt dizzy. I breathed some, and the dizziness receded. I saw a stained, white ceiling above with a fly-specked, plastic cover over a florescent light. I turned my head to look at the other side of the small room. A gurney was positioned there with an IV pole and a plastic tube running down to an arm. Three straps went around the gurney and over the body lying there.

A body. Memory returned with a jolt. This was the person who'd been brought in the ambulance.

I had to get up. I had to get untied. I felt the rising panic and breathed again.

Roll to the wall, I thought. Use the wall to push yourself up.

I rolled to my left side, and then on to my back in the direction of the wall. I rolled again to my side, putting my back against the wall, and then I scooted my legs around to try to get perpendicular to the wall. Too close. I felt like my neck would break. I used my heels to pull myself a short distance away. Pull. Rotate. Pull. Rotate. Finally I got enough purchase to push with my heels and slide my shoulders up the wall. It felt like my arms would pull out of my shoulder sockets. I breathed and rested and then pushed up hard. I was sitting.

Sitting up, I could see more of the body on the gurney. Black hair was visible and a brown arm into which some kind of fluid was dripping. As I'd suspected, it was Isobel.

I tried to push straight up the wall, but I couldn't get more than a few inches. I rotated my aching shoulders and got on to my knees. Then I rocked back on to my feet and, using the wall along my side to keep from falling over, I stood up, panting, my wrists and ankles rubbed raw. I looked down at my feet. White, plastic zip cuffs encircled my ankles.

I had to get out of the zip cuffs. I looked around the room. There wasn't much to work with. Isobel seemed to be unconscious. I called to her, but her eyes stayed closed, and her face was slack. There was the gurney, the IV pole, the drip line and the bag of fluid. The only other object in the room was a battered, metal cabinet about five feet high. It had double doors and one was slightly ajar. The inside edge was jagged in places from wear and, I thought, some rust.

I hopped over and turned my back to it. I had to hop around a bit more to get my hands in position to open the door completely. Luckily it opened against the far wall. Good. That would give me purchase. I looked at the ragged edge of the door, and then I hopped around so my bound hands were next to the edge. Up, down, up, down I slid the zip cuff, trying to use the jagged, metal edge to cut it. A couple of times, I caught my wrist instead. I tried to remember when I'd had my last tetanus shot. Finally, I could feel the zip cuff weakening, and I wrenched my wrists apart. They were slippery from blood, and I was able to pull them free. I sagged from relief as the pressure on my shoulders released, and I almost fell.

Using my aching hands, I steadied myself and opened both doors of the cabinet. The inside looked like it had been stocked for a 1930's horror film version of a hospital. There were surgical knives, but they had elaborate, engraved handles with gothic script writing. German, I thought, though I didn't bother to try to translate. There was a selection of long, thin scissors with blunt tips that were likewise engraved. Next to them were a couple of surgical saws that had some odd curlicues on the ends. These surgical tools looked almost antique, and they were clearly German. And there was a group of hammers of various sizes. They looked newer.

Other shelves contained boxes of sterile gloves, a pile of gowns, some sheets and some bandaging.

I selected one of the scissors and in less than a minute I was free of the ankle restraints. I gingerly put the very sharp scissors back and got out a box of the bandaging. I quickly bound my wrists. They were bleeding freely now, and I had to stop losing blood. I was already much too woozy.

I patted my pockets, vainly hoping my cell phone and key fob would still be there. No, whoever had hit me and tied me up had taken them.

I turned my attention to the gurney.

I had no trouble recognizing Isobel. She was pale and still. I opened her eyelids, and she appeared comatose. I looked at the bag hanging from the IV pole. Along the bottom of the bag was the word "Benzodiazepine." Serious sedative, I thought. But there was also a piece of tape stuck below it with some writing so small I couldn't make it out. A knock-out cocktail? I couldn't tell.

I guessed that Isobel was in a medically induced coma. Why? And why was it so bitterly cold in this room? I had warmed up with my gyrations getting the zip cuffs off, but now that sweat was evaporating, and I was chilled to the bone.

I went back to the cabinet and took out the stack of gowns and put them all on. It helped a little. I went back to Isobel and unstrapped her. I looked under the sheet, trying to see if she were injured in some way that would explain the need to render her unconscious. Oddly, she was wearing her prison pants and shirt, not one of the surgical gowns. I felt her skin. It was like ice. Well, no wonder. I was still shaking from cold myself.

I got out the pile of sheets and spread all of them over her. Then I sat on the foot of the gurney and thought.

The fears of the women prisoners, the gossip about "giving a piece" of yourself, and even Officer Jackson's suppressed horror at the gurneys leaving the medical building at the prison—there was no other conclusion. This little shop of horrors was a place where women were taken involuntarily and their organs removed. Had to be. Isobel was literally being "kept on ice" until they would cut her apart.

I got off the gurney and gently removed the long needle from her arm that was attached to the IV tubing. I just propped the needle, tip up, at the top of the gurney so it wouldn't drip. I couldn't see how to stop the flow, but I wasn't exactly at my sharpest right then. I didn't know how long it would take for her to regain consciousness, but I thought it was the right decision to stop the knock-out fluid mix. I hoped it was. I got some gauze and tape from the cabinet and taped Isobel's arm where I'd removed the needle. Then I sat back on the gurney at the bottom.

Now what? I was freezing, hurting and getting more dehydrated by the minute. I wanted to lay down next to Isobel and sleep.

Don't do it, my mind warned.

I got up and walked around the room flapping my arms and thinking.

They'll come back, and I'd better be ready, I thought, my fear returning. That was good. It was breaking through my numbing mind.

I went back to the cabinet of German surgical tools and selected a hammer and one of the long-handled surgical knives.

Then I sat back down on the foot of the gurney and waited.

❄ ❄ ❄

I'm so cold. So cold. My mind was sluggish. They'd taken my watch and my cell phone. It seemed like hours. I was so cold.

Then I heard a noise out in the hall that caused a jolt of fear. I got up off of the gurney, taking the hammer and surgical knife with me. Isobel had not stirred, though I thought her eyelids had fluttered some and her breathing seemed a little more normal, but what did I know?

I moved so I'd be behind the door when it opened. Footsteps approached the door, and I heard the sound of the electronic lock being disengaged.

The door opened slowly, and a short, balding man in a dirty, white coat entered. Before he could even react to the fact that there was no body tied up on the floor, I hit him over the head with the hammer. I aimed for his bald spot, and he went down like a bag of wet cement.

Right behind him, beefy, white guy #2 charged in and made a grab for the hammer. I stabbed at him with the surgical knife, but he knocked it out of my hand. My reflexes were too slow from the cold and the dehydration. We struggled for the hammer and then he threw me against the gurney. My left hand came down next to the tubing connected to the IV needle that I'd taken out of Isobel. I grabbed the long needle and stabbed it into beefy, white guy #2's chest as hard as I could. I aimed for where I thought his heart was. He roared and took his hands off me, trying to pull it out. He was gasping in pain, and then he wobbled a little. Either it was incredibly fast-acting stuff, or I'd really hit his heart, or both.

I pulled the hammer out of his hand and hit him on the head. He staggered, but didn't go down. I hit him again, and he fell backward on top of the little guy.

The warmth from the open door felt so good, but I didn't want to risk the two on the floor waking up on me. I took one of the sheets off of Isobel and used the lethally sharp scissors from the cabinet to cut off some strips. I tied their wrists first, and then their ankles. I fumbled a lot as my hands were so cold and aching.

I wheeled Isobel's gurney out into the front room so she could warm up too, and then I went back and searched the two men for a cell phone. The guy I took to be the doctor had one, and I pressed his thumb to the fingerprint pad on the phone, and the screen opened. I pressed the phone icon and dialed 911. No signal. All the cinderblock was impeding the call.

I limped out to the front room and over toward the double doors. One door was open. I tried dialing 911 again and a woman said "911 Operator." I almost sagged with relief. With chattering teeth I described the location as well as I could and also asked them to send an ambulance. It took a couple of tries, but I thought I got the message across. I heard Isobel moving on the gurney. Good. She was coming around. I went out the doorway and dialed Tom's cell. It went to voicemail. I managed to say "Tom, I need help, in Indiana . . . " and I felt Isobel come up behind me and grab the cell phone.

And then I knew no more.

21

Most middle-class whites have no idea what it feels like to be subjected to
police who are routinely suspicious, rude, belligerent, and brutal.

—DR. BENJAMIN SPOCK

"I want my lawyer, my kids, my fiancé, my dog and my wedding
planner," I said as loudly as I could as the door to the interrogation
room opened. I hated that my chattering teeth made me sound weak.

Two men entered but did not answer me.

"And let me make a phone call," I said, trying to control my shivering.

I was freezing, and it wasn't just from having been locked in an ice
cold room for half a day. The cold came from inside.

I wrapped my arms around myself and felt a twinge in my bandaged
hands. My cuts had been stitched and my bruises examined in an emergency room, and then I had been whisked away by what I assumed were
local cops and taken to this interrogation room.

I had no purse and no cell phone.

I was getting very angry. That was good. It was warming me up
some.

The two cops continued the silent treatment, taking chairs opposite
the small table in the interrogation room. I had been walking around the
small room still trying to warm up. I remained standing, even though I
felt a little dizzy. I'd been hit on the head and knocked out twice within
hours. I'd asked the ER doctor, who seemed to be about nine-years-old, if
I needed a brain scan to check for concussion.

"No," he'd replied. I assumed he'd heard of brain scans, but the clinic
where I'd been taken was so tiny and so poorly equipped, even if he had

thought I needed a scan, there was no chance I could get either a CT or an MRI. I hadn't even been able to get a Tylenol for my splitting headache.

I stood, swaying a little, and looked at the two men seated in front of me. Did they think this silent treatment was intimidating?

Pink, my weary brain registered. These two guys weren't so much white as pink. They had pink faces, pink scalps visible through their light, blond buzz cuts, thick pink necks and what I could only assume were big, pink stomachs under their shirts.

I squinted at their name tags. "H. Voss" was printed on one and "E. Voss" on the other. Great. Probably brothers like beefy, white guys #1 and #2. Voss. Likely German ancestry. Or twins. Did Germans run to twins? I wondered. Their arm patches read "Dyson Police Department." The prison address was Dyson, Indiana.

"Were you hoping to find drugs when you broke into the clinic?" "H" asked, adopting what he likely thought was a menacing tone. He looked so much like a big, pink baby, the intended menace seemed more like a whine.

"I want my lawyer," I said.

"Look, blondie, we got you dead to rights," "E" snarled, slapping a pudgy, pink hand down on the rickety table. It rocked but stayed upright. "The doctor and the clinic attendant have both filed charges against you. You are in deep shit. Breaking and entering, assault, unlawful imprisonment, and those are just for a start. So start talking."

Beefy, white guy #2 had said he was a "clinic attendant"? And these guys had believed him? I wondered if there were a connection between these local yokels and the highly illegal organ trafficking that was likely being run out of a prison in the same, tiny town.

"Come on. Give," "E" yelled.

"Lawyer."

"Listen, baby, we can keep this up all day," "H" said in his whiny tone.

I entertained myself by wondering how much I would finally be able to sue them for. Lots and lots, I thought vaguely.

Suddenly there were raised voices outside the door.

"We demand to see our client!"

Anna. That was Anna's voice. When she was angry she had this tone that could cut glass.

But who was "we"?

The door to the interrogation room opened, and a sallow-faced woman stuck her head in.

"Her lawyers are here," she said flatly.

Lawyers? Did she say lawyers? My ears felt like they were stuffed with cotton. I'd better sit down, I thought, and then I seemed to just fold so I was sitting on the floor.

"Kristin!"

I looked up and saw Anna in the doorway with a man I didn't recognize.

"H" and "E" got up and spun around angrily. Then their round, pale blue eyes opened wide at the sight of Anna. From her smooth cap of hair, to her laser eyes, to the bronze, Armani suit and gold jewelry, she seemed just to stun them. I'd seen that effect she had before. It was kind of like a Flash Gordon ray gun or something. My bleary eyes made it seem like their stomachs deflated a little. There was a tall, older man with her, standing slightly to the side. He and Anna stepped aside, and "H" and "E" slunk out.

"Kristin," Anna said coming over to me and crouching so she could look me in the eyes. I tried to focus on her, but my vision did seem to be getting fuzzier and fuzzier. "Do you need medical attention?"

"Anna," I said.

"Howard," she said over her shoulder. "Will you go get Dr. Grayson? He is in the outer office. Tell the officers we think Ms. Ginelli is in need of medical attention, and he is a physician."

"Tom?" I said, thinking I was hallucinating.

"Yes, he's here," she said, still crouched in front of me. She was gently rubbing my hands below the bandages, I realized.

"How?" I asked. There were raised voices again. The deepest voice was Tom's, I could tell.

"Apparently, you left a partial message on his phone," Anna said, and she moved her hands up to rub my arms. "When he couldn't get you, he searched for clinics and hospitals near the prison and found you in the system of one nearby. He called the clinic, and when he found you were under arrest, he called me, and I called Howard Carson. He's a well-known attorney here in Indiana, and his firm and mine have done some work together in the past. We met up outside this police station."

She stopped rubbing my arms and put a hand on my shoulder.

"Do you understand me, Kristin?" she asked, her gaze softening as she looked intently at me.

I nodded and then really wished I hadn't.

The noise from outside the door was getting louder. I could just make out the words.

"Arrest me if you want to, but I am going to look at Ms. Ginelli and determine her condition. If I have any concerns, I am calling an ambulance." Tom's voice.

I heard a polished, older male voice saying, "You are running a considerable risk of a lawsuit something, something, something."

Anna stood up as Tom came in.

Tom kissed my forehead and simultaneously lifted my wrist. Then he shone a light in my eyes.

"I'm going to call an ambulance," he said to Anna. "Can you get them to agree to that?"

"Absolutely," Anna said, turning sharply on her Ferragamo heels and marching out. I felt bad about those beautiful shoes having to touch the disgusting floor of the interrogation room. I was sitting on that floor and could see the yellow and brown stains up close. And I could smell them.

I WAS SITTING UP in a hospital bed, chained to the railing.

On the plus side, I felt a lot better. I had an IV in my arm and was getting intravenous fluids. Tom was almost asleep in an armchair next to my bed. He had this way of resting while not quite sleeping.

I knew I was at Mercy Methodist Hospital, right outside Gary, Indiana. The curtains were closed over the small window, but I knew it was very late. The CT scan had taken a while, even with Tom working the doctor network at this hospital. I had no bleeding into my brain, thank heavens, though I did have a mild concussion. Mostly I was dehydrated.

Anna had been in earlier along with her Indiana colleague, Howard Carson. She introduced him and gave me his credentials. Founding partner of Carson, Hayes and Moody, located in Indianapolis. Northwestern Law School, former Indianapolis prosecuting attorney, founded his own firm 20 years ago. He was a tall, distinguished man with a full head of thick hair, slightly greying over the ears. He had "high-powered attorney" written all over him from his clearly bespoke suit to his Patek Phillipe watch. Those watches were very expensive, I knew. I had wanted to get Tom a really nice watch for a wedding present and had priced one of those. I'd considered it briefly as they were so beautifully made, but I realized Tom would never risk wearing it and leaving it in the surgery locker room.

As I took Howard Carson's card from him, I realized he was a male version of Anna. Of course he was, I thought. Anna would only get me the best. I started to relax a little. Maybe I wouldn't go to prison despite the handcuffs.

Anna and Carson took seats on either side of the bed, and she put a very small recorder on the tray in front of me.

"We need a record of what happened, Kristin," she said firmly. "Are you up to telling us? We'll have the recording transcribed."

I nodded and again wished I hadn't. My head felt wobbly on my neck and moving it had caused a stab of pain.

"Yes," I said.

She hit a tiny button and asked me to state as precisely as I could what I had done that day and why. I began with my being asked to teach a class at the prison to substitute for a woman professor who had died. Over my time at the prison, I'd become increasingly worried because women prisoners would disappear from my class, I'd be told they were "sick," and then they'd not return. Ambulances left the medical building at the prison far too frequently in my view.

Anna stopped the recorder for a moment and asked me to explain in more detail why I had come to suspect that the women being taken away in ambulances was suspicious. She'd started the tiny machine again.

I did, summarizing the way in which I'd become increasingly alarmed, including a note from a student in the prison asking for help, though I did not think it wise to name Fabiola. I even mentioned Dr. Ivy Mercer. I said I was not persuaded now that her death had been due to natural causes. When another woman was said to be "sick," I said, I had become very concerned. When I'd left the prison, I'd followed the prison ambulance in my car and seen a figure on a gurney being taken into a cinder-block structure not too far from the prison. The person on the gurney had just been left there, unattended. I said I'd been concerned for her welfare. I'd looked in a window to try to find her and had been very alarmed by the operating room I'd seen there, so I had decided to break in to try to find her.

Carson's dark, thick eyebrows had gone up nearly to his well-cut, greying hair when I'd described the operating room, but Anna had merely nodded, gesturing me to go on.

I described being hit from behind, tied up and left on the floor of a freezing cold room. I'd waked up, freed myself and identified Isobel Rivera, a woman who'd been in my class at the prison. She had been strapped to a gurney in what seemed to be a medically induced coma. I'd said I'd removed the IV and then defended myself from two men who'd charged into the room, trying to attack me.

"Just a moment," Carson had interrupted at that point. "Defended yourself? How?"

Anna reached over and stopped the tape.

"She was with the Chicago police, Howard, and she has a black belt in Tae Kwon Do. Not as surprising as it seems." She turned to me.

"Just go over it one more time for us, will you, Kristin?" she asked and turned on the small recorder again.

I described the contents of the small, metal cabinet, including the German writing on the surgical tools, and how I'd used the bent, sharp edge of the cabinet door to saw through the plastic cuffs on my wrists.

Anna paused the recorder again.

"Describe the injuries you sustained from that, Kristin." I did.

Then I went on to how I'd heard the door being unlocked and how I'd used a hammer and a surgical knife to defend myself. I repeated "defend myself," knowing it would be crucial.

I said I had not known the man who'd worn the white coat, but the other one I'd met several times as he was a guard at the women's prison right down the road where I'd been teaching. I'd subdued both of them and tied them up with strips of sheeting.

Carson cleared his through at that, but Anna left the tape running.

Then, I went on, I'd called 911 using the cell phone of the guy wearing the white coat, and I'd also asked the 911 operator for an ambulance. I emphasized there should be a record of my 911 call. I'd heard Rivera getting up from the gurney behind me. She had grabbed for the cell phone while I was leaving a message for Dr. Tom Grayson, my fiancé, and then I'd lost consciousness. I assumed she'd hit me. I had waked up in the ambulance and been treated at a small clinic for my scrapes and cuts though not for the two blows I had taken to the head that had rendered me unconscious. I couldn't remember the name of the clinic. Then, I said, I'd been cuffed, placed in a police car and taken to an interrogation room in the small police station where they'd found me.

Anna had nodded to Carson, and they'd had each followed up with questions to confirm I'd been trying to save a woman who had been taken from the prison, that I'd been hit and tied up, and I'd been defending myself from attack.

"Excellent," Anna said after she had turned off the recorder. She turned to Carson.

"Howard, I think your associate is outside, correct?"

"Yes, I believe he is," Carson said, rising and taking the tiny recorder from Anna before walking to the door. He opened it and sure enough a baby lawyer stood outside, his very nice suit not completely drawing attention away from his round, unlined and freckled face. He looked about twelve-years-old.

"Harold," Carson said briskly, "take this and transcribe it as quickly as you can."

Harold took the small recorder and almost ran down the hall.

I leaned back against the pillows of the bed, exhausted. Tom had been silent the whole time I had been dictating the narrative. I hadn't dared look at him as I knew he'd find what had happened to me, well, and really, the risks I had taken and what I had done, very hard to hear.

He merely came over to the bed, lowered the rail on the side where I was not cuffed, and sat on the bed next to me leaning back and putting his long arm completely around my shoulders.

"Oh, Kristin," he breathed into my ear.

Anna and Carson left the room, and I think then I dozed.

After a while, Anna had come back, and I'd waked up. She said Howard had managed to get a hearing with a judge to get bail so I could get uncuffed and back to Chicago. But it wasn't until tomorrow morning.

"I'll stay close by," Anna had said to me, her hazel eyes snapping with an anger that she thought she was keeping from me. She had patted my arm above my bandaged wrist, the one that did not have an IV tube taped to it. The other one. "These cuffs are not a good look for you, Kristin. We need to get them off as soon as possible."

I was touched, and yet that made me more worried. It was probably only a forty minute drive back to her lake-front condo, but she was staying in Indiana. Why? Would "H" and "E" storm into the hospital and take me away if she wasn't actually in Indiana?

"You have my cell number, Kristin," she said, correctly interpreting my anxious face.

"We do, Anna," Tom had said. He had stayed on the bed beside me.

He was here. Anna was close by. I'd be okay. I wrestled up a smile. It probably looked like a grimace, but it was the best I could do.

She'd left then, a whiff of Chanel Coco perfume lingering near my bed. I took a big sniff of it before it vanished into the predominant smell of disinfectant that didn't quite cover the regular hospital smell made up of vomit and feces.

Then I must have slept.

※ ※ ※

The next thing I knew, Anna, Carson, and a large, horse-faced woman wearing a jacket that said "Sheriff" across the front were talking in quiet voices to Tom.

The woman in the sheriff's jacket approached the bed and unlocked the handcuffs.

"There you are, honey," she whinnied, or was that my imagination?

Whichever it was, she took the cuffs, put them in her back pocket, turned and walked out of the room on leather shoes that did make a distinct clopping noise on the linoleum floor. And what was with these cop-types that they didn't identify themselves?

"The charges have been dropped, Kristin," Anna said. "Howard is bringing the paperwork. He's right behind me."

"What?" I asked, still a little groggy. "Why?"

"Well, it seems that there is no one to press charges against you. The so-called doctor gave a false name and address to the responding police, as did the guy who said he was a clinic attendant and that you described as a guard working at the prison. The guy in the white coat called himself Dr. Richard Wagner, and the guard gave the name Peter Schmidt. No record of either. And apparently they both just took off after the cops took you away. The police also called the warden's office, and he denied emphatically that any such person as Peter Schmidt worked there. There are now warrants out for both of them, and for Isobel Rivera."

Wagner, I thought, still groggy. German, but probably not related to the composer. All the fancy, surgical tools engraved with German must have been his. Nazi doctors flashed through my mind, and I shuddered. I'd bet when they caught up with Wagner, he'd have been stripped of a medical license in his career. Maybe more than once if he changed names. And the prison warden was denying he'd ever heard of beefy, white guy #2? I wondered how long he thought he could keep that up. And Isobel was on the run.

"Wait," I said, starting to really wake up. "Does Isobel Rivera have my purse?" I sure didn't want her running around the Midwest with my ID. "And what about my car?" I added.

Carson was in the doorway, and he heard me. Behind him, baby lawyer came in, carrying a sheaf of papers and a paper bag. Harold, I remembered. His name was Harold.

"Your car had been impounded," Carson said. "We have gotten it released, and we obtained your purse and have it here," he announced, taking the paper bag from Harold, removing my purse and handing it to me.

I took it and just hugged it to my chest.

Harold coughed.

"You need to check the contents and sign for them," he said softly, smiling a little at my hugging my purse. What a nice person baby lawyer was. Harold, not baby lawyer I told myself.

I did as requested and everything was there. Including my cell phone.

"We will see that your car is driven back to your home in Chicago," Howard said.

In a very short time, or short for hospital time anyway, I had been discharged.

Anna had already summoned her limo service and been on her way.

"Howard and I will stay on this, Kristin," she said from the doorway as she was leaving. "There is a lot that needs further investigation."

Without a doubt.

As soon as I got into Tom's car, I fell deeply asleep and did not wake until we pulled up to the Chicago house.

Kid hugs, dog kisses and resounding versions of "Welcome home!" from Kelly, Carol, Giles, Nonna, and, yes, even Victoria, made me feel like I was back to 100%.

Tom rejected that argument, and I was hustled into bed.

I slept again.

22

The most painful state of being is remembering the future,
particularly the one you'll never have.

—SØREN KIERKEGAARD

"What do you mean, I can't look at the computer screen?" I yelped as Tom was reminding me about the do's and don'ts to recover from concussion.

"Kristin, you know perfectly well the neurologist said you should not look at a computer screen for at least four days while you are recovering. I know you heard him," Tom said, getting ready to leave for work while trying for his patient, compassionate voice. But there was a distinct undertone of irritation.

"How am I supposed to finish my dissertation? I'm so close to being finished," I whined. I knew I was being unreasonable, but it was early in the morning, and there had also been an "absolutely no caffeine" ban instituted because of the concussion, so even decaf coffee was out of bounds.

"You can use computer software to read to you, and you can talk into it," said a kid voice from above us. Mike was in the upper hall, apparently. Tom and I were right below him, arguing by the front door.

"There, you see, there's a computer fix for that," Tom said as he finished buttoning up his coat. He kissed me soundly, though I thought pretty much to shut me up, and he left.

"Mike," I called up the stairs. "It is not nice to eavesdrop on a private conversation."

"Couldn't help it," he said while thundering down the stairs. "You guys were so loud."

He must have been dressing for school as he had on a long-sleeve shirt with his pajama pants.

"Come on! I'll show you. It's really easy." He dashed into my study room and stood beside my desk. I sat down and used my fingerprint password that I'd had the computer tech install to open it. I did not want to get hacked by my own sons.

Mike nudged me off the chair, took my place and in an astonishingly short time a text-to-voice program was downloading, and a dictation program was waiting its turn.

I couldn't help it. I gave his sleep-tousled hair a rub.

"Hey!" he protested. The text-to-voice program finished loading, and the dictation program began its downloading journey across my screen. A sleepy Sam and Molly joined us.

"Whatchadoin'?" Sam said around a yawn. That made Molly yawn too. I smiled.

"See," Mike said in his explaining voice, "Mom can't read or write on the computer for a few days because she got a bump on the head. Tom said. So all she has to do is use this program to read stuff to her," Mike pointed at the download icon, "and this one," he pointed to the one crossing the screen, "Mom can use to just talk and the computer program will type it."

I had told the boys merely that I'd hit my head. The rest Tom and I had kept to ourselves.

"Cool!" Sam said. "Try it, Mom. Try it!"

"Okay," I said, hesitantly. "Let me try the reading program. Open that file there, Mike."

I pointed to my dissertation file and with a few clicks, Mike had the computer reading it to me.

"Write that down, will you, what you did there?" I asked.

A sigh.

"Sure." He scribbled on a pad.

"Now," he said importantly, "click that." There was an icon that looked like a head with an open mouth.

I obeyed my son.

"Now, talk."

I recited the first few lines of "Goodnight Moon."

Sam giggled as Mike tapped the icon again, and those words appeared on the screen.

"Now," Mike said in a voice that had a suspicious similarity to Tom, "you need just this blank screen with the two icons below. No reading the screen."

And my computer screen went blank.

"You guys should get finished dressing and ready for school," I said firmly. I had to take back some parental control. They ran back up the stairs.

"That was so GOAT," I heard Sam say to Mike.

GOAT. "Greatest of All Time" I translated from kid-speak.

Then Molly and I both heard the rattle of a pan in the kitchen, and we headed there. Nonna and Giles were sharing the tasks of getting breakfast on the table. Neither looked happy about it. I let Molly out and left them to it. I had a lot to do today no matter what doctors or family members in my life said.

❉ ❉ ❉

At 8 am I called the FBI offices and left a message for either Agents Paul Lindsay or Kamal Nadar to call me back. I had a strong suspicion that the remnants of the El Chapo gang were now trafficking in human organs, though that was such a horrifying a thing to contemplate. With the rise of new diseases around the world, as well as more social unrest, I had reasoned, people who didn't want to wait on an organ donation list in the US also might not feel they could safely travel abroad for what was commonly called "transplant tourism," that is, flying to a poor country to get a local organ. I thought the vicious entrepreneurs who had made up the El Chapo gang had seen a market for domestic organs.

I'd had plenty of time to think about the whole pattern while locked in the freezing cold room with the unconscious Isobel. She had been stored like so much meat. Just kept alive to be carved apart when there was an order for her organs. It was disgusting. But what would you put past the kind of drug traffickers who killed babies and stuffed their little bodies full of drugs?

Within minutes, Agent Nadar called me back.

"Ms. Ginelli," he said, his deep, measured voice sounding urgent, "I was going to call you today and ask you to come in to the office. There have been developments." I knew it was pointless to try to get him to elaborate on a phone line.

"I'm afraid you'll need to come to me," I said. "I have a concussion. When you get here, I'll explain how that happened and what I think I have found that might relate to your investigation."

"Hold on," Agent Nadar said, and the phone was muted.

"Agent Lindsay and I will be there in less than an hour," he said briskly when he came back on the line, and he hung up.

I knew they knew where I lived. They were the FBI.

❀ ❀ ❀

IT WAS MORE LIKE thirty minutes when my doorbell rang. I had barely finished yanking on some yoga pants and a big shirt.

I opened the door, and they came in quickly and stood in the hall. I guessed the FBI didn't like to linger on doorsteps. I quickly closed and locked the door.

We exchanged nods, and I gestured toward the front room. They each took a chair and took out their phones and started to scroll.

I waited, my stomach starting to churn. They always looked serious, but both men were frowning deeply as they looked down at their devices.

Agent Lindsay looked up first and cleared his throat. Agent Nadar nodded. I sat like I was made of stone. Lindsay took out a small recording device like Anna and Howard Carson had used to take my statement in the hospital. I started to wonder if I should call Anna and ask her to be here.

"Please tell us about your teaching at the private women's prison in Dyson, Indiana, what happened there and how you were injured," Agent Lindsay began.

I kept thinking.

The two agents looked at me.

"Ms. Ginelli?" Agent Lindsay finally said.

I had an electronic copy of the statement I had given to Anna and Howard. I decided the best plan was to simply share that.

"Let me get you the statement I gave to my lawyers for a judge in Indiana, though that proved unnecessary as no charges were actually ever filed."

Lindsay nodded. Nadar's dark eyes were scanning me. It was disconcerting.

I took out my own phone and went to email. Anna had sent me a copy. I asked each of them their email addresses and pressed send. I guiltily realized reading the tiny phone screen email was likely forbidden as well given my concussion. Well, it was done.

They both immediately opened their email programs and began to read.

I went to the kitchen to make coffee for them and the dratted chamomile for me. I had confined Molly to the kitchen before I'd gone to get dressed. She was not happy about that, but the best I could do was give her a dog cookie.

When I brought the tray of mugs back to the front room, Lindsay and Nadar were conferring in low voices.

I put the tray on the coffee table and waited.

"How were you hired to teach that prison class?" Nadar began.

I explained about Jane, the university chaplain, the consortium of seminaries and their prison education programs and that Dr. Ivy Mercer had thought she had gotten a severe flu and that they'd needed a substitute. Then Dr. Mercer had died and I'd continued the teaching.

"Did Dr. Mercer say anything to you when she called you the evening she died?" Lindsay asked.

"How do you know about that?" I asked, startled.

"This is part of a wide-ranging investigation," Lindsay replied shortly, and then he asked again, "Did she say anything?"

I thought back to that horrible call, trying to remember every nuance. It was clear to me they didn't think she'd died of flu.

"No, she seemed to think she had called 911, and she was barely coherent," I said.

They took turns going through the copy of the dictation I'd just emailed them, clearly probing more deeply in certain areas.

"This warden of the prison," Nadar asked, tapping a finger on his phone. "What is your impression of him?"

"I think he's nutcase," I said, shortly.

"Could you elaborate?" Nadar said, a flicker of irritation showing briefly on his bronze features.

I quoted the warden as accurately as I could, and I added my own QAnon interpretation of his odd questions and statements.

They nodded and then asked me to go through my growing suspicions about women disappearing and the growing tension in the class. I'd covered that in my statement, I said. We'd been at this for nearly an hour. I let my impatience show. I was doing all the telling, and they were giving me nothing. Typical FBI.

"Tell us your impressions of Isobel Rivera and what happened at that so-called clinic," Lindsay said.

I went back over that and I shared my anger that after I had effectively rescued her from death, she'd hit me and run.

Lindsay reached out and turned off the recorder.

"This will be hard for you to hear," Nadar said, and his stone face softened. He glanced at Lindsay, who nodded.

"We have determined from the enhanced dash cam photo of the driver of the van your husband stopped that the person who shot and killed him is Isobel Rivera."

I saw double. Then the top part of Nadar disappeared into a mist. I felt myself sway in the chair.

"Drink this," I heard Lindsay say. "You need fluid and sugar. Come on, drink."

I obediently sipped the tepid tea. They must have added a ton of sugar it while I was, what would you call it, swooning? The tea was so sweet it made my teeth hurt. But it helped.

The room came back into focus.

"Tell me," I said in a voice that sounded far away even to myself. "Tell me everything."

"I will tell you what I can," Lindsay said. And he recited Isobel Rivera's history of being a part of the El Chapo gang primarily as a driver for the Midwest distribution of the drugs that came in the big trucks from Mexico. After the breakup of the gang, she had re-located to Indiana and had been involved with drug distribution there. She had been arrested and imprisoned in Indiana for that crime.

"We surmise that she was part of a kind of spy network in the prison, helping the warden select women as candidates for organ harvesting. Given her history, it is possible she started to blackmail the warden either to get paid more, or even get released and instead found herself strapped to a gurney."

Harvesting? I thought. What a term. I thought of J.C's comment about a "body farm." I shuddered.

"There is now a wide-spread hunt for this Rivera woman. We'll get her, and she'll go down for your husband's murder and another that we suspect," Lindsay said confidently.

I have a name, I thought dully. I know who killed Marco.

And I had saved her life.

I ran for the downstairs bathroom and was thoroughly sick.

23

Bitterness is like cancer. It eats upon the host.
But anger is like fire. It burns it all clean.

—MAYA ANGELOU

"How much are you still bleedin' inside?" Alice Matthews asked, the skin around her eyes creased into narrow lines as she sat facing me, staring at me so hard it felt like she was trying to see under my skin.

She was right. That's just what it felt like. And how much was I still bleeding inside? I asked myself silently. While telling her the whole story, I'd tried not to relive it, but that had been impossible. And one thing I knew Alice knew well was the pain of loss, and she knew how having saved the life of Marco's murderer had cut me up inside like I'd had surgery without anesthesia.

Yesterday, after the FBI agents had left, I had sat in our front room in silence for an hour. Then the boys came home, and I had walked and talked and eaten though I had little memory of it. Then I had gone back to sitting in silence, waiting for Tom.

He had come home late, taken one look at my face and walked me upstairs. I had started from the end, what the agents had said, and then I'd broken down completely, sobbing until I was exhausted and had fallen asleep in his arms.

Broken down, I thought now gazing at Alice. I had broken last night, and today the shattered pieces inside were still cutting me. It was true. That's why I'd called her this morning, asked her to come over. She hadn't even asked me why, just heard the tone of my voice and replied "Yes."

"A lot really, Alice. Just what it feels like," I said, my head bowed forward like it had gotten too heavy.

She reached over and patted me on my knee. I looked up, startled. Alice was not a person who gave out pats.

"So, how are they gonna get her?" she asked sternly.

Maybe that hadn't been a pat, but more of a poke.

"I don't know," I said slowly, realizing I hadn't asked that question. I hadn't asked about anything. I'd just been stunned.

"Can't have that bitch running around loose, now can you?" Alice said sternly. "You need to call those agents, find out. You might know somethin' from that class, or other that could help them find her. And what's happening with that cesspool they call a prison? Is it still open?"

Right. Right. I felt rising anger, and it was cauterizing the bleeding.

I sat up straighter and let the fury fill me. Marco's murderer was running around free, and I was sitting here wallowing.

I looked over at Alice. She looked formidable. Righteous. And focused.

"Thanks, Alice," I said, thinking of the information I had on Rivera in my class file. "Get her. That's the job now."

"Damn straight," she said.

❉ ❉ ❉

AFTER ALICE HAD LEFT to continue keeping the campus safe from what she called "the educated idiots," I called the FBI offices and left a message for Agent Lindsey to call me. He called back immediately.

"What is it, Ms. Ginelli?" he asked, his voice low. I could hear some traffic noise in the background.

"I have some notes from my class in the prison, and some are about that person we discussed the last time."

"Just a moment," he said. Then he spoke again.

"Agent Nadar will have someone send you a secure computer link. Log on to it and write up what you have in your notes. The link will be good for only one use. Clear?"

"Clear," I said and hung up. I felt like a junior Fed.

I went to my study and got my class file out. I had typed up notes after each class about every student's interests and comments, printed them and added them to the file. I remembered Isobel had been told to be quiet by Officer Jackson for one of her contributions. There had been something in what she had said that had alerted Jackson, caused her to interrupt.

I flipped through my printed notes and saw "Rivera." Yes, it was about what she'd liked about Ivy's class. I read the few words about "Moses," by whom I thought she'd meant Harriet Tubman, the woman who had been enslaved, escaped and then come back and led others to freedom. Yes, I'd noted "places to run to" that would have had to be "close by" and a peculiar reference to Tubman not having a car. Then Jackson had interrupted.

I turned on my computer. I'd need to violate the "no screen time" dictum. I went to my email program and saw a new message headed "Savings for You." They were such jokers, these FBI agents. Yes, perhaps this would be a saving.

I clicked on the link and quickly typed up what my notes indicated Rivera had said. The memory of that moment became clearer as I typed.

"And I like that Moses woman. There's places to run to. People to help you on the way. And if that Moses woman had had a car, well then, good help would be close by."

That was it. There was some kind of a safe house near the prison that she knew about. She'd thought she could get a car there. I pressed send and guiltily shut down the computer.

Just then my phone rang. It was Tom. As I pressed "accept," I thought he couldn't possibly know about my using the computer for a few minutes.

"Hello, Kristin. I only have a second. Dr. Patel called from the rehab facility, and Vince is well enough to be discharged tomorrow. They want to know if he can stay locally, but I'm concerned about the additional stress on you."

Of course Tom was concerned, but Vince and Natalie needed to be here. I told him that.

"I'll make a few calls, Tom," I went on. "I can hire help and get that side parlor on the first floor fitted up with a hospital bed, a chair with a hoist and a wheel chair."

"Well, okay," Tom said slowly. "Just don't tax yourself. Rest is important."

So is catching Rivera, I thought, but I said nothing about that.

"Absolutely."

The thing was, I knew exactly whom to call. The only woman cop friend I'd made while I was on the force had gotten married, quit, and with her new husband opened a medical supply company in what was called the "South Loop," an up and coming neighborhood only a little north of the university area.

I thought I still had her number in my phone. I did.

"Shandra," I said warmly as she picked up on the first ring.

"Kristin, is that you?"

We chatted for a while about how happy we both were not to be cops any more, and then I explained the situation.

"We have plenty of stock. No problem. I can have those items moved in for you this afternoon. What about home health aides, though? Do you need them as well?"

"Yes, I do, Shandra. I was just going to ask you for recommendations."

"My little sister does that. I'll call her and get her to send some people by. They can also help with the set-up of the room. Do you want men or women?"

Good question. I thought about Vince and whom he would like to help him to the bathroom and so forth.

"Men, I think, Shandra. I think you might even have met my father-in-law before he retired from the force. Vincent Ginelli?"

"Oh, yes. Old school guy. Sure. I'll have Chanice send Albert, and he can alternate with his brother, Michael. You'll love'em. Terrific guys. They were professional weight-lifters before they got their LPN's."

I couldn't help thinking of beefy, white guys #1 and #2. I hoped Albert and Michael were strong guys without the paranoia. I was sure they would be, knowing Shandra.

"Perfect," I said, and we agreed on two o'clock for the delivery.

I texted Tom back that we were all set, and then I called Natalie. She had been spending her days at the rehabilitation hospital. When Vince was exercising, I had been told she was volunteering in the crafts room. Her phone went to voicemail, and I left a message we would be all ready for Vince to come home.

Molly had been sleeping on my feet while I had done all this, but she got up immediately when I went to the kitchen to get a snack. I was hungry. That was a good sign, I had been told.

Molly and I shared my snack, and I let her out into the yard for a short while.

When I let her back in, I headed upstairs for a nap. I set my phone to wake me at 1:30 pm in time to meet the delivery.

I stretched out on the bed and shut my eyes. I felt the mattress next to me shift. I opened my eyes and saw Molly was already sleeping next to me.

Dogs can always nap. Me too.

❈ ❈ ❈

I SURVEYED THE PARLOR. We were pretty much all set there. There was a hospital bed all made up. A lift was pushed over into a corner. There was a portable toilet also pushed back in that corner with a portable screen to hide it. A chair that had its own lift that operated with a lever on the side was in front of one window, and a comfortable arm chair for Natalie that converted into a single bed was in front of the other. There was a third chair for the health aide. I'd asked Shandra's movers if they could bring down the small television from the master bedroom. Tom and I never used it. That was set up on a small table across from the chairs. I'd also asked them to roll up the oriental carpet that covered most of the floor and take it upstairs and just put it along the wall in the master bedroom. The floor needed to be free of such obstructions. The wheel chair I'd ordered and the walker were in the center of the room, and I pushed them over past the TV. The movers also had brought the portable ramp Shandra had reminded me we needed, and they'd set it up out the kitchen door that led to the path to the garage. Molly had followed them and after sniffing it thoroughly and walking up and down it, seemed to approve. The movers had laughed. Dog people.

I tipped them generously as they prepared to leave. Good timing. Natalie was coming up the front walk as they were walking out.

"Kristina," she said as she came in. "So much trouble, and you head still hurting?"

"Those men did all the work, Nonna, and come see. I think you will like the place we made.

I was showing her the parlor when the doorbell rang.

It was Albert and Michael. They looked to be in their twenties and, as advertised, they were quite muscular; their copper-colored muscles sticking out of their short-sleeved shirts almost gleamed. Their smiles were warm. They introduced themselves, and I took them to the parlor to meet Natalie.

Introductions made, I left them to it. Natalie had to be comfortable with them. As I was walking away, I heard Natalie say solemnly, "My Vince, he no like help."

"Well, ma'am," I heard a deep voice reply, "we'll just have to help him think things are his idea, right?"

"*Giusto*," Natalie said, her voice more cheerful. That's right, in Italian.

I let Molly in from the backyard. She still seemed entranced with the ramp, and she ran up and down it twice before bounding into the house. I had forgotten to close the kitchen door, and she got past me and down the hall to the parlor before I could stop her.

I heard "hello, dog" and a rumbling chuckle. Then I heard Molly's whine of pleasure. Either Albert or Michael must be scratching her ears.

Good enough.

Then I heard the front door open and close and the boys calling "Mom!"

Good thing I'd taken that nap.

24

I learned that courage was not the absence of fear, but the triumph over it.

—NELSON MANDELA

The ambulance pulled up to the front of the house. Natalie, Albert, and I went down the walk to meet it. Albert was carrying the new wheelchair and a blanket. Natalie was a little teary, and I put my arm around her. She's lost weight, I thought as my arm nearly encircled her.

Albert clearly knew his stuff. He had the wheelchair open and ready as the ambulance guys lowered Vince on a lift out the side. He was strapped in, and he looked grim.

The transfer to the new wheelchair went like clockwork. Vince was raised to a semi-squatting position by Albert putting his arms under Vince's armpits and lifting with his legs. That's what people always said, lift with your legs. I saw what that meant. Vince took a couple of steps sideways, and Vince was lowered expertly. Not his first time being transferred into a wheelchair, I thought sadly.

Suddenly I became conscious I was holding my breath, and I exhaled.

Albert tucked the blanket he'd been carrying around Vince. I realized it had gotten quite cold, and there was a stiff wind from the west. Albert didn't waste any time. He immediately started pushing the wheelchair down the side path toward the back door. They were followed by Natalie who was uncharacteristically silent. One of the ambulance guys lifted out Vince's rolling suitcase, and the other handed me a clipboard to sign. That taken care of, I thanked them and they sped away. I took the handle and rolled the little case around to the back.

Up the ramp and into the house took little time, and I heard Albert down the hall telling Vince, "Easy does it."

When I got to the renovated parlor, Vince was sitting in the recliner chair, and Natalie was seated just on the edge of the convertible chair next to him.

"How'bout some water, you two?" Albert asked.

"Nah," I heard Vince say, and Natalie must just have nodded no.

"Okay, then," Albert said in a level tone. "Lunch in about an hour?"

"*Si*," Natalie said. "I fix."

"Alright, Nonna," Albert replied. "That's okay with me. I heard you a wonderful cook. But I do the carrying, right? You tell her, Vince."

Nonna? I thought to myself. I guessed Natalie must have asked Albert to call her Mama in Italian.

I heard the rumble of Vince's voice and though I couldn't quite make it out it seemed he was agreeing with Albert. Smart of Albert to make it about him and Vince taking care of Natalie.

I left the rolling suitcase at the foot of the front stairs. It was probably full of dirty clothes, and the laundry was on the second floor.

"So, what you folks like here on the television?" I heard Albert ask.

I went in to my study room, shut the door and exhaled again. This was working.

Just as I was about to try to get the software going to read the last pages I'd written on my dissertation, my phone buzzed with a text.

Oh no. It was a reminder from Adelaide about the two o'clock lecture today by our second candidate for the new ethics position, Dr. Sandra Ellen Parker. She was Adelaide's preferred candidate, the environmental ethicist who had trained both at the University of Colorado and at Vanderbilt. I was torn. I thought her work enormously important, especially since the destructive effects of climate change were creating literal climate emergencies in our own country and around the globe.

And, I sighed to myself, I had not told Adelaide anything about getting injured.

Maybe I could make it. I opened the door of my study room and listened. I didn't hear anything, and I looked down the hall to see the sliding door of the parlor had been pulled shut. I tiptoed down there and listened. I heard the sound of a game show punctuated by snores. I pulled the door open slightly, and I could see Vince was tilted back in his recliner snoring away, and Natalie had her head back and her eyes closed. A small footstool was under her feet. Albert was sitting in another arm chair on the far side of the room, reading on his phone. He lifted his head and gave me an "OK" sign.

I silently slid the door closed.

I walked down to the kitchen wondering if it would be safe for me to walk to campus. I doubted I'd have to read any computer screens along the way, and I was feeling a lot stronger. I'd just need to bundle up. I came into the kitchen and found Victoria and Kelly were sitting at the table, each working on a portable computer.

They looked up when I entered. I knew Victoria liked to come by and work at our kitchen table. I was glad she felt comfortable doing so. I was still worried about ole Trevor making a comeback with her if she was too lonely. And she and Kelly had become friends.

There were two "hi, Kristins" and I hi'd them back.

"Nonno and Nonna doing okay?" Kelly asked.

"Yes, they are snoozing away in the parlor. One of the home health aides is with them."

"That's good," Victoria said, smiling. "I could fix them some lunch if you'd like."

"Right," Kelly chimed in. "I could help."

"Let's play that by ear," I said slowly, thinking about Natalie wanting to fix lunch. "Nonna had said she wanted to do it."

"I am excellent at helping her while she thinks she's teaching me how to cook," Kelly said wryly. She smiled at me and suddenly looked so adult I swallowed. I would miss her so much when she went off to college.

"I'm sure I can do that too," Victoria said sweetly. Well, I chuckled to myself, at least I'd have Victoria as an adopted daughter when Kelly started college.

"Okay, fine. You two work it out. I'm going to walk down to campus to go to a lecture."

Kelly got out a "But," and I cut her off.

"I feel fine. Don't worry. And don't call your Dad," I said.

"Okaaaay," Kelly said slowly. God she was like Tom.

✿ ✿ ✿

Students and faculty were lined up outside the larger auditorium next to Myerson where Dr. Parker's lecture would be held. "Our Current Extinction Event" was her title, and it was certainly packing them in. I went around to a side door and went in through the stage entrance. There were seats reserved for me and the colleagues. Aduba and Hercules were already there, chatting away. They seemed to have become good friends. Donald and Adelaide had not yet arrived, Adelaide because she would be escorting the speaker. If Donald blew off this guest lecture, Adelaide would make him pay. I didn't think Donald was brave enough to risk that, but who knew?

I sat down next to Hercules and got his usual warm welcome. Aduba said "Good afternoon, Kristin" in his British/Nigerian-accented English. I said hello back. I didn't have to even turn to feel the auditorium filling to capacity. Voices, breath, bodies, backpacks, and the clicking of cellphones made the human volume felt.

Then a rustling of turning bodies told me Adelaide and the candidate had arrived. I turned like most of the audience and saw our department chair accompanying a tall, thin woman with what I could only call a buzz cut dressed in a light-grey, ill-fitting suit. Dr. Parker did not waste her time on hair or dress apparently. Adelaide's royal blue, flowing dress billowed out beside her. Parker looked like a shadow that had fallen across a blue sky. Probably an apt metaphor I sighed as I turned back toward the front. There was a looming, grey shadow over the blue planet's future. I periodically felt a deep dread about the planet the boys would inherit, and often I ruthlessly suppressed it because I also felt powerless to change it.

Adelaide and the candidate ascended the stairs to the stage in this auditorium where there was a podium and two seats. A large screen was hanging in front of the curtains.

Adelaide stepped to the podium and introduced Dr. Sandra Ellen Parker. She listed her impressive training and then the various parts of the world where she had done field research, most recently in Siberia where temperatures above the arctic circle occasionally reached above 100 degrees Fahrenheit.

The dread I was feeling increased. No wonder people were sleepwalking through this disaster. Who wanted to feel dread all the time?

Parker took the podium and began to talk about "climate grief." Behind her a series of photos of empty lakes, ground that had become so dry it had cracked into fissures, and flaming forests rolled forward like a news reel from the future, except it was now.

Then she paused the photos and asked us each to examine how we were feeling. I personally wanted to get up and leave the auditorium. I thought if I'd been sitting toward the back I might have left at that point.

I just didn't feel I could take an hour of this unrelenting reality that made me feel worse and worse.

"Feel bad, don't you?" she asked, in a tone that I could only describe as brisk compassion.

She had that right.

Then new photos went up of some of the indigenous peoples of the Amazon. She described how the people who have been experiencing some of the worst effects of climate change have found many ways to take action and lessen the harm.

Her calm, steady voice went on. "These approaches include selecting and growing seeds that are more resistant to drought and heat, investing in frontline firefighters and even a smartphone app that offers information about climatic variations."

The rest of the lecture followed in that vein from Siberia to the Navajo Nation to central Africa.

The message was clear. People who are on the front lines of climate catastrophe are doing better at coping with climate grief through action than more privileged, largely white communities that have more physical insulation from its effects.

When she finished, the applause was loud and sustained. Hands went up all around the big auditorium. I stayed for a little while and then started to really feel fatigued. But not any longer so grief-stricken and depressed.

I slipped out a side door while someone in the back was asking about the permafrost in Siberia.

Walking back, I didn't think as much about the lecture itself as about how much we needed both Womanist scholarship and environmental ethics in our department. And then I focused in on possible strategies I could use to blackmail the administration into giving us both positions.

GILES HAD FIXED A WONDERFUL casserole with chicken and all kinds of vegetables in a spicy tomato sauce. He and Carol had taken their portions upstairs. Kelly was out for the evening with Zeke. Tom was still at the hospital. Natalie and Vince had eaten on trays in the parlor. Albert had been replaced by Michael who seemed just as competent and caring as his brother.

So the boys and I had enjoyed a meal together, and I got to hear all about this "new kid" who was from Japan. His parents were going to teach at the university starting in the fall. "Science stuff," Sam specified. The new kid was pronounced "cool" as he knew karate.

I listened to them chatting happily and tried not to fall into climate grief once again. After checking homework, I read them some of *The Call of the Wild*. We were working through it chapter by chapter before bed.

I tucked them in and went back downstairs to see how things were going there. Michael met me in the hall and whispered that Vince was already asleep in the hospital bed and Natalie was upstairs in their bedroom. All was well.

Well, except for Tom not being home yet. I headed for the stairs and saw the little rolling suitcase still sitting there. I'd better get these dirty clothes in the washer, I thought, so Vince will have some clean clothes tomorrow.

I carried the little bag to the second floor laundry and dumped the contents on the folding table that ran along one wall. As I thought, it was all in need of a thorough wash.

As I sorted, I checked the pockets to be sure they were empty. Not quite. I pulled an envelope out of one of the pants pockets. It was still sealed. I looked at the address. It was to Vincent Ginelli at the trailer park address. But what shocked me was the return name. Y. Kelly. This was a letter from Yitz. Yitz who had been murdered according to Vince.

I just left the pile of dirty clothes and took the envelope to my bedroom. I sat down on the bed and stared at the wrinkled paper.

To open it or not? Vince could not take a shock right now, and the contents of this letter might very well be shocking, at the very least coming from someone who was dead by violence.

I tore it open.

Vince, I think I found the warehouse where they bring the coolers and then there's pickups. I am going to stake it out tonight. The warehouse is north of Dyson in a place called Wishott, stashed in some woods off of 29. But you have to get on a dirt road where there is an abandoned Esso station and then go 4 miles. Well hidden in the trees on the right. I will come and tell you what I find. Yitz

Yitz had been caught on his stake-out and likely killed there. Vince had said his dead body been moved to the Chicago alley where he'd been found.

So horrible. And coolers. God almighty.

I called the number Agent Lindsay had given me for emergency contact. The phone was answered on the first ring.

"Yes," a toneless voice said.

"This is a message for Agent Lindsay or Nadar. I found evidence of the location of a warehouse in Indiana that is likely being used. They should come pick it up."

"Thank you," the voice said. Toneless, but polite.

I looked at the envelope and paper in my hand and then thought dully, "I should have worn gloves."

I held the papers by the edge and went downstairs. I made a copy on the small printer in my study room and then went to the kitchen for a Ziploc plastic bag. I slid them in and sealed it.

I waited in the front room with the lights off. My phone rang.

"I'm right outside," Agent Nadar's deep voice said.

"I'm coming out," I said and hung up. I went on to the front porch, leaving the porch light off. I could see him in the light from the streetlamps. I kept the plastic bag down by my side.

"I want your promise I will be informed of how and when you move on this. It's a warehouse in Indiana," I said flatly.

"You know that's not possible," Nadar said, as tonelessly as the voice on the phone.

"Then I will stake it out myself and wait. You know me. You know I will do it. And you don't want to take the chance of me messing up your operation. I need your word, Agent."

Nadar sighed but did not say anything.

"Your word?" I insisted.

"Yes, but you will be ride-along only, nothing more. You stay in the van. Got it?"

"Got it," I said, and I handed him the bag.

Just because I "got it" didn't necessarily mean I would do it.

25

Boards don't hit back.

—BRUCE LEE

The next three days were outwardly calm and inwardly excruciating. Vince was taken to the rehabilitation institute each day by either Michael or Albert. Natalie went along and volunteered in the crafts room. Vince was visibly getting stronger, though his speech was still halting, and he had emotional swings from angry to withdrawn to a little of his former self. There was no way I thought it was a good idea to tell him about Yitz's letter and the FBI operation against Isobel and the other traffickers.

Tom operated. Kelly attended high school and studied. The boys walked to school with Carol. Carol and Giles went to class, and Giles cooked. Victoria worked at the kitchen table between client visits. Molly continued to run up and down the ramp.

And I was in a constant state of anxiety about when the FBI operation would take place.

The ban on screen time for me was lifted, and I was able to do more work on my dissertation. The audio program had actually helped some with organization as I had been able to sit and listen to how I was constructing my argument. But now I typed furiously. Was there ever a more powerful metaphor for what was happening in our country now with the rising hostility of white supremacists against racial/ethnic minorities? White supremacists denied these so-called "minorities" were equally human with the same rights as whites. Cutting these women prisoners up for parts and selling them demonstrated how much their lives could be reduced to just things. It reminded me, in a way, of that movie "Get Out" and the wealthy white people stealing the bodies of black people so they could insert their own brains.

But I also obsessively checked in several times a day with the FBI using the confidential link Nadar had sent for me to communicate. Our exchanges were so short they were microscopic.

Ginelli: "When?"

Nadar: "Not yet."

I met Alice several times at her preferred coffee shop. We sat outside at my request because I wanted to tell her everything that was happening.

"You know, gettin' angry and chargin' in to get them traffickers, two different things," Alice said, sitting at the outdoor table we liked, twirling her stick of gum so fast it was blurred.

I thought she was regretting telling me to go get Isobel.

I took a long look at her over the rim of my cup of decaf coffee.

"Don't look at me like that," she said, getting irritated. "I know you gotta get her. Stands to reason. Just don't be stupid, okay?" She wagged her stick of gum at me like it was her baton.

"No, I won't be stupid," I said slowly, but I feared I was lying to her and to myself. The hatred I felt for Isobel was like acid, corroding my impulse control.

Alice snorted so loudly it would have cooled her tea if it had not already been stone cold.

❄ ❄ ❄

THE OTHER PROBLEM WAS I hadn't told Tom that I was planning to go with the FBI on their sting. He'd been operating almost around the clock. There seemed to be so many elective surgeries that had piled up, and then he had the regular demand of emergencies.

But I had to do it. I couldn't just disappear when the FBI van showed up at the door.

Tonight, I told myself.

Fortunately, Tom got home earlier than usual, if you can call 10 pm early. I sat with him in the kitchen while he ate the meal I had warmed up for him.

"So, Kristin. You have that look. What is it? What's the matter?" Tom asked, and he carried his plate over to the dishwasher, giving me a little time.

"There's a warehouse in Indiana, not far from the prison," I said slowly.

Tom turned at the sink and looked at me, braced, I thought, for what was coming.

"The traffickers use it as kind of a way station before they do the distribution," I continued, picking up speed. "The FBI plans a sting, though I don't know when. I do know they want to get as many of the key players as possible, including Isobel Rivera."

Tom walked back to the table and sat down across from me, a grim expression on his face.

"And you want to go along, right?" he said.

"Yes. They want me to stay in the van, of course."

"Of course," Tom said dryly.

"I know, Tom. I know. But she's out there, free, and I can't stand it."

"Yes," he said, and he reached across the table and put both his hands over my fists that I had clenched with the huge emotion I was trying to control.

"Just be careful, okay?" he said, and I was stunned to see his eyes tear up slightly. "It does no good to trade your life for hers. Then she'll really have won."

Oh God. He was so right.

❁ ❁ ❁

THE OILS OF FAST food and the sour sweat of countless bodies tainted the air of the closed van. The side windows were blacked out. The windshield was darkly tinted. There were three agents seated in oversize swivel chairs. Their tactical gear took up a lot of room. Three computer screens on retractable arms were spaced along the right side. Below them was a shelf with keyboards and microphones bolted to it. Electrical outlets were spaced between. I assumed the monitors were connected to cameras concealed on the outside of the nondescript van. I was relegated to a narrow, back bench that was probably used for storage.

At 11 pm that evening my cell had rung, waking Tom. I had been awake, staring at the ceiling, so I was able to pick it up immediately.

"Out front. Half an hour," Nadar's deep voice said, filling my ear and ratcheting up my blood pressure.

"You're going on the Indiana raid?" Tom asked softly from his side of the bed.

"Yes. Now. I need to get ready," I said, already out of bed and heading toward the closet. I'd assembled my bullet-proof vest, the one I'd lent to my Muslim colleague when he'd given a public speech despite threats against him. I also had gotten out my retractable baton, a pair of handcuffs, and my opera glasses. Regular binoculars would be too big, and the agents would perhaps get suspicious. I attached the baton and the handcuffs to the outside of the vest. To go over this gear I had selected a black, bulky sweatshirt to hide it all. I put the opera glasses in one pocket. I put my cell phone in the other. I had black jeans ready and a black watch cap.

Tom was standing by the door when I emerged from the closet.

He looked at my bulky form, but said nothing more than "I love you. Be careful."

I hugged him tight and then tiptoed down the stairs and out the front door. The van pulled up immediately. A sliding door opened, and I crawled in, making my way between the big chairs and all the way to the back where Nadar, who was in the front passenger seat, pointed.

We rode in silence, I assumed toward the Indiana location of the warehouse, but since I could see nothing, I took out my phone to see if I could use my map program to locate us.

My phone said, "No Signal." Not surprising, really. I shut it off.

I had started to doze when the computer monitors lit up. They had map programs with small red dots moving and white dots following. They were not all displaying the same locations, I saw. All three agents in the chairs swung to the right to look at the screens.

"On track?" asked Nadar from the front.

"Yep," said the bulkiest looking agent, leaning forward to tap the keyboard in front of him.

"ETA twenty minutes."

I kept still, but I could feel my heart rate accelerate.

Soon we turned off of a smooth road that I assumed was the highway and took a left turn. That road was also fairly smooth, but the van had slowed some. Route 29? I wondered. Likely.

After about five minutes we turned right, and the van bumped and rocked. We were moving very slowly. I doubted this was even a road. Were we making our way through the trees? I thought so. The double dots on the screen were moving more slowly as well, but I thought there was also a pattern of convergence.

The van stopped.

A radio crackled in the front.

"Hold," a voice said. "Not in position."

We sat silently for what seemed like an eternity, but was probably only about twenty more minutes. I had on my watch with the illuminated dial, but I didn't even want to move enough to look at it as I was totally here on sufferance and wanted to draw no attention to myself.

"Go!" the radio voice said.

"Go," Nadar said. The doors flew open, and the agents stepped out making remarkably little noise.

"Ginelli, you stay put," Nadar said as he turned to exit. "You can come up here to look through the windshield, but that's it."

I nodded.

They were gone.

I squeezed past the swivel chairs and got to the front. Ahead, through the trees, there was what I thought was the warehouse. I had spent a lot of time on Google maps looking at this location, and I knew it was a long, low building with trees surrounding it and vines crawling up its side. It seemed to be cinderblock with moss coloring it green, though in the dark it was hard to tell. I could see only one of the agents, out to the right, behind a tree.

"First car arriving," the radio crackled, causing me to jump a few inches in the seat.

I wondered if Nadar realized he had left it on. Perhaps he had, knowing me and knowing that if I did not get some information, I would leave the van to try to get it. Between my promises to Tom and to Nadar, I was going to do my best to hang back. I did not want to do anything to screw up what was plainly a sting designed to get as many of the players in this trafficking operation as possible.

"Second, third cars coming up the road now. Hold your positions."

Silence.

Then I saw a flash of light and heard a muffled gun shot. I opened the passenger door to hear better. Definitely gunfire. Automatic weapons. Lots of shouting. "You're under arrest."

I stepped out of the van and shut the door, but I stayed right by the front fender. There was more gunfire, but now it sounded like all automatic weapons. Then I saw a light appear in the side of the warehouse. A door had opened. A short figure appeared. It shut the door quickly, looked around and ran for the trees. Right toward me.

One of the traffickers was making a break for it.

I wiggled my baton out from under the sweatshirt where it was attached to the vest. I slid it open and ran sideways to try to intercept the escaping figure. I caught a glimpse in the light from the windows that ran along the top of the warehouse and saw a tell-tale, patterned scarf tied around the figure's hair. I'd seen that scarf before. This was Isobel.

A rage so powerful swept me I nearly growled. But I held it in. Time for that when I caught her.

I stopped behind a tree and peeked around. I saw I needed to move further right to intercept her. I ran not only sideways but backwards a little. I risked another look. Yes, unless she swerved, she'd run right past this tree.

I heard her footfalls, and I took a batter's stance, the baton in both hands. As she got level with me, I swung it with all my might at her neck. I hadn't calculated quite right. She was so short I hit her head and only a glancing blow. But I knocked her sideways, and I jumped out and swung again. She lifted one arm to block the blow while her other hand went to her back. There was no doubt in my mind she was armed. I heard her forearm break from the force of the blow, and she screamed, but she was still on her feet and still reaching for her back.

I kicked her in the knee, and she fell, but I saw she now had the gun in her hand, though that hand was shaking. I swung down at her wrist and connected. Another crack, and she dropped the gun.

I jumped across her legs, hoping to get to the gun that was lying a few feet away on some leaves, but the devil woman that she was, she kicked out at me with her other leg, the one I had not kicked. I fell, and I felt her climb on to my back, her hands around my throat.

She cried out "arrrah" as she realized I was wearing a vest with a collar, and she could get no purchase on my throat. With the injuries to her arm and wrist, it must have been excruciating to try to choke me, but she was giving it her best shot.

I bucked my back and let loose with the scream I had been holding, holding in for years actually.

I bucked again, hard. Isobel was now trying to get at my eyes. I flipped her off, on to her back. I swung the baton toward her face and connected, but not as hard as I'd hoped. I thought I had just broken her nose as blood streamed out of it.

She would not stay down. She scrambled to her feet and tried to kick at my head as I was getting up. But she couldn't keep her balance with only one good leg. She staggered back.

"*Coño! Puta Madre!*" she spat. "You bitch! I kill you like I kill you husband. You think I no know? I know name. I saw his handsome face blow up when I kill. I enjoy. I enjoy now kill you."

Then she made a big mistake. She looked toward the gun. In one big stride I had it, and I leveled it at her.

"Take one more step, Isobel, and I will take great pleasure in shooting you," I said through clenched teeth.

"Shoot! Shoot! *Cobarde!* Coward. I not go back to prison."

She took a step toward me, taunting me, wanting me to kill her.

I trembled with wanting to kill her. I wanted to kill her so much I screamed inside with the wanting. But now I knew how bad it was in prison, even if you were a stooge. So instead I just swung the baton with my left hand and knocked her out.

I flipped her over and pulled off the handcuffs I had fastened to the other side of my vest and cuffed her hands behind her back. Then I sat back on my heels, closed my eyes and hissed curses at her.

"Ginelli!" Nadar's voice seemed to come from a long way off. I opened my eyes and was surprised to find he was only about four feet away.

"Did you kill her?" he asked.

"No," I said hoarsely, my throat sore. "She's just unconscious."

"Good work," Nadar said, bending down to feel Isobel's wrist.

"Here's her gun," I whispered, holding it out butt first to him as he stood back up.

"Thank you," he said. He paused. "I bet you were a hell of a cop."

I just bowed my head.

26

The old law about an eye for an eye leaves everybody blind.

—MARTIN LUTHER KING, JR.

I walked away from the van, looking for a signal. I found one and called Tom. It was after 3 am, but I knew he'd want to know immediately.

He picked up on the first ring.

"Kristin, are you okay?"

"Yes, Tom, I'm fine. We got them all. We got Isobel Rivera."

"Thank heavens," Tom sighed.

"There's cleanup here. I think the FBI sting was very successful," I said as I watched. "It will be a couple more hours though."

"As long as you're safe. I love you," Tom said in his rumpled, sleepy voice. He was dozing off even as he hung up.

I walked closer to the circle of SUV's, vans, and floodlights on stands. I watched as at least two dozen, handcuffed people were loaded on to a prisoner transport. Isobel was not among them. I had seen she had left earlier under guard in an ambulance.

Other agents were carrying out computer equipment, tables, chairs, some cots, and various boxes. I saw an agent carrying two small coolers. I shuddered.

As I pieced it together, it seemed the FBI had identified as many of the gang members as they could and had followed them for several days. It must have become clear the traffickers planned to shut down their operation and empty the warehouse tonight. The FBI was able to scoop them all up and also raid their distribution center.

Agent Nadar walked up to me, carrying two bottles of water. A little while ago another agent had moved the van forward into the circle around the floodlights, and I had seen Nadar enter it while looking at his phone.

He handed me one of the waters.

"You could go sit in the van if you like," he said as he stood beside me. "We'll be a while yet."

"Where is Isobel Rivera?" I asked. "I saw the ambulance."

Nadar sighed. "She's dead," he said, turning to look at me. "There were two agents in the ambulance with her, and she was restrained, but somehow she got a hand on the throat of a paramedic and was choking him. The agent pulled him away from her, but she went for the agent's gun. She actually had gotten a hand on it when the second agent shot her in the chest. She died instantly."

"She wanted to die rather than go back to prison," I said slowly, looking at the low, concrete block warehouse instead of at him.

"I think so," Nadar concurred. "We got some of the higher ups, though, so we're not hurting for evidence."

"I'd like to attend the debriefing if that's okay," I said, feeling oddly empty inside.

"I think I can swing that," Nadar said, and he walked back toward the circle of SUV's, vans and lights.

She was dead. We got her, Marco, I thought. Your murderer is dead.

I turned, walked a little ways away, bent over and threw up on a pile of leaves. I stood up and wiped my mouth with a tissue from my pants pocket. Then I walked over to the area by the tree where I'd finally subdued Rivera.

Was I sorry I hadn't been the one to kill her? I asked myself as I looked at the blood-stained ground. No, I thought. Someday I would have to tell the boys that their father's murderer had been captured by me. I would not have to tell them I'd killed her.

But, I thought as I continued to stare at the blood on the ground, I hoped there was a hell. I wanted to believe she was there by now.

❄ ❄ ❄

I HADN'T BEEN ABLE to sleep well for a few nights after the raid. I'd finally called Jane and gone over to her office to talk through how for years I had worked to find Marco's murderer and now that I had there was what felt like a constant emotional storm inside me. The grief and anger at his murder was still there, but the target of it was dead.

"What do I do with all this, Jane?" I asked her, my arms literally circling my chest where all the emotion felt like it might burst out at any moment.

"You give it time, Kristin," she had said softly. "It's the only thing that works. The only thing that ever has. And you are doing well not to hold it in. That is the route to depression."

We'd made plans to talk again, and oddly enough, I'd slept better that night. She was right. Just giving voice to the turmoil inside me had helped.

But I was still anxious about the upcoming FBI briefing and what I might learn from that. Finally, I'd gotten a call from Agent Nadar telling me the briefing would be in three hours. I'd raced downtown.

Even so, I was late. I had to wedge myself into an empty wall space at the back of the windowless briefing room on the top floor of the downtown FBI offices.

It was not my fault I was late. I had been stopped six times as I tried to get in to the office downstairs, and I'd been detained for a short time when I had tried to get up to this room. Agent Nadar had finally been reached on his cell phone, and I was escorted up with a badge that said "GUEST" pinned to my dark, ill-fitting suit jacket. I'd thrown on that ugly suit from my cop days. I had tried to look like an FBI agent, but it clearly had not worked.

It was a large meeting, I realized as I scanned the packed room. An agent was speaking into a microphone at a long table that ran across the opposite end of the room.

"Yes, the body was exhumed, and it was determined that Dr. Ivy Mercer died of acute arsenic poisoning," she was saying.

My stomach turned over. It was as I expected, but terrible that it was confirmed.

"Acute arsenic poisoning is associated initially with nausea, vomiting, abdominal pain, and severe diarrhea, thus giving the appearance of serious flu," she went on in the kind of curious monotone law enforcement often adopted when stating even hideous facts. "We assume the arsenic was administered in water while she was in the prison, perhaps by the warden himself. Dr. Mercer had made a call to this office two weeks before her death, asking for a time to come in. Unfortunately, she died before she could get an appointment."

Why? I wondered. A shortage of agents? An African American woman wanting to speak to the FBI wasn't a priority?

Dr. Ivy Mercer had suspected something was wrong at the prison and had been killed before she could report it. But, I thought regretfully, I could tell no one of her bravery, or even how she died. Jane would never know, I thought. Her colleagues would never know. I had been cautioned that revealing anything from this briefing to anyone could result in my prosecution.

That agent, having dropped a small grenade about agency incompetence, was passing the microphone to another agent sitting down the table. I thought I recognized him from the van. He looked smaller without the tactical gear.

"The Federal Bureau of Prisons has taken over the prison facility in Indiana. An arrest warrant had been issued for Herbert Snyder who had fled, along with two of the guards employed there, Axel and Finn Becker." He consulted some notes. "His office was raided and his appointments schedule shows he had met with Dr. Mercer two days before she reported to her institution that she was starting to feel sick and could not come in to teach." He paused again as he was handed another piece of paper. "This is an update. I see that all three have just been arrested near the Canadian border."

Well, good, I thought, but poor Ivy. Suffering alone at home, thinking she just had bad flu. Though arsenic poisoning in a big dose could not be treated, except for the dehydration. She had been dying. I shuddered.

The Becker brothers must be beefy, white guys #1 and #2. And QAnon Snyder had fled with them, but not for long. He and the beefy guys had not seemed clever enough to evade the FBI. I was glad to hear the prison was under new management, though I was certain the rumor mill was working overtime among the women.

I quit speculating as I heard a familiar name.

"Officer Quisha Jackson surrendered voluntarily and has been co-operating with authorities. She has already named several of the local police as persons of interest, and that is being investigated."

It had been Officer Jackson who had warned me not to drink or eat anything while in the prison complex. Had she suspected what had happened to Ivy Mercer? And her face when she had seen gurneys at the medical building had been grim. I hoped she'd get a good deal. She'd been at the prison longer than Snyder, and I'd bet he'd been key to setting up the prison end of the organ trafficking. Had she been threatened just to go along? I doubted I'd ever find out.

Suddenly I stood up so sharply I banged my head a little on the wall behind me. The agent was describing the more than 100 pounds of meth and opioids that had also been taken from the warehouse. The gang had not given up on its traditional drug trafficking, apparently, but had just added organs to the list.

Another agent took the microphone and read out a list of those who had been arrested at the warehouse and the plans for their prosecution.

Then I felt like I'd received a small electric shock, even though I had been waiting for it. Agent Nadar took the microphone, and I heard Rivera's name.

" . . . who was already a fugitive having escaped from the organ procurement facility. She was captured at the warehouse, and she sustained several injuries. She was shot by Agent Harrison in the ambulance taking her to a hospital when she attacked the medical technician and attempted to steal Agent Gomez's weapon. She died of that injury."

He coughed and glanced across the whole room at me, and then he dropped his gaze.

"Isobel Rivera had been identified through enhanced facial recognition we recently acquired as having shot and killed Chicago Detective Marco Ginelli seven years ago when he stopped the van she was driving . . . ."

I leaned back against the wall, and the room seemed to expand and contract with my labored breathing. There it was. Official confirmation.

I realized I had to tell Vince and Natalie everything now. The fogged up room receded even more, and I felt myself being helped to a chair.

"Just breathe," someone said, and I think I did.

The room came back into focus after a while, and my hearing returned.

"Dr. Helmut Granger, aka Dr. Richard Wagner, aka Dr. Herman Wagstaff, and we think several other aliases, has been apprehended. The doctor had lost his medical license several times, it seems mostly from trafficking in pain medications, and re-applied with other names. He is now claiming to be Dr. Richard Strauss." There was a slight chuckle around the room. There must be classical music fans among the FBI.

Soon afterwards Paul Lindsay took the microphone and dismissed the room, reminding various task forces they should check for their continuing assignments.

I waited until the room was nearly empty, and then I got up to leave. Both Lindsay and Nadar were still at the front, conferring. They turned as they saw me looking at them.

"Thank you," I said.

They both came over, and each one shook my hand.

"No, thank you," Nadar said.

"You got her," Lindsay said. "Your husband would be proud."

"I know," I said and walked heavily toward the elevator banks.

Closure. I'd always thought it would feel better than this.

✿ ✿ ✿

I GOT HOME IN the mid-afternoon. The house was quiet except for voices from the parlor. I went down the hall and knocked on the sliding door.

Michael opened it, an inquiring look on his face.

Vince and Natalie were seated, watching a game show. They looked up.

"Michael, could you take a break in the kitchen? I need to talk to Vince and Natalie."

"Sure," Michael said. "No problem."

I went in and turned off the TV. I pulled the spare chair over to face them.

"Nonna, Nonno, I have something to tell you," I began.

27

One of the hallmarks of white privilege is the casual ability to ignore or
avoid race at one's whim."

—SHARON H. CHANG

Natalie and Vince had left. The day after I had told them about what
had really happened to Yitz and how Marco's murderer, Isobel
Rivera, had been identified, captured and then killed, they had both become very withdrawn. I found out that evening they had called Vince
Junior to come get them. Natalie told me they would stay with him until
they could get home health aides for Vince at their own home and a rehabilitation schedule set up. With Vince Junior's rambunctious kids and his
wife's history of coolness toward her in-laws, I was betting that transition
would happen very rapidly. She'd want them gone as soon as possible.

They'd said good-bye to everyone at breakfast. As Michael helped
Vince walk to Vince Junior's car, Natalie had murmured to me, "We back
for the wedding, Kristin. You no worry." Vince did not speak to me.

I knew Vince was angry at me for keeping so much from him, but
I also knew that his anger came from his frustration at the limitations
posed by his stroke. I watched them drive away, knowing a chapter in my
life with them had just closed. But they would stay close to the boys. I was
certain of that.

That evening I sat in the circle of Tom's arms and grieved.

"They have been my parents, really from shortly after I started dating Marco. And when he was killed, they, and the boys, were my only
family. But, I couldn't have told Vince what was going on. I couldn't. And
now I'm losing them, losing Vince especially."

"I'm your family, Kristin, along with the boys and Kelly. And I doubt you are losing them, as you say. They are fully mourning their son now. It's a lot for them."

It was a lot for me too. I realized he was right. I was fully mourning Marco for the first time. Tom pulled me in closer and held me, silent and yet deeply present. But loss is loss. There's no getting around that.

❀ ❀ ❀

WORK ON THE DISSERTATION helped. I wrote and revised furiously for two weeks, and I finished it. I alerted my advisor it was done, and a tentative date was set for the oral examination.

I'd called it "Frozen Hearts Burning With Fear: Physicality in the Abuse of Power."

One thing I had learned from the time I had spent in the women's prison was how much the physical control of the human body was at the root of how power was maintained and expanded in this society. Many had written on the way in which the exponential increase in what was now called "the prison-industrial-complex" was the latest version of the way power and control was asserted, especially over Black bodies. But the literal carving up of bodies to sell the parts drove home to me the way in which the hearts of those who could do such a thing were frozen, frozen to absolute zero, devoid of an acknowledged human connection with those women as even human. And yet, those frozen hearts could still beat, could still perpetrate great evil because they burned with fear of the other, the one different from them.

This is an aspect of power and control that I thought had been less explored. But it is what drives whites to demand, even crave such visceral evidence of their superiority. As Ta-Nehisi Coates had written, "White America is a syndicate arrayed to protect its exclusive power to dominate and control our bodies . . . the power of domination and exclusion is central to the belief in being white, and without it, white people would cease to exist for want of reasons."

And that perceived existential threat is the root of the fear that drives white America to try to contain the bodies of the frightening "other" within prison walls.

Now, I thought, if I could just get my doctoral committee to accept that argument. My finger hovered over the keyboard, twitching with tension. Finally, I just did it.

I pressed "Send."

❉ ❉ ❉

I LOOKED OUT OVER the standing-room-only crowd packed into the larger auditorium. Students, faculty, staff and a few people I recognized from the neighborhood were waiting to hear from our third and final ethics candidate. It was my turn to present. I took a deep breath and began.

"It is my pleasure and privilege to introduce Dr. Nia Zendaya Turner, Womanist Ethicist and candidate for the Ethics position in the Philosophy and Religion Department. Dr. Turner holds a BA and a JD from Harvard University, and she has a PhD from Claremont. She is a prolific writer and speaker and has been interviewed numerous times on major television networks, especially about her prize-winning book, *Survive to Prevail: Womanist Ethics and the Politics of Death.* She is also an author and the editor of the widely used textbook, *Womanist Ethics: A Reader.*

"Please join me in welcoming Dr. Turner for her lecture "Seeing the Evil and Telling the Truth: Womanist Ethics Today.""

Dr. Turner, who was seated on the stage with me and Adelaide, rose. She was a tall, willowy woman wearing a flowing, white silk overshirt, leggings and short boots. I couldn't help mentally noting the contrast of her elegant garb with the ghastly tweed jacket of our first lecturer. Her short hair was curled on the top of her head and the sides cropped. Her eyes twinkled behind her wire-rimmed glasses as she shook my hand and said a warm "Thank you, Professor Ginelli." I was somewhat startled to see both her hands were empty. She was apparently going to speak without notes.

As she began, her measured voice, magnified by the sound system, seemed to fill the huge room from wall to wall and floor to ceiling.

"Toni Morrison, in her novel *Beloved,* has a main character ask 'Would it be all right? Would it be all right to go ahead and feel? Go ahead and count on something?' This masterpiece of what I would call 'magical realism' shows, no, really, performs the risks to African Americans of remembering. But without remembering, the very prospect of prevailing in life, in changing the present and the future, is in peril."

Oh, too close, I thought. Memory was not my friend these days. But I cautioned myself. This trauma is not my trauma. I shouldn't take it over. As a white person, I had more permission from society to remember, to know my history. I sighed a little, acknowledging the hurt I felt and yet putting it aside.

Dr. Turner was still speaking in a calm and yet relentless voice about the way in which slave narratives had recounted the horrors of slavery, but in a descriptive way. Those writing them knew that white America was rejecting the truth of what slavery was like and for them to put their own feelings into the narrative would perhaps have pushed even the staunchest white allies over the edge.

"So now we have to remember for them, otherwise we cannot achieve the moral autonomy needed to do the complex tasks of ethics today. African American women occupy a particular place in doing this work, but it is not exclusive to them. That place is made up of economics, laws, religion, and culture that demands they stay at the margins so the rest can function comfortably, seeing them and not seeing them."

I thought of the political manipulators and the ordinary morons who were railing against Critical Race Theory without having any idea what it was. And here Dr. Turner was showing how ethics without such a critical tool was not even possible today. But surely that was the goal of the political manipulators, I thought. They don't want truthful ethics to be possible.

"To become a moral agent then requires breaking free of those constraints while daring to imagine a world, a society, that does not depend for its raison d'être on the ability to oppress others."

The examples that followed were incisive and cut right through our current easy acceptance of lies and hypocrisy all in the name of not letting anybody remember anything really important.

The applause when she finished was thunderous. Hands went up all over the room. I looked over at Adelaide, and we both nodded.

Clearly, Dr. Turner was our first choice. But why should we be forced to choose? The reality of our times, as she was arguing, is so constrained from the top. It was the university that was forcing a choice, but maybe we could counter it somehow. I once again pondered strategies of a Machiavellian nature while the audience asked question after question.

Then I surfaced as I heard an aggressively loud, male voice shout out a question.

"So what you teach is Critical Race Theory, right? And so if you're hired, this university is going to brand all of us white males as evil and force us out."

I looked and saw the guy who was yelling way in the back. He actually had a sign that he now raised. "Critical Race Theory is Communism."

"Tell me what Critical Race Theory is, sir, and I will tell you whether I will teach it," Dr. Turner replied in a confident and yet carrying voice.

There was no reply.

The audience started to titter and then laugh as the demonstrator lowered his sign.

"That's just a trick!" he finally shouted, but by then the laughter was louder, and Dr. Turner called on someone else who had her hand raised.

I was reminded of Giles and how he had helped campus activists learn to use humor to counter white supremacists last year who had been threating a rally for peace and justice.

※ ※ ※

THE COLLEAGUES AND I trooped up the stairs with Dr. Turner for a reception and informal discussion with her. The same selection of tea, coffee, cheese and crackers was spread out on a table in the hall. I hoped the cheese and crackers were at least newly purchased and not saved from the last reception.

In any case, Dr. Turner avoided that part of the table like the experienced academic she was. She poured herself a cup of coffee and was immediately greeted by Hercules. He had apparently risked the elevator again and already had a cup of tea.

"Docteur Turn-er, what a pleasure to hear your lecture. I could not help but wondering about the role of memory in post-Holocaust philosophy and its relationship to your work."

And they were off and running on the works of Elie Wiesel.

Well, that was going well, I thought, as I put a chamomile tea bag into my cup and filled it with hot water.

I noted Donald had just come up the stairs and was hovering against the wall. I thought about going to talk to him about what he'd thought of the lecture, and I realized I just didn't have the energy for that. There would be time for that when we convened in the seminar room.

But curiously enough, the faculty discussion with Dr. Turner did not include Donald. He slipped away as we moved from the hall with its table of embarrassingly meagre snacks to the seminar room. Aduba asked about the influence of African history on Womanism. Hercules remarked on how Womanism was being taught in French universities, and Adelaide and Dr. Turner had a spirited discussion on the role of Womanism in the teaching of feminist philosophy today.

I asked about Dr. Judith Herman, the famous Harvard psychiatrist, and her observation that articulations of trauma in the public square were subject to "episodic amnesia," the willful social suppression of traumatic memories that get too close to the surface in our culture.

"Her work is important in my theory of ethics," Dr. Turner replied. "I got to know her when I was at Harvard. The mechanisms of suppression of historical trauma are very strong and have multiple sources. This makes any progress in the advancement of Womanist ethics be constantly be under threat. Live threat. It is, in short, risky business."

I didn't think she meant just theoretical threat. I looked over at Aduba, and he nodded back at me. He was constantly threatened by white supremacists on campus for his work on Islam and American culture.

Here was another colleague who might need to borrow my bulletproof vest.

28

Sitzfleisch: the ability to sit through any task, to do it again and again until the job is somehow done. Those who give out PhD's are human too - sooner or later they give in.

—LEON M. LEDERMAN

Doctor Kristin Ginelli, I thought to myself as I drove down Lake Shore Drive. It was a rare moment of little traffic. That was good, because I hardly saw the road.

I'd passed my doctoral exam. There had been a few aggressive questions. Chiefly, I'd been asked to explain why I had had so much trouble deciding on a dissertation topic.

I had wanted to say, "Because I was thinking about it," but I refrained. Snark did not seem like a good idea in that important examination. I think I said something about the value of exploration in philosophy, or some drivel like that.

I'd called Tom immediately after I'd left the building where I had had my defense. The sky over the lake was remarkably blue, and the vast body of water sparkled back in reply. Or perhaps that was just my mood. I was sparkling with happiness. I'd done it.

I held on to the ringing phone, but disappointingly it went to voice-mail. I still left a happy-voice message. "Passed!" I knew Tom had ordered a chocolate cake to celebrate tonight. He thought it was a secret, but the boys had ratted him out.

My next call had been to Adelaide. Fortunately, she picked up; so quickly, in fact, it seemed like she had been waiting for the call.

"I passed, Adelaide," I said, practically singing it.

"Oh, congratulations, Kristin. You did fine work in getting that done with everything else that has been going on."

Yes, I thought, as I simultaneously said, "Thank you" and listened to Adelaide congratulate me some more. There had been so much turmoil these past months.

At the last minute, before I'd pressed send on the dissertation copy to the examining committee, I had dedicated it to "Marco Ginelli, friend, husband, and a courageous man." Maybe someday I would give Vince a copy. But I thought it would be a while. Perhaps, I sighed, a long while.

Adelaide continued to talk gleefully about the future of the department. A promotion for me was on her schedule, she said. Then her voice dropped.

"But, we have to decide on the new appointment, and I tell you, Kristin, I am really conflicted. Two such outstanding candidates."

I muttered something about "We'll work it out" and then disconnected saying I had an appointment downtown.

I did. I had a meeting with Anna.

❉ ❉ ❉

ANNA'S OFFICES ALWAYS SOOTHED ME. Her executive assistant had come out to tell me she was finishing up a call and would see me shortly if I'd please wait. That was okay with me. The outer reception area with its soft colors, tasteful arrangement of actually comfortable furniture and the few, very intriguing, original paintings always combined to tell me "Don't worry so much, we've got this."

I heard the clicking before I saw her, and I looked up. Anna herself was coming down the marble floored hallway in her sky-high, Louboutin heels. Her pale grey, silk and wool Armani faux wrap dress was a new look for her. She usually wore tailored suits. I had actually considered the same dress online for the honeymoon, but I'd thought it would make me look like a beanpole. It looked fabulous on Anna.

"Hello, Kristin," she said warmly as I rose. "Come on back."

"That's Dr. Ginelli, now," I said as I came alongside her.

"Really wonderful, Kristin." She paused and chuckled as she opened her office door. "And now we won't have to sue them for not passing you."

"True," I replied, "though that could have been fun."

"So," Anna said when we were seated at her elegant office conference table, and she had a fresh legal pad and a fountain pen in front of her. "How can I help you?"

"Two things, really. Number one is I want to endow a chair in African American Studies at the university, but I want to do it anonymously. I'd like to name it after Ida B. Wells-Barnett and have it dedicated exclusively to the Philosophy and Religion Department. I want to tie up the endowment money in perpetuity so the chair cannot be yanked away and given to the Business School or some such and remade into economics, or worse.

"Will you draft that up for me and then negotiate the transfer of the funds? It needs to be done quickly, actually, as we have a good candidate for the first appointment."

Anna made some notes in her flowing shorthand, and then she looked up at me.

"How much?"

I told her and her left eyebrow went up slightly.

"Really? Are you sure you don't want to spend a few dollars more and just buy the university?"

Anna was joking, of course. At least I thought she was joking.

"I want the chair to be able to attract the absolutely topnotch people, and it should have travel and research funds attached."

More shorthand.

"Okay. I have it. I can email you a draft by this evening." She paused. "What is item number two?"

"There's a woman at the prison where I volunteered whom I think is wrongly imprisoned. What I have read about her case indicates that she acted self-defense. I'd like to see if, with proper legal representation, we could get that conviction overturned."

"Tell me some about her," Anna said softly.

"Her name is Fabiola Aime. From what I've been able to glean from the Internet, she was born in Haiti and sex trafficked from there at 14. That seems to have been about two years after the earthquake. She was passed around by pimps and finally sold to a suburban brothel in an Indiana suburb at 16. News reports indicate she attacked the man guarding the young women at the house. She escaped, but she was injured. She lost an eye. She was arrested for assault, and at 17 she was given a ten year sentence." I paused. "I think this was a travesty of justice, and I have wondered what role the traffickers might have played in getting this victim of sex trafficking imprisoned as a warning to other young women who would try to escape."

"Phew," Anna said as her pen flowed across the pad. "No wonder you want to see what you can do."

She tapped her pen on the pad.

"We can get Howard and his firm, of course. I'll get him to start working on this and get back to you."

"Thanks, Anna. I want to go out to the prison and get Fabiola's permission to hire her a lawyer, so please don't do anything until I have been able to do that. It's her call, of course."

"Right. Of course," Anna said.

THE PARTY TO CELEBRATE my passing my doctoral exam was excellent. When I'd gotten home, a big banner saying "Congratulations Dr. Ginelli" was hanging over the dining room table.

Tom got home in time for dinner, and we sat down to Thieboudienne, the national dish of Senegal we all loved. By "we," I had come to realize, I meant Tom, the boys, Kelly, Carol, Giles, Victoria and Zeke.

The dark chocolate cake with the dark chocolate icing was incredible.

On the dark as night surface of the cake, white icing spelled out "Dr. Ginelli!"

I had three slices. I didn't even try to count how many the boys had.

I WAS DRIVING EAST again along the expensive toll road toward the prison. I wondered suddenly if these tolls were tax deductible since I had been volunteering at the prison. I'd have to ask my accountant who was not going to be happy with the amount I was taking out of my investments.

Anna had come through both with the document for the donation for the named chair at the university, and with information on legal representation for Fabiola to re-open her case.

For the donation, I'd need to set up a revocable trust at my bank, Anna had written. Then the trust is the donor, and I could remain anonymous. Okay, not that hard. I'd called the banker I'd worked with over the years and told her to work with Anna to set that up quickly. I'd need to run down to the bank tomorrow and sign those documents in front of a notary.

Anna's communication on the options for Fabiola was interesting and complex. The best bet would be to hire a private investigator and try to uncover new evidence, information that had not been available at her first trial. If new evidence could be obtained, she could get a new trial and that evidence could be used. Just going for an appeal meant new evidence would be excluded. Since judges are notoriously loathe to grant new trials in criminal cases, the new evidence needed to be solid and compelling.

I had called ahead to the new warden's office and asked for a private visit with Fabiola Aime. The nasal warden's secretary seemed to be gone too. The new person who answered the phone was male and quite efficient. He asked me to wait for a call back, and shortly I had received permission.

The Federal Bureau of Prisons had recently stepped up both their oversight of private prisons, and in extreme cases, as I assumed was true for this one, they could send in their own team of temporary staff while an investigation and mandated overhaul could be conducted. The prison corporations were not happy about that, and they were lobbying to get rid of that oversight, of course.

I pulled up to the gate, and a forty-ish white man in a brown uniform stepped out of the guard house. He looked like the antithesis of beefy, white guy #1 as he was trim and fit. He came through the door in the sliding gate, took my license and when I presumed he had checked it, the gate started to open, and he waved me in.

I opened my window to get back my driver's license and astonishingly, trim and fit guy identified himself.

"Terrence Hathaway, Federal Bureau of Prisons," he said politely.

"Dr. Kristin Ginelli, visitor," I said. It still felt so odd to use that title, but I had to confess to myself I really liked it.

Hathaway waved me toward the parking lot, and I drove over there and parked. Another trim and fit guy was approaching, though he was a little younger and African American.

"Jamal Niang," he said pleasantly. I recognized his last name as of Senegalese origin. He wore the same brown uniform.

I was escorted into the building and down the corridor. The receptionist had changed too. I wondered if all the staff of the prison had been replaced. It was probably wise, but such turnover would be difficult for the women.

A young, Hispanic-looking woman appeared with a clipboard.

"I am Maria Hernandez. Follow me, please," she said, and I did.

We actually stayed in the administration building and just went to the second floor. I was ushered in to a small room with a table and several chairs. The window was high in the wall and screened with wire mesh.

"Please wait," she said and left. This staff was certainly polite.

After about fifteen minutes the door opened, and Hernandez appeared escorting Fabiola.

Fabiola looked frightened, though she smiled a little when she saw me.

"Use this phone when you are finished, and I will return," Maria Hernandez said indicating a wall phone.

"Certainly," I said, and, when the door closed, I was quickly embraced by Fabiola.

"I miss you," she said.

I patted her back. "I missed you too."

29

What were you hoping, when you removed the gags that stopped up
these black mouths? That they would sing your praises?

—JEAN PAUL SARTRE

I had done my best to explain to Fabiola what would happen if she
chose to try to get a new trial. I had thought the private investigator
might be a sticking point, especially if there was more to her story than
she had shared in class. The problem was not that, but the reach of the
traffickers even into the prison.

"This private man, I tell him all, he go talk to people?" she asked in
a quavering voice.

"Yes," I said as we sat across the table from each other.

"They tell me I tell all, they cut me," she said, her head hanging down
and her shoulders slumped.

"Fabiola, I will tell your new lawyer that, and he will need to see if
we can arrange protection for you first, you understand?"

"*Oui. Je sais.* They very *dangereuse.*"

I had noticed Fabiola reverted to French when she was stressed.

"You can decide after you talk to the lawyer, okay? You don't need
to decide now. But do not tell anyone here in the prison about this. I am
sure there are spies among the women prisoners."

"*Espionnes,* yes. All know this. Keep quiet always," she said. "You
know this too, *non?* From the class."

"Yes, I know it," I said steadily. "So, it is your decision. Do you want
to talk to the lawyer?"

"*Oui. Certainment.* It is no life here," she said, her one eye tearing up.

"Okay, I will tell him," I said.

We hugged again, and I left, my heart heavy. The drive back to Chicago was a blur as I wondered if I had done the right thing.

Should I just quit meddling? I asked myself. I was meddling in our department appointments, I was meddling in Fabiola's life. I could hear Alice in my head. "You think you know everything, but you don't."

I didn't know all the consequences of what I had put in play. That was true. But should a likely innocent person be left to rot in that private prison hell? Shouldn't students be taught as much about the major crises of our time, the rise of white supremacy and the acceleration of climate change, that were clear and present dangers to us all?

But who did I think I was, the white Fairy Godmother who could wave her magic wand and fix all this?

It started to rain, and the road was slick. I should pay attention to my driving, I thought, but I kept up the interior monologue just the same. The junctions of the road caused a steady beat of questions. Selfish? Caring? Whitewashing? Acting for justice? Bump. Bump. Bump. No good answer came. Or none I cared to listen to.

❀ ❀ ❀

THE FIRST THING I had done when I reached home was to go into my study to call Anna and explain that any representation of Fabiola would have to make her security a priority. She had said, "I'm on it," and hung up.

But then I made the mistake of leaving my study room and entering the kitchen. The wedding planning crashed over my head. Now that I had finished my dissertation and had "some free time" as Victoria put it, I was bombarded with questions. When was Tom's brother arriving? Was he bringing a suit? What would the boys wear? Would the matron of honor dress and bridesmaids dresses arrive on time (and how could I know that?)

Escape. I needed to escape the house or I'd go crazy.

Then an email alert came from Adelaide.

"Emergency Faculty Meeting. Noon today. Attendance mandatory."

She must have been informed of the endowment for the new chair for our department. I stuck my head into the kitchen where Victoria was laboring away over the wedding crises and told her I had to run to the university as we had our own crisis.

I almost jogged over to the campus I was so glad to get away.

I WAS A LITTLE EARLY, and I stopped into my office for a minute to take a breath. As I sat behind my desk, I gazed over at the divider that made this small office into two shared offices. Where were we going to put two new hires?

Unintended consequences were already raising their ugly little heads.

I could hear muffled sounds coming from the open door of the seminar/meeting room. As I got closer I heard, "Just wait until everyone gets here." That was Adelaide's rumbly voice.

The room contained the colleagues, though they had not yet taken seats. There were extra chairs along the wall, chairs that represented the ghosts of the positions we'd lost over the years. Two could be moved back, I thought as I walked toward the table.

"Okay, good. You're here, Kristin. Let's get started," Adelaide said briskly and took her customary seat at the head.

The others sat as well. Aduba and Hercules sat next to each other across the table from me, and Donald sat at Adelaide's left hand, his usual, likely unconscious desire to be close to what passed for power in our little clan in evidence.

"First," Adelaide said warmly, "I want to congratulate Dr. Kristin Ginelli for passing her doctoral exam. Dr. Ginelli, we will have a reception for you shortly."

Adelaide's broad face simply beamed.

"Thank you," I said, "and truly, Dr. Winters, I have to credit you for scaring me into finishing it."

I smiled back at her, and there was a little ripple of laugher from both Aduba and Hercules. If only they knew how true that was.

"That said, let me tell you there has been a development that directly impacts our search," Adelaide said in her no-nonsense, administrator voice. "We will need to act immediately."

She tapped a pile of papers in front of her.

"Our department has received a gift of a named chair, and we are entitled to fill it immediately. This gift specifies that this endowed position is in addition to the other position we currently have open. That means we can offer two candidates positions.

Donald sat up like his chair had suddenly been electrified.

"Really?" he said. "That means we can certainly expand the scope of what we teach. Adding Moral Philosophy, for example . . . "

"Let me finish, please," Adelaide said sharply.

"The new chair is named 'The Ida B. Wells-Barnett Chair in African American Studies' and it comes with the restriction that it is dedicated to Philosophy and Religion in perpetuity, and the person who holds the chair should be a recognized expert in the field of African American Studies."

I'd never seen a clearer example of the phrase "he had the wind taken out of his sails" than Donald's body language at that moment. He seemed to literally "luft" as those of us who sailed called it when full sails lost the wind. He almost flapped.

"Well, this is *merveilleuse*," Hercules exclaimed. "So very good. "We can hire the incredible Dr. Turner and the incredible Dr. Parker, both at the same time."

I smiled to myself. That was Hercules. He never held back from stating what was what and who was who.

"Wait a minute," Donald said, puffing back up again. "Just wait a minute. There are three candidates to consider. And, and, who gave this money anyway? Do we know the source? That should be investigated."

"It was an anonymous donation, Donald, but the university lawyers are satisfied, and there is no need for further investigation," Adelaide said sharply. Then she glanced down the table at me.

She suspects, I thought. But I was very good at keeping secrets. She'd never know for sure.

"Aduba," she went on after that brief pause, "I'm going to turn over this meeting to you as chair of the search committee. Donald is right, we have three candidates to consider."

"Ah, yes," Aduba said, putting on his reading glasses and turning to the pile of papers in front of him.

"I suggest we vote on the Wells-Barnett Chair first, and then move on to our other open position." He turned to me and smiled.

"Dr. Ginelli, would you like to make a motion?"

"Yes, thank you. I nominate Dr. Nia Zendaya Turner for the Wells-Barnett Chair, and I propose we approach her immediately."

"Second," Adelaide said quickly.

"All in favor?"

Four ayes followed.

"So ordered," Aduba said.

"Now to the open position. Do I hear a motion?"

"I propose Dr. Nigel Wilson for the open position!" Donald fairly shouted.

"All in favor," Aduba said without glancing up from his papers.

There was one loud "aye."

"All against?"

Four quick "nays" followed.

"I would like to nominate Dr. Sandra Ellen Parker for the open position," Adelaide said in an even tone.

"All in favor?" Aduba quickly asked.

Four ayes followed. When Aduba asked if there were any nays, Donald was silent.

"Let the record show Dr. Parker has been selected for the open position."

I had to hand it to Aduba and his British education. He certainly knew how to run a faculty meeting.

❈ ❈ ❈

THAT EVENING, I DROVE over to pick up Kelly and the boys at Tae Kwon Do class. It was raining again, and besides I had been too tired to take the class with them. As we headed home, I gathered there had been successful board breaking among all three, and they were hyped up on the excitement.

I pulled into the alley behind our house and used the automatic door opener to open the garage door. We all exited the car, but before I could close the garage door a harsh voice startled us.

"You stop! Kids come here. Now or shoot you."

In the garage overhead light I could see a short, Hispanic-looking woman with a black gun trained on us. I ran directly at her, startling her while yelling, "Kelly, get the kids in the car. You too. Lock the door."

Behind me I could hear the car door open and a couple of grunts. Then I heard the locks.

My run had startled our assailant, and she'd instinctively moved back. I didn't stop. I kicked as hard as I could at the gun in her hand, and it went flying.

I dove at her, the heel of my hand aiming for her face. I connected, and I heard a crunch.

"*Puta sucia!*" I heard in a suspiciously familiar tone.

Isobel? No, she was dead, my mind told me. I flipped this assailant on to her stomach and kneeled on her back. She was a small woman, but she bucked hard underneath me, still screaming Spanish obscenities. I grabbed her arms and pulled them back so sharply she screamed. I yanked off the belt from my raincoat, and I tied her hands behind her. She wasn't done by a long shot though. She kept bucking, and I feared she'd throw me off.

I put my hands around her throat and applied pressure to her carotid artery. I choked her enough that she lost consciousness.

"Kelly," I yelled. "It's okay. Could you come here? And boys, just stay in the car until the cops come."

Kelly jumped out of the car and ran toward me.

"Get my purse, will you, and use my phone to call the police? I will need to hold this woman until they get here."

Kelly responded quickly. She got out my phone and put it in front of me so facial ID would open it. She called 911 and explained succinctly what had happened.

"Hurry!" she said briskly and hung up.

"Get a cloth from the shelf over there, will you, and use it to pick up that gun? Just carry it out of the middle of the alley and leave it over there. Be very careful." I used my shoulder to indicate the side of the garage wall. She did what I asked without question.

We heard sirens in what must have really been just a just a couple of minutes, though it seemed like ages.

"Mike! Sam! You okay?" I called out, never moving from holding down our would-be attacker.

"Yeah!" I heard. "We're in the back, and we can see everything," Mike said. "Good work, Mom!" Sam added.

A campus police car with flashing lights pulled up, and Alice jumped out.

"Kristin! You okay? What happened?" she called as she ran toward me. I could see her partner, Mel Billman, exiting the other door.

"Well, sort of," I said. "Bring your cuffs."

"Got 'em. Whadda you think?" Alice said roughly. I knew how dangerous this must look.

"Hi, Alice!" the boys chorused from the back of the Subaru.

"Sam, Mike, you stay there, right?" Alice called out.

"We're okay!" they called. Still, I saw Mel move over, pat Kelly on the arm, and then move toward the back door of the car.

Alice had our attacker cuffed in seconds. It was a good thing as she was coming around and starting to spit obscenities again.

Alice sat back on her heels.

"Who the hell is this? Somebody else wants to kill you now?"

"I don't know, Alice. She just jumped out at us, waving a gun. The gun's over there," I said and pointed.

Mel went over immediately and took out an evidence bag.

Alice glared at me.

"Seems like old times, Alice," I said trying for a little humor. Alice and I had met when I been mugged in this very same alley a couple of years before.

Alice just snorted, but behind me I actually heard Mel chuckle. That's when I'd met him too.

❀ ❀ ❀

The Chicago police had arrived not too long after Alice and Mel, and they'd taken charge of the small, and obviously very vicious woman.

One cop had reached into the pocket of the assailant's jeans and pulled out a battered wallet.

"Maria Rivera," he read out. "Mean anything to you?"

"Are you Isobel's sister?" I asked Maria.

"You kill her, I kill you all," she said.

Yes, she was clearly related to Isobel.

"You need to call FBI agent Kamal Nadar," I told him. I used my phone to scroll to Nadar's number, and I read it out to him.

"It is likely she is part of a trafficking ring they have been breaking up."

"Yeah, well, okay," he said. "You know the drill, right? You need to come in, give a statement. We'll take her to Branch 30."

"I will," I said, taking one of my cards out of my own wallet and handing one to him. "I need to get my children into the house and calmed down first, however."

"Sure. Don't worry." He handed me his own card.

Sargent Murray Hicks.

I tucked his card in an empty slot in my wallet and went to put my remaining cards back.

I need to get new ones, I thought. These don't say Doctor. Then I thought, I must be losing my mind if that's a concern right now.

The boys jumped out of the car when I opened the door.

"Wow. Just wow, Mom. You did great," Mike said. "Yeah, kapow!" Sam added.

"Mel, I'm stayin' here some," Alice called over her shoulder.

"Okay, just call me," Mel's deep voice said from the alley.

Alice pushed the button to close and lock the garage door, and she followed me into the house.

30

Holding on to anger is like grasping a hot coal with the intent of throwing it at someone else; you are the one who gets burned."

—BUDDHA

Kelly was already on her phone when Alice and I entered the kitchen. "Zeke, OMG, you won't even believe it," we heard her say as she ran up the back stairs.

Alice and I looked at each other.

"You better find out if there's more of them gang members gunnin' for you," Alice said severely, her eyes following Kelly up the stairs.

"Yes, you're right," I sighed. "But first I'm going to call Tom and then go talk to the boys."

"Good idea," Alice said turning toward the stove. "I'll make you some of that chamomile tea you hate."

Great.

The call to Tom went to voicemail. He must still be in surgery. I left a brief message for him to call me.

Then I took a moment to scoop out some vanilla ice cream into two bowls, and I grabbed a dog cookie as I assumed Molly had followed the boys. I could hear their voices in the TV room.

"Hey, guys," I said as I entered, trying to keep my voice from cracking. They were sitting on the floor, facing each other, Molly between them. They were both petting her. Petting Molly was my go-to stress reliever too, though it hurt my heart to see how clearly they needed that.

I sat down on the floor with them, gave them each a bowl of ice cream and Molly her cookie.

"That was pretty scary," I said as they held their bowls, not eating, just looking at me, their round, normally soft, kid faces tight with fear. The fist-pumping "hurray, Mom!" was over and normal fear reaction was setting in. My stomach clenched.

"Yeah," Mike said. "I mean like you got her Mom, but that was a gun."

"You kicked the gun, Mom. You kicked it right away. And she's in jail now, right?" Sam said seriously, all his usual smart-alecky tone gone.

"Yes, she's in jail, and she's not going to get out," I said firmly, reaching out both hands to stroke the two tousled brown heads.

"Never?" Mike asked, his lawyer's mind kicking in, even as he leaned his head into my stroking hand.

"Never," I said. Anna and I would make sure of that.

"Okay, then," Sam said, taking a small bite of ice cream.

"And hey, Mike," Sam added. "Wait 'til our friends hear tomorrow. They'll be so jealous."

"Oh, right," Mike said, taking a big bite of ice cream and swallowing it slowly, probably thinking how much this would raise their stock at school.

I would ask Jane if she thought they might need to see a child psychologist. Right after I told her how much I wanted to kill Isobel's sister for scaring my children like that.

I told them to bring the bowls to the kitchen when they were finished, and, as I left, I heard the TV turn on.

"Oh, Alice," I said as I walked back into the kitchen.

She was standing by the counter, stirring sugar into our tea.

"It's okay, honey," she said, looking at me, her brown eyes narrowed with concern. "Drink this now, and then I'll go with you to Branch 30."

I knew it was probably the end of her shift, and she was bone tired from patrolling all day. But I could only bless the friendship that caused her to make the offer. And she'd never called me anything but Kristin before.

"Thank you, Alice," I said. Then I couldn't help it. "But since when do you call me honey?"

"Not gonna happen again," she said gruffly. "You are staying out of messes from here on, you hear me?"

"Yes, Alice," I said meekly, and I obediently took my tea off of the counter and drank some.

After I'd finished it, I had called up to Carol and Giles and asked them to come down. Alice and I then filled them in on what had happened in the garage and alley, and that I had to go file a police report.

"This one is the sister of the one who killed your husband?" Giles asked, his brown eyes both shrewd and concerned. "Are there more in this family?" Giles knew from his home country how often violence was perpetrated by family groups.

Carol looked horrified.

"I don't know, Giles, but you can be sure I will find out," I said.

Alice and I took my car to Branch 30, our local police station. Fortunately, as these things go, they were not that busy, and I was able to give my statement fairly quickly. I think having Alice in her uniform with me helped some.

I drove Alice back to campus and waited until she got in her car and drove away. Then I drove slowly home, but as I approached the garage that opened on the alley, I froze. I didn't want to go into that enclosed space and risk having someone come up on me from the alley. I drove around to the front of the house and luckily there was a parking space on the street right there. I parked and breathed a sigh of relief as I turned off the engine.

"Kristin?" Tom asked from the sidewalk as I opened the driver's side door. "Why are you parking on the street?"

I just threw myself into his arms and held on.

"Let's go inside," I said into his coat. "I have a lot to tell you."

❊ ❊ ❊

I OPENED THE FRONT door the next morning and bizarrely, Victoria, Agent Lindsay and Agent Nadar were all standing on the porch looking at each other.

Late last night, after I had finished talking to Tom, I had emailed the agents at the address Nadar had given me before the sting.

Tom had been very proud of how Kelly had handled herself, and I had too, but I told him in the morning he should talk to her. She was sure to have a reaction.

My email to the two FBI agents had been very pointed. "Isobel's sister Maria attacked me. My house 9 am. Urgent."

I hadn't emailed Victoria, but since she spent most days at my house, her presence wasn't unusual.

I just stood aside and let everyone troop in. This is my life these days, I thought as I shut the door behind them. FBI investigations and wedding planning.

Victoria jumped in first as soon as the door was locked. You had to hand it to her if she could beat the FBI to the punch in terms of interrogation.

"We have a million details to go over, Kristin," she said firmly, using her small, thin body as best she could to block out the agents from getting to me.

I gestured for Lindsay and Nadar to head to the front parlor, and I turned to Victoria.

"I know, Victoria, but I have to talk to these men first. Why don't you head to the kitchen and make a list for me?"

Her face brightened. She loved lists.

"Yes, good idea," she said and hustled down the hall, her shiny hair bouncing on her neck.

"Hello, Molly. Good dog," I heard her say.

I entered the parlor. The two agents were seated, but I stood and glared.

"Why was this nutcase Maria Rivera not rounded up with the others? How many more Riveras are there? You are endangering me and my family by trickling out only the information you think I need to know. After last night, I need to know it all, and I need to know it now." I was breathing hard when I finished my tirade, but it also felt good to release some of my anger. The boys, and Kelly too, would remember the sight of that gun for the rest of their lives.

Lindsay looked at Nadar and nodded. He nodded back. I had to clamp my lips together to keep from yelling some more.

"We have taken custody of Maria Rivera," Nadar said in his deep, measured voice. "She was not on our radar. Apparently she traveled by bus to Chicago from Nogales, Arizona when she heard of her sister's death, or so she says. We called the FBI office that deals with that area. I got a call back on our way over. According to the agent there, she's also into drug trafficking, but mostly Mexican black cocaine that is distributed locally in Arizona and adjacent states." Nadar glanced at Lindsay again, either for permission or confirmation.

I realized I was grinding my teeth.

"Maria Rivera has been in and out of prison her whole life and has been diagnosed by prison officials as paranoid schizophrenic," Nadar went on. "She and her sister were thought to be sworn enemies since they had gotten into a bitter dispute over a kilo of cocaine over fifteen years ago. Maria shot Isobel in the leg, and Isobel beat her unconscious. They both recovered, and Isobel moved to the Midwest. In sum, they are thought to be the last of their family." He stopped his monotone recitation and looked at me.

I looked back at them. The repetition of "they are thought to be" was enraging. That was FBI-speak for "we don't really know."

"So, you don't really know if there is more threat to my family and me or not, right? That's what you're really saying."

"We are telling you as much as we know," Lindsay said, his dark brown eyes carefully assessing me, probably to see if I was going to take a swing at either of them.

"I want surveillance on the house, and I want daily reports emailed to me with updates on your threat assessment to me and my family," I said coldly.

I'd managed to knock Lindsay out of his cool detachment. He looked taken aback.

"There's no way we have the manpower for that," he said through his teeth.

"Then who is next up the chain of command? I'll talk to that person. Or better still, I'll have my attorney ask. I know there have been mistakes in this investigation, and I think those should be looked into as well." Mistakes like not getting back right away to Dr. Ivy Mercer, I thought.

Lindsay's mouth drew into a hard line, but I thought Nadar looked resigned. The FBI protected their little compartments of information, and they sure wouldn't want any dirty laundry to be passed up the chain of command.

They both sat in silence. I stood still in front of them. The silent treatment was not going to work on me. I was the mother of two young boys. I could outwait the FBI.

Finally, Lindsay sighed and said curtly, "We'll make it work."

"Starting today," I said. "If there is going to be retaliation for my role in the arrest of Maria Rivera, it will come quickly."

Nadar's nearly black eyes bored into me, his face set in unreadable stone. Then he turned to Lindsay.

"I will take the first shift, starting now."

I nodded and escorted them to the door.

❀ ❀ ❀

I ENTERED THE KITCHEN, and Molly wagged her tail from under the table where Victoria was laboring away over a list. Quite a long list, I thought despondently, and I headed to the counter.

I put the kettle on with shaking hands and got out the decaf French Roast I had purchased. It was pretty good. I ground some fresh, put it into the French Press and poured boiling water over it when the kettle steamed. The swirling, dark grounds mirrored my swirling, dark fears. I had walked Carol and the boys to school earlier this morning and made arrangements to pick them up this afternoon. I had concealed my retractable baton under my coat for walking them to school, the same baton I'd used to take down Isobel.

Finally, the timer I had set for brewing the coffee dinged. I pushed the plunger down and the thick, sable-colored liquid filled the top. I poured it into my mug and drank, trying very hard not to think.

"Kristin," I heard Victoria say from behind me. "Can we go over this list now?"

"Yes," I said dully. At least wedding details would be mind-numbing.

"Now, about suits for the boys and Tom," she began. I looked up at her deceptively Bambi-face and thought she'd make a good FBI field agent. She never gave up.

Two hours later I had my own list and one for Tom. Lists begat lists I had begun to realize.

I took my lists, went in to my study room and shut the door. I called Jane and asked her if we could meet. Anger, fear, grief, and a deep-down, murderous rage were not exactly the emotions best suited for my approaching nuptials. I had to talk them through again as I could feel them burning me from the inside out.

"Yes, Kristin. I can see you in an hour," Jane said in her soft voice. Good.

I sat at my desk and stared at the wall. An hour.

31

Kristin Ginelli's guide to wedding planning: Listen. Smile. Agree.
Then do whatever you were going to do anyway.

Several weeks had passed since anyone named Rivera, or anyone else, had tried to kill me. I had finally agreed with Agent Lindsay that the daily surveillance could cease. I did ask to be copied on any further activity relating to the former El Chapo gang.

"Within reason," he countered. I'd pointed out my requests were within reason, the reason being I wanted my family to be safe.

I also wanted Fabiola to be safe. Howard Carson had gotten right on the case, and an investigator had been hired. That meant a drive out to the prison to see about Fabiola's safety. The new warden had been very cooperative, and she had been assigned to a "private" suite in the main building. I had been very afraid protective custody would mean solitary, and that was unacceptable.

I met Fabiola in the small suite, and she seemed happier than I'd ever seen her. I'd be happy too, I thought as I drove away, if there was a real prospect of getting out of that prison.

There was still a lot of stress to go around, however. Perversely, the wedding planning had helped, in fact, as there was so much busy work for all of us it was hard to keep obsessing about the clean-up of the investigation.

I took the boys for a session with a pediatric psychologist who specialized in trauma, as Jane had thought it was wise. They'd not been impressed.

"He acted like we were babies," Mike stated in an outraged voice when we'd left the office, and they'd gotten into the car.

"Puppets, can you believe it?" Sam added in the same outraged tone. "He had puppets, and we were supposed to make the puppets talk about how we were feeling!"

"It was embarrassing," Mike added.

"Can we stop for ice cream?" Sam said, clearly done with the psychologist.

"Sure," I said. They seemed fine to me.

Kelly had had quite a different reaction. She had approached me a few nights after Rivera had pulled a gun on us and asked if we could spar together some. She wanted to learn that disarming kick and also the blow from the heel of my hand that had broken Rivera's nose.

I said sure, and we'd gone off together for a couple of sessions at the university gym, not telling the others. It helped me too, I found, to reinforce that I could protect myself and those I loved.

Tom had taken the boys out on a Saturday, and they had gotten matching suits. It seemed to have worked very well for bonding, and the hamburgers and ice cream on the way home had been a great idea of Tom's. When the suits had been delivered, the three of them had modeled them in the parlor, taking turns coming down the stairs and turning around like male models. The sharkskin fabric and pale grey color was elegant, and when I saw they had matching ties and pocket handkerchiefs, I cried.

Kelly and I had gone out together to buy dresses for the wedding rehearsal. I'd called Anna ahead of time, and she'd directed me to the private salon where she brought most of her clothes. She had even called ahead to make sure we got her preferred fitter.

We'd gotten some really elegant and yet simple outfits that I thought looked spectacular. I picked a Chanel, cream-colored dinner suit with cap sleeves and pearl buttons and trim. Kelly chose a pale, rose-colored mini-dress with lace applique on the bodice. She looked so grown up.

"Zeke is going to swallow his tongue when he sees you," I joked with her back in the fitting room.

She turned to me, her eyes brimming.

"Kristin, may I call you Mom?" she asked, her eyes welling up.

"Oh, Kelly," I said, wrapping my arms around her. "Of course. I'd love you to call me Mom."

Then we were both crying.

This wedding business was turning me into a fountain. I cried so easily now.

When I got home, I got a text from Adelaide. Both Dr. Turner and Dr. Parker had accepted the offers to join our faculty in the fall. "Wonderful news!" I texted back.

Then I cried again.

Three days until the wedding

Tom's brother was due at the airport in a few hours. I hoped Tom would make it home in time to go with me.

I'd heard nothing directly from Vince and Natalie. Vince Junior had called and let me know they were back in their own home with day and nighttime help. Vince Junior reported that Vince was grumpy both health aides were women. "He liked those guys you hired better."

No doubt.

"You'd better go to the airport without me. Got another short case." Tom texted a little later. Then I saw there was a picture attachment.

"My brother," he had written underneath.

Well, this wouldn't be hard. His brother looked like a younger Tom with slightly lighter hair and a beard. Just like Tom, David Grayson was very handsome.

I had no trouble picking him out at International Arrivals, and we chatted like we'd known each other for years on the way home.

As we entered the kitchen through the back door, Molly, Sam and Mike raced into the room. Molly kept coming and put her head between David Grayson's legs, nearly unbalancing him. But he had eyes only for Sam and Mike.

"Hi, guys! I'm Tom's brother Dave," he said. "I brought some stuff from Africa for you."

"Wow, really?" they chorused.

"Yeah, really. Come on. Show me my room, and I'll give you your presents right away."

"Cool!" Sam said, and the three of them headed up the back stairs.

"You wanna just call me Uncle Dave, get that out of the way? We're all gonna get married soon, right?" Dave said.

Oh, lord. More tears.

Two days until the wedding

I was hiding in my study room when I heard crying and laughing coming from the kitchen. Not all that unusual these days, but I thought one of the voices was Giles's.

I hurried down the hall and looked.

Giles was, in fact, laughing.

Victoria and Carol were dancing around in a circle while normally reserved Giles was watching them and laughing a deep, sonorous laugh.

"Oh, Kristin!" Victoria said when she saw me. "Carol and Giles want to get married, and they want me to do their wedding!"

"Really?" I said, stunned. Not that Carol and Giles would get married, but that they'd want the wedding planned by Victoria.

"That's wonderful," I quickly added and went over and hugged them both.

"What's up?" I heard a man say from the kitchen doorway. I turned. It was David Grayson, now widely known as Uncle Dave.

Victoria just sang out the news again.

"*C'est vrai*," Giles said happily. Carol was crying too hard to speak.

"And it's going to be a human rights festival on the Midway at the end of the summer, and people can sign up to volunteer, and there'll be some musicians and singers too!" Victoria trilled as Carol and Giles nodded.

"Now that's a wedding!" Uncle Dave said warmly and looked very appreciatively at Victoria. I didn't think it was just the idea of the human rights festival slash wedding that interested him.

"Well, it was their idea," Victoria said modestly, gesturing at Carol and Giles, "but I have lots of contacts to help set it up."

"I'm Dave Grayson, by the way," said Uncle Dave, holding out his hand to her.

"I'm Victoria Layne," Victoria said, blushing prettily as she shook it.

Was it my imagination or was her hair getting bouncier by the minute?

It crossed my mind that we'd have Victoria with us most of the summer.

Oh well.

That evening after dinner and many toasts to the newly engaged couple, my cell phone rang.

It was Natalie.

❉ ❉ ❉

"KRIS-TIN-A?" MAMA GINELLI DID not fully trust cell phones and always spoke slowly and loudly.

"Yes, Nonna, I'm here. I can hear you. Where are you?"

"We at hotel." She paused. I could hear Vince in the background.

"Yes, yes, Vince, I tell her. We are at HY-ATT. Hyde Park. Vince Junior he drop us off. That young Michael? He come to help. We call him."

"You're not staying with us?" I was taken aback. They always stayed at the house.

"No is necessary. We come wedding. You have much to do." A growly voice in the background again.

"Yes, Vince. I tell her. So, Kris-tin-a, Vince he want meet you for coffee tomorrow morning here at hotel. Talk. Is okay? When, Vince?" I could hear the shout of "Nine!"

"Nine in morning. Coffee shop here. You good? You come?" Natalie was getting agitated from being Vince's mouthpiece.

"Yes, sure. Tell Vince I'll come."

"Is good. Kiss boys."

AT 9 AM ON the dot I was sitting in the Hyatt coffee shop. It was a new hotel only a few blocks north of the campus. It was part of a neighborhood renovation and seemed always to be full. I wondered how Vince and Natalie had gotten a room.

Vince appeared with a walker in the door of the coffee shop and spotted me. He moved slowly and carefully across the crowded space. There were lots of chairs that could trip him up, but I stayed seated suspecting that jumping up and helping would not be welcome.

He finally lumbered up, held on to the table and the walker, and he got seated. Then he flipped the walker closed and hung it on the back of his chair. He'd clearly practiced this a lot.

Vince breathed heavily for a few seconds while he looked at me with his sad, Italian Buddha-face that now only drooped slightly on one side.

"Hi, Vince," I said in as casual a tone as I could.

"Kristin. Thanks for meetin' me," he breathed.

He had always called me kiddo. My heart sank a little.

"It's okay, Vince. I really want to talk. I want you to know I'm sorry for not telling you everything as it was happening. Perhaps I should have," I said.

"Nah," Vince said. "I was out of it. I get that now. But I was pissed when I found out. I gotta tell you that."

"I know, Vince," I said softly.

"Not now. Just wanna fill in a few missing pieces, you know."

"Sure. Understandable. And you have to know it was your friend Yitz who broke the whole thing open. If he hadn't found that warehouse and staked it out, I don't think the FBI could have cracked the case," I said firmly.

"It's good. It's good. Sorry he had to go like that, though," Vince said, his whole face drooping now. I realized the effort he was putting in to talking so clearly.

The waitress interrupted. We both ordered decaf.

"Decaf, Kristin?" he asked with a crooked smile.

"Decaf, Vince?" I joked back.

That broke the ice.

"So let me fill you in on the whole thing then," I said, and I went through everything in as much detail as I could.

Our coffees came, but we hardly noticed.

"So, like it was suicide by FBI agent, she did?" he asked flatly.

"Yeah. Just like that."

"And they sure? The FBI. They sure this Rivera, she killed Marco?"

I knew it would hurt him to hear it, but I said it anyway. "She bragged about it to me, Vince. Right before I knocked her out cold."

"Good. Good," he growled. "Glad you got a shot in."

I could see his energy was flagging, though. I needed to hurry up.

"She had a sister, tried to threaten me with a gun. I broke her nose, had her arrested. The FBI has got her now. She's a nutcase, apparently. Had nothing to do with the Midwest operation."

Vince reached over and patted my hand.

"You done so good, kiddo. Marco'd be proud," he said, his eyes filling with tears, his good hand now grasping mine.

I put my head down on our linked hands while I cried, and he patted my head.

❀ ❀ ❀

THE REHEARSAL WENT SURPRISINGLY smoothly. Jane had everyone lined up and ready to go in a matter of minutes. She might be soft-spoken, but apparently she was a drill sergeant when it came to wedding rehearsals.

We all piled into limos and were driven in style to a private room in a lovely downtown restaurant that overlooked the lake. Victoria had booked it, and I must say it worked really well.

I hadn't had a private moment to tell Tom about my conversation with Vince, but I did as we sat up in bed together that evening.

"See?" Tom said a little smugly. "They love you. That relationship is going to be fine."

There was a small knock on the door.

"Come in," I said.

It was Sam and Mike. They were in their pajamas but looked very serious.

"Yes, guys? You okay?"

"We need to talk," Mike said.

"Is it true Kelly is calling you Mom?" Sam asked, looking hard at me.

"Yes, I said, that's true. She asked, and I said okay. Is that okay with both of you?" I realized I should probably have told them first.

"Yeah, yeah. Fine. Whatever," Sam said impatiently. "That's not what we wanna talk about."

"So, Tom," Mike said quickly. "We got a Dad, and he died, but he's still our Dad you see, but we wanna, well . . . "

"We wanna call you Pop!" Sam burst out.

Tom immediately slid out of his side of the bed, hurried over to the boys, knelt down and hugged them.

"That's perfect!" he said, kissing the cheek of each one in turn.

I cried again. I have to get through this wedding before I turn completely to mush, I thought.

"So, this Pop is going to tuck you guys back in bed, okay?" Tom said, standing up and taking their hands.

"That's good, Pop," Mike said, taking it out for a test drive.

"Yeah," Sam said. "That's good, Pop."

❋ ❋ ❋

Wedding Day

TOM AND I STOOD in the back of the small chapel. We had elected to walk in together after the attendants were all in place. The chapel really was lovely, I thought, as the sunlight pouring in through all the stained glass illuminated the pews and the people in them. I knew it was a tableau I would never forget.

As I gazed over them, all the people I loved, liked, and a couple, like Donald, whom I barely tolerated but had had to invite, I felt content for the first time in many years.

3 2

At 40,000 feet on the way to Paris

Tom and I stretched out in our first class seats. The seatbelt sign was off, and an attendant was approaching us with two flutes of champagne.

"You are the newlyweds, yes?" she asked with a charming French accent, starting to hand us the drinks.

"We are," Tom said smiling, taking his.

"Yes," I smiled back, "but could I have sparkling water instead?"

"*Certainment*," she replied and returned to the front to get my drink.

Tom looked at me quizzically.

I smiled back at him.

"I'm pregnant, Tom."

"Oh, Kristin. How wonderful," he said and kissed me.

After three months I'd finally realized what all the crying all the time and throwing up could mean. Some former detective I was. I'd gone out and gotten a home pregnancy test, and it had been positive. I'd snuck off to the OB/GYN who'd delivered the boys, and I had a copy of the ultrasound picture. I slipped the photo out of my purse and handed it to him.

"Here you go, Pop. Your wedding present. To be delivered in October."

Tom took the picture from me.

"Twins????"

Acknowledgments

F amily and community have become so intensely important in these
years of the pandemic. I want to acknowledge that without the love
of my husband, adult children, and grandchildren, I could not have continued to be creative in this time. We have been separated far too much,
but we have also grown closer.

I have made the decision to ignore the pandemic in this novel. The
reason is simple. I am tired beyond words of these waves of infections and
the failures of many people to live up to their responsibilities to their own
families as well as to neighbors and the larger community by getting vaccinated and wearing masks. I certainly don't want to write novels about
it. It's clear: get vaccinated and boosted, wear a mask, social distance and
take care of one another.

Organ trafficking tragically exists around the world and should always be illegal. The US has crafted and sustained strict ethical guidelines
and laws for organ procurement and distribution and this has enabled
this life-saving treatment to continue and to grow. I urge you to become
an organ and tissue donor, as I am, by signing the consent form on the
back of your driver's license if you have not already done so.

In this novel, however, I have also employed illegal organ trafficking
as a metaphor for the objectification and commodification of primarily,
though not exclusively, the bodies of women of color. Combined with the
terrible reality of the prison industrial complex, this is as close to writing
horror as I think I will ever venture.

Finally, I would like to acknowledge all those who actively work for
racial and gender justice in this society and who refuse to accept that
prejudice is "normal," or, God help us, something to be proud of.

I wish you health and safety in the coming years.

Recommended Reading

Womanism and Womanist Ethics:

Alice Walker. *In Search of Our Mother's Gardens: Womanist Prose.* New York: Houghton Mifflin Harcourt, 1983.

Katie Geneva Cannon, Emilie M. Townes, Angela D. Sims, eds. *Womanist Theological Ethics.* Louisville, KY: Westminster John Knox Press, 2011.

Racism and Gender Violence:

Traci C. West. *Solidarity and Defiant Spirituality: Africana Lessons on Religion, Racism, and Ending Gender Violence.* New York: New York University Press, 2019.

Climate Crisis:

Dina Gilio-Whitaker. *As Long as Grass Grows: The Indigenous Fight for Environmental justice from Colonization to Standing Rock.* Boston: Beacon Press, 2019.

Discussion Questions

1. Kristin Ginelli juggles her twin sons, her impending marriage, her aging, former in-laws, and her fiancé all while trying to volunteer teach in a women's prison and finish her doctoral dissertation. In other words, she lives the fragmented, stressful life most working parents face these days. How does that resonate with your own life, or the lives of people you know?

2. Illegal organ trafficking is not only a terrible reality some places in the world, but also, in this novel, a metaphor for how people, particularly women of color, are treated just as a means to an end, not as fully human in themselves. Depending on who you are, how did you feel about that metaphor?

3. How does your own identity inform you about ways to combat systemic racism? In what ways might your own identity limit your ability to understand and act against systemic racism?

4. How do you understand Womanist ethics? How is that perspective helpful for today's society?

5. Kristin's wedding planner, Victoria, is a victim of domestic violence. Was Kristin right to go confront her abusive boyfriend and in effect rescue Victoria? Did that further disempower Victoria or might it have saved her life? What other options might there be if this was someone you know being abused?"

6. "Climate grief" is addressed by one of the fictional guest lecturers. Do you feel climate grief? What helps you deal with that?

7. Kristin's anger and grief over the murder of her first husband, Marco, seems to intensify for a while when his murderer is captured. Often we can imagine when a terrible thing ends we will feel better, but sometimes it takes a while. Does that resonate with your experience?